The Bad Boys
Guide to
the Galaxy

The Bad Boys Guide to the Galaxy

KAREN KELLEY

BRAVA

KENSINGTON PUBLISHING CORP.
http://www.kensingtonbooks.com

BRAVA BOOKS are published by

Kensington Publishing Corp.
850 Third Avenue
New York, NY 10022

All Kensington titles, imprints and distributed lines are available at special quantity discounts for bulk purchases for sales promotion, premiums, fund-raising, educational or institutional use.

Special book excerpts or customized printings can also be created to fit specific needs. For details, write or phone the office of the Kensington Special Sales Manager: Kensington Publishing Corp., 850 Third Avenue, New York, NY 10022. Attn. Special Sales Department. Phone: 1-800-221-2647.

Brava and the B logo Reg. U.S. Pat. & TM Off.

ISBN-13: 978-0-7582-1769-1
ISBN-10: 0-7582-1769-2

First Kensington Trade Paperback Printing: July 2008
10 9 8 7 6 5 4 3 2 1

Printed in the United States of America

To Karl Kelley,
The love of my life.
Where would I have been without my hero?

Chapter 1

Sam Jones stepped on the elevator and pushed the button. His life was about to change for the better. *Rest and relaxation, here I come.* His only worries were going to be if the fish were biting and there was enough beer in the fridge.

He didn't want to think about the bad guys on the streets of Dallas. Hell, he and Nick had put away one of the biggest kingpins in the city and gotten commendations from the captain *and* the mayor.

With the help of Kia, of course. He couldn't leave her out. Man, she was something else. Nick had all the luck.

But they'd had to be extra careful where she was concerned. They'd shielded her from the press as much as possible. At the time, she'd come off as a happy but beautiful fiancée and nothing more. But then she didn't really look like an alien from the planet Nerak.

Now it was vacation time. He'd gone months without a decent day off, and he had a little two bedroom cabin in the piney woods of East Texas calling his name. He could almost smell the fish frying.

When the elevator stopped, he got off, whistling a jaunty tune as he strolled to Nick's apartment. Another fifteen minutes, and he'd be on his way.

He tapped on the door.

Nick opened it, then frowned when he saw who it was.

"Hey, buddy." Sam grinned.

Nick slammed the door.

Now that wasn't nice, and after everything he'd done for his friend. "Hey, did I say anything when you went on your honeymoon? No, not one word, and I had to partner with Hank the Skank. The man never bathes. He could stink a dog off a gut wagon. At least you're working with Trudy."

The door opened, and Nick glared at him. "You think Trudy's better than Hank?"

Sam stepped inside. "No." He chuckled. "You just have to tune her out. The woman never shuts up. At least with Hank, I could roll the window down."

"If I tune her out, then she pokes me in the ribs." He grimaced. "The last time I worked with her, I carried bruises for a solid week."

"I'll be back before you know it."

"Yeah, yeah."

Nick could complain all he wanted, but Sam was leaving on vacation and nothing was going to stop him. He dug in his pocket. "Here are the keys to my apartment." He dropped them in Nick's open hand. "Just put the mail on the table."

"You're too damn happy about all this," Nick grumbled.

His deep sigh was full of contentment. "Why shouldn't I be? I haven't had any time off in six months, at least none to speak about. I'm ready for a little fishing, tossing back a few beers, and a whole lot of peace and quiet. There's nothing like my cabin in the springtime."

Kia came from the back of the apartment, all four of her shih tzus following right on her heels. You'd think they were her babies the way they trailed after her.

"Sam, I didn't know you were here," she said, smiling.

"I was just dropping off the keys to my apartment," he told her. He couldn't stop his grin from forming when he thought of all the hell she'd put Nick through. He was glad everything had worked out, but he'd take single life any day.

He looked around at the garish colors on the apartment

walls. "By the way, I like what you've done with the apartment. Very psychedelic with the hot pinks and bright greens. Did Nick help you decorate?"

Nick shot him a look that said he was not amused. Sam kept his expression innocent—not that he thought Nick bought it.

"I did it while Nick was at work," Kia told him. "It was a surprise."

"Boy, was I surprised," Nick muttered, then quickly smiled at Kia. "You did a wonderful job. I love it. All our friends are envious."

"Oh, good! I was thinking about doing our bedroom next."

Sam smothered a laugh. If he didn't watch out, Nick would be poking him in the ribs.

"You're leaving for your cabin?" Kia asked.

He nodded as one of the pups jumped up, begging for attention from Nick.

"Have a good time, and try to relax. Nick said you don't relax enough. He said you should learn to bend the rules a little and let your hair down."

She studied him for a moment before looking at Nick, then back to him.

"I think that must be a figure of speech since your hair isn't long enough to let down. He also said you needed to get laid. Are you tired of standing?" She went on to the kitchen, not waiting for an answer.

"I'm not a bit tired," Sam called after her. "I think Nick needs to worry about his own life rather than mine." He looked pointedly at his friend. "And I do bend the rules. I just don't warp them completely out of shape like you do."

Nick cleared his throat and reached down for the pup. He picked up the ball of black and white fur, rubbing her behind the ears. For a man who'd sworn he'd never have a girly dog, Nick had changed his mind pretty fast.

And Nick thought *he* needed fixing?

He did sort of feel bad leaving Nick with Trudy. "Try to follow the rules while I'm gone, and I'll try to bend them a little."

Nick grinned. "You think I won't follow them?"

They both knew the answer to that. "Hell, no."

Nick shrugged. "I can't be like you. Life wasn't meant to be point A to point B. Sometimes you have to veer off the track to see what else life has to offer."

"That's why I worry about you, Nick. While I'm taking a little R&R, I won't be there to keep you out of trouble."

"Like Kia says, try to relax. You deserve it. I'll keep my nose clean, promise."

Sam chuckled. "I always relax at the cabin. You know me, I'm a natural born explorer." He could easily see himself traversing across new terrain in undiscovered lands. "If I'd been born a hundred years or so ago, I might've discovered all kinds of new countries."

Before Nick could comment, a loud rumble shook the apartment.

"Thunder?" Strange. He glanced out the window, but the sky looked bright and blue.

"Oh, no!" Kia rushed back to the living room, her face a shade paler. She grabbed the pup from Nick and hurried to the bedroom. The other three puppies followed.

"What is it?" Nick called after her.

Sam had never seen her this upset, except maybe when Nick had gotten shot. What was going on?

She hurried back into the living room after shutting the pups in the bedroom. "The Elders. I know the sound of their crafts."

"I won't let them take you," Nick said, his expression grim. "We've been through too much already. No one is going to come between us."

Her smile looked a little wobbly. "I told you that I wouldn't go back to Nerak, but sometimes we don't have a choice in what we want." She drew in a deep breath. "It sounds like they're landing on the roof. We'd better meet them."

"I'm not staying behind," Sam said and followed. Damn, after all these two had been through, this was the last thing they needed.

They quickly took the stairs to the roof.

"What about your neighbors?" Sam asked.

"Either working or old enough they probably didn't hear a thing."

Before Nick pushed the door open, he glanced over his shoulder with a troubled expression.

Sam's stomach churned. He'd heard about the Elders, the supreme rulers of Nerak. If they wanted to take Kia back with them, there wouldn't be a whole hell of a lot Nick and Sam could do. But he wouldn't tell Nick that.

"Don't worry, buddy. I've got your back," Sam tried to reassure him.

"I never thought you wouldn't." Their gazes met for a brief moment before Nick opened the door and they stepped out to the roof. Sam closed it firmly behind them.

"An Elder's craft," Kia breathed.

Sam had still been holding on to the belief they were worrying for nothing, and that it had been thunder . . . or a sonic boom. What he was looking at wasn't either one.

A billowing gray cloud enveloped the tube-shaped craft now sitting on the roof. The door swished open, and a woman stepped out. She wore an emerald green silk robe, and her pale blond hair reached to her waist. But he couldn't see her face.

Kia's mouth dropped open, then snapped closed. She quickly bowed before the woman. "Greetings, Healer."

"This is an Elder?" Nick whispered.

"No, my sister, but she's also a healer." She waved for Nick to bow. He looked at Sam before shrugging and bending slightly at the waist.

"It isn't an Elder then?" Sam asked. So it might not be as bad as they'd first imagined. Kia had a lot of sisters.

"No," she whispered, head still bowed.

He might have thought about bowing if it had been an

Elder, but one of Kia's sisters? Sam wasn't about to bow. Instead, he watched and waited to see what was about to happen.

The woman faced him as the rest of the gray cloud dissipated and looked Sam directly in the eye before one eyebrow rose disdainfully.

His stomach did a crazy flipflop as it hit him. This wasn't just any sister. This was the woman from the hologram. Kia had shown it to him when she'd tried to convince him that she was an alien.

Lara, her name was Lara. My God, she was more beautiful in person. In the hologram, she'd come across as ethereal, angelic, and pure.

But right now, she had her head held high and acted as if they should be paying homage since she'd gone to the trouble of gracing them with her presence.

Man, something must've happened on the flight here because she sure didn't act angelic.

"It's good to find you well, Sister," Lara said, turning her attention back to Kia.

"You stole an Elder's craft," Kia whispered. "You are in so much trouble."

Oh, great, Sam thought. They would have all of Nerak after them now. He raised his gaze to the sky but didn't see a legion of women warriors coming after them.

"Of course I didn't steal the craft," Lara said. "The Elders sent me to Earth. I'm here on a mission."

Kia stiffened. "I won't return to Nerak."

Nick draped an arm across Kia's shoulders. Sam stepped to her other side. They wouldn't let her go without a fight.

"I'm not here to take anyone home," Lara said. "There's trouble on our planet."

Kia squared her shoulders. "Someone has dared attack Nerak?"

"So, the warrior code enforcer still lives inside you. I would've hated for my sister to forget her heritage."

"Why have you come to Earth?" Kia asked, apparently deciding to let the chastising note in her sister's voice slide.

"There has been no attack . . . yet. When our cousin's craft returned, there were aliens from earth on board—three men and a woman. One became ill and infected an Elder. I must find a cure before it's too late."

"Cast the invisibility shield around the craft and come inside," Kia told her. "I found out the hard way it's not good for anyone to learn where we come from."

"There are men with you," she said, not leaving the safety of the craft.

Kia looked at Nick, then him. "They are good men."

Both Lara's eyebrows rose. "There is such a thing?"

"Yeah, there're a few of us left on Earth," Sam told her. She might be beautiful, but when she opened her mouth, she reminded him of one of his ex-girlfriends—real uppity. Now he remembered why they'd split.

She turned her gaze on him, studied him for a moment, then just as quickly dismissed him as she focused once more on her sister. "I will go with you."

It was no skin off his nose what she thought about him. Hell, the sooner he left for his cabin the better. Just as soon as he made sure Nick and Kia were okay. And he wasn't leaving until he did.

He let everyone go in front of him, watching Lara as she took in her surroundings. She seemed cautious but curious until she looked down at the floor. Then she quickly raised her hem.

Hell, the floor looked clean to him. He didn't see a problem. Apparently, Miss High and Mighty did, though.

Nick shut the door behind them after everyone was inside, and they all turned as one to look at Lara.

Man, he shouldn't have looked directly into her pale green eyes. He'd never seen eyes the color of hers. They drew him in, made him feel as if she were caressing his soul.

Maybe she was like Medusa because he was starting to feel

as if she could turn him to stone—at least one part of his anatomy. God, she was sexy as hell. He wouldn't argue that.

Not that he was even remotely interested since he'd witnessed firsthand her haughty attitude. Nope, he didn't want any part of that.

"It's imperative that I find a cure for the Elder," Lara repeated. She tilted her head to the side. "What *is* that scratching noise? It's very unnerving."

"The puppies," Kia said and went to let them out.

Lara took a cautious step back as they came barreling out from the other room and headed right toward her.

"They won't hurt you," Kia said.

Tentatively, Lara leaned down and touched one. When it licked her finger, she jumped. "It tried to eat me," she said accusingly, rubbing her finger.

"The puppy was showing you affection, that's all," Kia told her, picking one up and holding it close. She nuzzled her face in the softness of the fur.

Lara didn't look at all comforted by this knowledge as she straightened. "You've succumbed to Earth's temptations," she lightly scolded.

What person didn't want to pet a puppy? So what if Kia was tempted to cuddle them? What difference did that make?

"Which Elder is it, and what do we need to do to help find the cure?" Kia returned to the subject at hand, looking genuinely worried as she set the puppy back on the floor.

"Torcara."

Kia drew in a sharp breath.

Sam felt sorry for her. He knew the Elders were the ones who ruled Nerak. This one must mean a lot to her.

"The disease came from Earth, so this is where I'll need to find the cure," Lara explained. "I must test the plants and see if one of them will work as a remedy."

"Yes, of course. We have plants here." Nick said.

Lara looked at Nick, then just as quickly turned back to

Kia. Sam frowned. This Nerakian was starting to piss him off.

"I'll work here then. You'll take me to where these plants grow."

"We don't actually have a place here," Nick tried to explain.

"Then you lied?"

"No, not exactly," Nick said. "This is the city. Plants grow in the country, unless a nursery will work. That's a place where people grow plants from seeds and cuttings."

"You will take me to the country. I need to test them in their natural environment."

"Do you even know what you're looking for?" Sam asked. He wondered if she realized how many plants there were on Earth.

"I'll know it when I find it. I only need one that will react with the chemicals I will be adding."

Kia and Nick looked toward him at the same time and acted as if he was supposed to say something.

"What?" he finally asked.

"You can take her to your cabin," they spoke in unison.

"Me? Uh-uh. I'm not taking her with me." This was his vacation, and he damn sure didn't want to spend it with this . . . this Nerakian who thought she was better than everyone else.

"Please, Sam," Kia pleaded. "For me?"

This wasn't right. Not right at all. They shouldn't even ask. Not that it was going to do them a bit of good.

"I'm not taking her to my cabin."

"But . . ." Kia started.

He shook his head. "No way, nohow. It's not going to happen."

Chapter 2

"How much farther is this cabin?" Lara sat stiff as a board on the passenger side of his pickup.

Was she afraid she might accidentally touch him and soil herself? Oh, hell, he'd hate for that to happen. It would be a crying shame.

"Don't you ever get tired of asking the same question?" Sam glared across the seat at her.

"You keep saying the same thing, 'not long,' but I think you're lying because we're still not there. So, how long before we arrive at this cabin where I'll be able to do my research?"

"Not long . . . ." He watched her mouth turn downward.

What the hell was he supposed to say? She probably didn't know what a mile was. When she continued to stare at him, he decided he wasn't going to win this round.

"We're about to turn off the highway, then we'll go down another road until we get to the cattle guard and cross it. We'll go over a small ridge, and the cabin is sitting in the middle of a cluster of pine trees. There, are you satisfied?"

"Don't you have a craft that goes airborne?" she asked, changing the subject. "This ride is very uncomfortable. I can feel every bump. On Nerak, we have aero units. The ride is quite enjoyable."

"Well, you're not on Nerak. You're on Earth, and no, we don't have aero units for everyone to fly around in."

"That's because this is an inferior planet." She turned her gaze out the window.

He really liked his pickup and had gotten a sweet deal when he'd traded in his car. It was a rusty brown—more rust than brown—but he planned to have it sanded and repainted someday.

"Your craft appears quite antiquated," she continued, and he wondered if she got a kick out of irritating him. "Will it complete the trip?"

Sam gripped the steering wheel until his knuckles turned white. It was safer that way for Lara. He couldn't very well strangle her if he was choking the steering wheel.

"It will." He didn't add that she might find herself sitting on the side of the road, though.

Nick would owe him for this the rest of his life, and a few years after that. How the hell could he let himself get talked into taking Lara on his . . . *his* vacation? This had to be the most harebrained thing he'd ever been talked into doing.

He was a sap. That was his problem. Kia had kept looking at him with those beautiful deep blue, pleading eyes of hers, silently begging him to help.

He'd crumbled like a stale cookie.

"I have to use the elimination facilities," Lara said.

"You have to what?" It dawned on him that she needed to use the bathroom. "Why didn't you go when I stopped for fuel?" Exasperating woman—no, make that alien.

She raised an eyebrow. "I didn't need to go at that point in time."

"Worse than traveling with a bunch of kids," he grumbled but took the next exit.

When he stopped the pickup, she waved her hand as she had from the moment she'd arrived. At the apartment, whenever she'd waved her hand, Kia had rushed to open the door for her, treating her like royalty. Now she was doing it again, as if he was a damned flunkey or something. He gritted his teeth, then strode to her door and opened it. He should make *her* open it. Force her to wait on herself.

The bathroom was inside the gas station. He went with her, noticing how everyone stared. Why the hell wouldn't they when she wore her green robe thing that she held up so it wouldn't brush the floor, like she was a queen or something. She certainly acted like royalty.

A royal pain in the ass!

"There's the ladies' room. Just go in, and you'll see the . . . uh . . . toilets. You know how to . . . uh . . . use one of them?" This was damned embarrassing.

Her eyebrows shot up again as if he were an ant beneath her foot and she was about to squash him. He should tell her that he didn't squash quite so easily.

"I'm quite capable of understanding how to use the equipment, even as primitive as it must be." She waltzed toward the ladies' room, waved her hand, and then ran smackdab into the door.

"Ow." She reached up and touched her forehead, then looked accusingly at him. "The door is broken. Just like the door on your craft and the ones at my sister's dwelling."

"This is a primitive planet, Princess. You said so yourself." He pushed on the door. "You have to open it manually."

Okay, so maybe he'd been wrong about the waving hand thing she'd been doing. That must be the way they opened doors on Nerak. Must be nice.

The look she was giving him right now made him wonder just what she was thinking, though. He had a feeling her thoughts were about him, and maybe he didn't want to know.

Lara didn't care for Sam's attitude at all. She frowned. Why had he called her a princess? She wasn't of royal blood. She had a feeling he was being sarcastic. How rude of him. She'd only been pointing out the truth. Compared to Nerak, Earth *was* primitive.

It was as the Elders had warned before she left. Men would try her patience if she had the misfortune of coming into contact with them. How right they were.

"You going inside, or do you want me to just stand here holding the door open all day?"

She raised her chin and walked inside the facility without saying a word.

"A thank you would've been polite," he said.

She looked over her shoulder. "Thank you." She would not get angry with this man; instead, she would learn his customs while on earth.

As soon as the door closed, she bit her bottom lip and glanced around. Her nose twitched. There was an odor here that did not please her.

She quickly reminded herself why she was here. She would deal with doors that did not open, the smells, and Sam. It was her duty to the Elder, and Nerak, to face these hardships.

She barely managed to fit in the tiny stall with her voluminous robe. Maybe she should've listened to Kia and changed into something more earthlike. But she had refused to abandon the ways of her people. Still, Kia had placed Earth clothes in a carrier that she called a suitcase and sent them with her. Not that she thought she would need them. They'd looked quite uncomfortable.

She finished and moved to a counter imbedded with basins. But when she ran her hands beneath the spouts, nothing happened. There were no beams of light to rid herself of bacteria. How did one clean her hands on Earth? Or the rest of her body, for that matter?

A woman came out from one of the stalls and gave her a funny look before going to the counter where she turned a knob. Water poured from the spout.

"Water!" She turned her knob, and water poured from hers, too. Amazing. She rotated the handle again, and it stopped. She opened it, and once more, water came out, then she stopped it from flowing again with another turn.

"You okay, honey?" the woman asked.

The woman looked nice enough—for an Earthling—although she talked rather oddly. She'd drawn out the word okay so it sounded more like okaaay.

Lara turned the spout on, then off again. "Water."

"Yeah?"

"Isn't it wonderful?"

"You're not from around here, are you?"

"I come from Nerak."

"Thought as much. A foreigner. But that's okay. My name is Mary Lou."

"I'm called Lara."

"That's a pretty name."

Lara turned the water on again and splashed her hands beneath the flowing stream, then splashed it on her face. Laughter bubbled from her. Water was fun.

There was another spout, only smaller. She pushed it, and a blob of pink stuff dropped on the palm of her hand. She held it toward the other woman. "And what is this?"

"Soap. You rub it between your hands. It'll clean them, and it kind of smells nice."

She cautiously rubbed her hands together. Oh, this was marvelous. Tiny bubbles appeared, and when she blew on them, they floated away.

"You okay in there?" Sam called from the other side of the door.

"Yes," she called back.

The other woman handed her some brown paper. "This is to dry your hands." She smiled.

Lara took it from her and copied what the other woman had done. She remembered what she was supposed to say. "Thank you."

"No problem. Enjoy your time in Texas."

The woman tossed her paper in a can that stood in the corner and left. Lara tossed hers in the receptacle as well. It was going to be quite easy adapting to Earth. She left the elimination facility, remembering to push on the door to open it. Very primitive.

"You discovered water, I see," Sam said as she joined him.

She looked down at her robe. It was quite damp in front. She didn't care. The water had been fun.

But when she returned to the pickup, she realized she'd inadvertently enjoyed one of the temptations that Earth had to offer. The Elders had not mentioned how insidious these temptations would be when they'd briefed her prior to her journey.

No, they'd only discussed men and something called chocolate. Apparently, both could be very addictive, and she had to be careful.

She glanced across the seat. Sam had been infuriatingly rude. She didn't think she'd have any problem resisting him.

He was nice to look upon, though, with his dark hair, blue eyes, and wide shoulders . . . but he had a bad attitude, and she had a feeling he didn't like her. That was hard for her to comprehend. Everyone liked her on Nerak. What wasn't to like?

She was kind and generous and a healer. She could take care of Nerakians if they became ill. Except no one ever became ill on Nerak.

That is, until now.

It was quite an exhilarating feeling knowing someone needed her. Not that she wished the Elder this disease that wracked her body with chills and fever.

But Sam couldn't see how important she was to her people and that she was due respect. She had a feeling she would have to remind him often. How tedious.

He turned off the road he'd called a highway. Finally! Her backside was sore from all the bumping and jarring. She had thought the torture would never end. This other road would have to be smoother. It couldn't be any worse.

Or could it? Her eyes narrowed. "It isn't as wide as the other road," she said as he turned onto it.

"Wow, you're really observant."

"You're being sarcastic again, aren't you?"

"Ya think?"

She didn't say anything. What could she say?

He drew in a deep breath. "I'm sorry. I usually don't talk to women like this."

"Only me."

"You rub me the wrong way."

"I haven't rubbed you at all."

"It's a figure of speech."

"Oh." She thought about what he'd said for a moment. "How do I rub you the wrong way?"

He frowned. "It's your attitude. I guess I expected you to be different."

"How could you expect me to be different when we've never met?"

"Kia showed me a hologram. You looked very . . . very . . ."

"Very what?" She was curious to know what he'd thought of her.

"Very beautiful."

"And you don't think I'm beautiful?"

She noticed that his forehead wrinkled as he concentrated on what he would say next.

"Yes, you're very beautiful."

"I know," she preened.

"That's it!"

She jumped. "What's it?"

"It's your 'greater than thou' attitude."

"Earth people are so very confusing. First, you tell me that I'm beautiful, but I'm not supposed to agree with you. Yet when I look at my reflection, I know I'm beautiful. Am I supposed to lie and say I think I'm ugly?"

The creases in his forehead deepened. "No, but you don't have to be so thrilled when you're right."

Her head was beginning to ache. She needed a relaxing smoothie. Earthmen were so very difficult to understand.

And the road he'd turned on was worse than the last one. So much so that she thought her teeth would jar loose and fall out. But the passing scenery was beautiful. She couldn't deny that. The trees reached across like a canopy above their heads and cast patterns of light and shadows on the road in front of them.

Maybe there was something good about being on Earth. She would try to explore some of this land while she was here so that she might report back to the Elders.

But she would have to be very careful of temptation. Like the water and puppies.

They had been adorable. She'd wanted so badly to pick one up and cuddle it, but she'd quickly seen the puppies for what they were—a trap.

As was Sam. He'd made her body grow warm in a way she'd never experienced.

Until she'd been around him for a while. She wasn't sure he was so much of a temptation anymore. Unless it was the temptation to do bodily harm to him. But healers didn't cause bodily harm. They healed.

She'd have much to tell the Elders when she returned. About men, puppies, and water, too. Water was good, but it still wasn't enough to make her want to stay.

They went across a row of pipes that caused her to bounce on the seat. Thankfully, it didn't last long, or she wouldn't have been able to stand it. The Elders would certainly give her high praise for being so brave.

Maybe she would even get a shining star to hang on her wall. There was nothing better than a shining star. It didn't do anything, but it was pleasant to look at. She had many on her walls now.

"Listen," Sam began, "I haven't been the nicest person, and I know you don't have the same customs as we have on Earth. I'll try to be a little more understanding."

She respectfully lowered her gaze. "I accept your apology," she said. She would also try harder to understand this Earthman.

"Here we are," he said, his voice thickened with pride.

She looked up. Her mouth dropped open as she stared at the leaning structure. Maybe the cabin hid behind this atrocity of a building.

"Where is it?" She tried to see through the trees as she looked for the place where she would be living while she researched the plants.

He raised his hand and pointed with one finger. "Right there in front of us." He pulled up close to the wooden structure and stopped his craft—no, his pickup—then got out. He came around to her side and opened her door.

She got out, still staring at the structure. Surely, he wouldn't expect her to live in something that looked so deplorable.

"It leans," she said.

"Just the porch. I've been meaning to brace that side. The inside is level, though."

She wasn't sure she wanted to find out, but he grabbed her hand and pulled her alongside him. She tugged it free of his grip.

"What?" He looked genuinely surprised.

"You touched me."

"And?" He planted his hands on his hips.

"I'm a healer. No one ever touches a healer. It's not permitted."

"You've got to be kid—" He stopped, drew in a deep breath, then exhaled. "I'm sure I'm going to love this one. Okay, tell me why no one is allowed to touch you."

She wasn't sure she liked his attitude, but she would attempt to be more reasonable. He was, after all, an Earthman and therefore not as intelligent as she.

"By touching a healer, you can disrupt the flow of balance between her and the very air she breathes. A healer's equilibrium must stay equalized at all times." Anyone with any intelligence should know this, but then she remembered who she was speaking to.

He laughed.

She stiffened. "Did I say something that amused you?"

"Lady, you've been amusing me this whole trip." He bent at the waist and motioned for her to proceed.

She swept past, glad that he had the ability to understand her. When she came to the door, she hesitated. He reached around her and placed a metal object inside a hole.

She inhaled, closing her eyes—nice. His scent pleasantly teased. Not soft like the ones the Elders used to mist the bubble that all Nerakians lived beneath. No, this was different. It made her body tingle and her nipples tighten and started an ache deep inside her.

What could be causing this rush of warmth that swept through her every time he came near? It would bear further scrutinizing when she had a moment.

He turned the knob at the same time he pushed on the door. "Home sweet home," he said as he stepped inside.

Against her better judgment, she followed. It didn't look sweet to her, as he'd claimed. Her nose wrinkled at the musty smell. A layer of grime covered everything. The room was dark and stuffy and completely unappealing. She tentatively reached out and touched a table. Her finger came away dirty.

Sam removed a filthy cloth that draped a lounging sofa. The cloth might have once been a lighter shade but was quite despicable now. He shook it before tossing it into the corner.

She coughed, almost gagging as the dust stirred up around her. No, this wouldn't do at all. Already she could feel her body reacting to this environment, and not in a good way. She needed pure, filtered air.

"Sorry about that. It's a little grubby," he told her. "I haven't been here in a while."

A shudder swept over her. "It's quite deplorable. If you diligently apply yourself and clean it properly, then I might be able to function in this hovel while trying to find a cure."

Sam's face turned a deep shade of red. He sputtered and coughed.

There, he'd just proved her point. The filth was affecting him, too.

Chapter 3

Deplorable! Hovel! The cabin was his pride and joy.

"Don't hold back, lady," Sam told her. "Go ahead, and tell me what you really think."

"But I just did." Her forehead wrinkled. "It's wrong if I perceive myself as beautiful. And yet, I'm supposed to lie and say your cabin is quite wonderful when in reality it's the opposite. Is that correct?"

Sam opened his mouth, then snapped it closed. He turned on his heel and marched back to his pickup. Once there, he rested his palms on the side of the bed as he fought to regain control of his anger.

Take a deep breath. Don't explode.

He wouldn't kill her. Kia would never forgive him if he killed her sister.

Lara came to the door. "You *are* going to clean the cabin, aren't you?"

Okay, maybe he would kill her . . .

No, he had a better idea. "If you don't like my cabin, then *you* clean it. The cleaning supplies are in the kitchen under the sink."

He reached in the back and retrieved his fishing pole, tugged his hat further down on his head, and glared at her as he grabbed his tackle box.

"I'm going fishing. This is still my vacation."

"You expect *me* to clean your cabin?"

"Lady, I don't give a . . . a . . ." He looked at her as she stood on the porch looking so damned regal and—sexy. How could he be attracted to her when he didn't even like her? "Do whatever you want to do."

He took off on foot. There was a narrow river that ran through the woods not too far away. Maybe a little fishing would calm him down. That, or maybe a little Valium would be nice.

Damn, where the hell was his temper coming from? He'd never acted like this. He stomped through the woods, not even looking twice at the squirrel that scampered away. He usually liked watching the animals and exploring the woods that surrounded his cabin.

As soon as he got to the river, he let out a deep breath, then another until finally he began to feel like a human again.

Lara wasn't at all like he'd expected. She'd seemed so angelic in the hologram. Well, hell, of course she would. It was a hologram. Kia said they used them rather than writing a letter. And just like a letter, she'd put her best foot forward. Man, he'd really been taken in. Maybe that was his problem. He didn't like being made a fool of.

He cast his fishing line in the water and slowly began to reel it back toward him. The last time he'd been here, the bass weren't biting, but he'd put a new lure on his line that was supposed to be good.

Nothing.

He cast the line out again and reeled it back in. It didn't look like the fish were tempted to bite today, either. Had he ticked someone off upstairs?

Ah, man, he knew what his problem was with Lara. He'd fallen a little in love with her when he'd watched the hologram. She'd been safe. It wasn't as if he'd ever see her in the flesh. No, she was someone he could put on a pedestal and never worry that she'd fall off.

Boy, she'd shot that image out of the water. Hell, what could he expect when she came from a planet of all women?

He realized his line was out of the water, the lure dripping water onto the ground. He frowned. Fishing was supposed to relax him, but all he could think about was Lara.

He tossed his line out a little too hard. It spun across the river and tangled in a fallen branch on the other side.

Damn, was nothing going right in his life? Apparently not. He tugged. Did the branch move? He moved closer to the bank, leaned his pole out over the water, and jiggled it.

This time, he saw the branch move. A little more, and he could probably pop the line loose or at least jar the branch enough that it . . .

His feet went out from under him when the bank gave way. He landed in the water with a big splash and came up sputtering and spitting.

"Son of a bitch!" He sucked air. Damn, the water was freezing! It was only chest deep, but man, was it cold.

Hell, he was already soaked. He damn sure wasn't leaving without his new lure. He waded across the narrow river and grabbed the branch, untangling his line, then waded back to the other side.

A hell of a way to start a vacation.

He climbed out of the water, stomping toward a large rock, then leaning against it. A squirrel chattered at him from an overhead branch as if it were laughing at him. He glared at the rodent, but it just sat there, staring.

"I'm the talk of the woods. Great, just great."

He removed first one boot, then the other, dumping the water out of them. Nick would owe him the rest of his life for this. He'd take Talking Trudy any day.

He tugged his boots back on. Damned hard, too. It wasn't good to get leather wet. Man, he really liked these boots. He'd had them for fifteen years and only resoled them four times. He grabbed his pole and tackle box and headed back to the cabin, squishing with every step.

Back to Lara.

Ethereal goddess, his ass.

She'd talked about his cabin, for Pete's sake. No one talked about his cabin. He'd scraped and saved for years to buy it. She could sleep in the pickup if she hated it that much.

When he got back, Lara wasn't in sight. He'd figured she'd be sitting on the porch waiting for him. A twinge of uneasiness swept through him. He went around to the back. She wasn't there, either. He set the tackle box down and propped his fishing pole against the cabin.

He hoped she wasn't walking back to her sister's because he'd have to go after her—probably.

Did she hate his place that much?

What wasn't to love about the piney woods, the deer, the squirrels, even smart-assed ones. A fishing pole in one hand and a can of beer in the other. Total relaxation.

He grimaced. At least, it used to be.

He cautiously opened the back door. Hell, he didn't know what an uppity alien would do. She might just zap his butt. He should've asked more questions before he left Dallas with her.

His nose wrinkled as he stepped inside. He sniffed again. It smelled . . . soapy.

His eyes adjusted to the dim interior. When he could see, his mouth dropped open. Oh, man, this wasn't right, not right at all.

It looked as if she'd dumped all the powdered detergent on every surface in the kitchen and part of the floor. He must've really pissed her off for her to get even like this.

He ran a finger through the muck on the counter. It wasn't just dry detergent. She must've poured out the liquid first. Yeah, he'd really pissed her off.

There was a noise from the other room. He followed it, then stood in the doorway and watched.

Lara sprinkled dry detergent on the floor, then stooped over, looking down at the floor as if something major was supposed to happen.

What the hell was she doing?

She stomped her foot. "I don't know how I'm expected to

clean when the dirt will not go away!" She turned and screamed, throwing the box of detergent at him.

He dodged. Good thing he had quick reflexes or it would've hit him square in the face.

"What the hell are you doing?"

"You frightened me." She glared at him. "You could've let me know you'd returned."

"Yeah, I could have."

"I don't understand you, Sam Jones, and I don't understand how to clean."

"That's obvious." He waved his arm. "Why are you destroying my cabin?"

Rather than answering, her eyes narrowed. "You're all wet. While I cleaned, you were having fun playing in the water."

He frowned. "I was not playing in the water. I . . ." Oh, yeah, she'd have a field day if he told her that he'd fallen in the river. "Just answer my question. Why the hell are you destroying my cabin?"

She raised her chin. "I cannot survive living in dirt. It upsets my inner balance. You said to clean, so I was cleaning." She frowned. "You have inferior products. I read on the bottle of liquid detergent that it removes dirt and grime, so I poured it on the counters, but it just sat there. Then I found the powder that said it would get rid of dirt and grime, but it sat there doing nothing. Nerak's products are much more superior."

He laughed. Oh, God, he was going to kill Nick for getting him into this mess. Torture first, then a slow, painful death.

"Why are you laughing?" She planted her hands on her hips and pursed her lips.

He only laughed harder.

She wasn't nearly as uppity as she had been earlier. Maybe it was the smudge of dirt on her face.

It was time to call a truce.

"Come on." He walked back inside the kitchen and grabbed some cloths from under the sink. "Just pouring the cleaning product on a surface doesn't make it clean."

He glanced over his shoulder. She arched a haughty eyebrow.

"But I guess you figured that one out." He ran water over one of the cloths, then rung it out. "This is how you do it." He wiped it across the counter, rinsed it, then repeated what he'd just done.

She ran her hand over it. "It's clean."

"Who cleans on Nerak?"

"Companion units."

"Like Barton?"

"You know Barton?" Her eyes widened. "Mala's companion unit?"

"He's married to Carol, actually. I don't think he knows he's a companion unit, and Carol doesn't seem to care."

"Married?"

Of course, she wouldn't know what married meant. There weren't any men on Nerak. "Joined." She still looked confused. "Took vows. Mated."

"Mated? Ridiculous. I'd heard Barton was . . . different, but mated. It's unheard of."

"Don't tell them. They seem happy enough."

"You will make the cabin clean?" she asked, looking hopeful.

"On Earth, we each do our share." He went to the closet and grabbed the broom, then motioned for her to follow him into the living room. "Brush this back and forth across the floor. It's called sweeping. Aim toward the front door, and when you've done all the room, sweep the dirt outside."

This was about the easiest job he could think to give her. Maybe she wouldn't screw it up.

She arched an eyebrow. "You think I can't do it, don't you?" she asked, correctly reading his thoughts.

He forced himself not to smile. Okay, she was kind of cute, looking very affronted as she stood there with the smudge of dirt still on her face.

"Let's just say I have my doubts."

She grabbed the broom from him. "I can do anything you can do, only better. My race is much more superior than yours." She marched to one corner and began to sweep. When he continued to stare, she stopped. "Are you going to help or just stand there?"

"I'm going, just as soon as I change into dry clothes." He was smiling as he went into his room. He was just careful she didn't see it. He wouldn't want her to think he was starting to like her.

Maybe she wasn't so bad. She only needed to learn how things were done on Earth. She might be from Nerak, but she was in his neck of the woods now.

His grin widened. He could hear her grumbling in the other room. He wondered what was giving her fits now. Whatever it was, at least she was out of his way. He'd get the kitchen cleaned so they'd have a place to eat tonight. He'd worry about the rest of the house later.

Companion units. It must be nice to have someone waiting on you all the time. Every demand met. No wonder she was so uppity. Before Lara left Earth, she'd see how other people lived, and he'd almost bet she wouldn't be the same.

Lara's robe dragged through the dust and dirt she'd swept into a pile and scattered it about—again. How did Earthmen get anything done without getting dirty?

She glanced at the hem of her beautiful green robe and saw how soiled it was getting. Deplorable. She marched to the other room and pulled the top bedcloth back, exposing the clean one beneath it.

After untying her robe, she slipped it off her shoulders and carefully laid it across the bed. She smiled as she went back to the other room. Now at least, she wouldn't ruin it.

There was much more freedom cleaning without clothes to hamper her progress. She would show Sam exactly what she could do, and more!

She had all the dirt in front of the door when she heard a strangled cough from behind her. She turned. Sam stood in the doorway.

"There, it's finished." She glanced around the room. The floor fairly sparkled—she'd done such a wonderful job.

"Where's your dress . . ."—he waved a finger around—"thingy . . . robe, whatchamacallit?" He finally pointed toward her.

She raised an eyebrow. He didn't seem to notice the clean floor. Disappointment filled her. She'd hoped for more. Silly, she knew. After all, he was an Earthman, and she shouldn't care what he thought.

"My robe was getting dirty along the hem, so I removed it."

Her gaze traveled slowly over him, noting the bulge below his waist. It was quite large. Odd. She mentally shook her head.

"Your clothes are quite dirty. Once again, I've proven that I'm superior in my way of thinking," she told him.

"You're naked."

She glanced down. "You're very observant," she said, using his earlier words. "Did you know there's a slight breeze outside? It made my nipples tingle and felt quite pleasant. Not that I would be tempted to stay on Earth because of a breeze."

"You . . . you . . . can't . . ."

She frowned. "There's something wrong with your speech. Are you ill? If you'd like, I can retrieve my diagnostic tool and examine you." He was sweating. Not good. She only hoped she didn't catch what he had.

"You can't go around without clothes," he sputtered. "And I'm not sick."

"Then what are you?"

"Horny!" He marched to the other room, returning in a few minutes with her robe. "You can't go around naked."

"Why not?" She slipped her arms into the robe and belted it.

"It causes a certain reaction inside men."

"What kind of a reaction?"

What an interesting topic. She wanted to know more. Maybe they would be able to have a scientific conversation.

Kia had only talked about battles, and Mala had talked about exploration of other planets, but Sam was actually speaking about something to do with the body. It was a very stimulating discussion.

He ran a hand through his hair. "I'm going to kill Nick," he grumbled. "No one said anything about having to explain the birds and bees."

"And what's so important about these birds and bees?"

He drew in a deep breath. "When a man sees a naked woman, it causes certain reactions inside him."

"Like the bulge in your pants? It wasn't there before."

"Ah, Lord."

"Did my nakedness do that?"

"You're very beautiful."

"But I'm not supposed to think so."

"No, we're not talking about that right now."

She was so confused. Sam wasn't making sense. "Then please explain what we are talking about."

"Sex," he blurted. "When a man sees a beautiful and very sexy naked woman, it causes him to think about having sex with her."

He looked relieved to finally have said so much. She thought about his words for a moment. A companion unit did not have these reactions unless buttons were pushed, and even then, their response would be generic. This was very unusual. But also exciting that her nakedness would make him want to copulate. She felt quite powerful.

And she was also horny now that she knew what the word meant. She untied her robe and opened it. "Then we will join."

He made a strangled sound and coughed again and jerked her robe closed. "No, it's not done like that. Dammit, I'm not a companion unit to perform whenever you decide you need sex."

"But don't you want sex?"

"There are emotions that need to be involved. I'm not one of those guys who jump on top of a woman, gets his jollies, and then goes his own way."

"You want me on top?" She'd never been on top, but she thought she could manage.

He firmly tied her robe, then raised her chin until her gaze met his.

"When I make love with a woman, I want her to know damn well who she's with, and there won't be anything clinical about it." He lowered his mouth to hers.

He was touching her again. She should remind him that it was forbidden to touch a healer. But there was something about his lips against hers, the way he brushed his tongue over them, then delved inside that made her body ache, made her want to lean in closer, made her want to have sex other than just to relieve herself of stress.

When he pulled back, she stumbled forward.

Why had he stopped? She didn't want him to stop. Maybe he remembered that he should ask for permission before he touched her.

She puckered her lips. "You may touch me again."

He gazed into her eyes. His were filled with need. Yes, he would want to copulate now, and she would have the release she required.

He shook his head. "I don't think so. You're not ready."

She nodded her head. "Yes, I'm very ready to have sex."

"But, sweetheart, you're not ready to have sex with me."

"I don't understand."

He studied her face. "When the time is right, then we'll make love, not have sex. There's a big difference." He turned and went back to the other room.

Frustration filled her. An Earthman who did not want to have sex with her, someone of superior intelligence? Ridiculous!

She raised her chin and glared in the direction he'd gone. It didn't matter. She didn't want to copulate with him, either. In fact, the need had already left her.

She bit her bottom lip. Now he had her lying to herself. She wanted to join with Sam very much. Her body burned to feel his touch again.

Temptation wasn't good. Not good at all. The sooner she found a cure for the Elder the better.

Chapter 4

Sam scratched his head. A beautiful woman had just asked him if he wanted to have sex and he'd turned her down. What was wrong with that picture? Had he finally lost his mind? Man, he needed some air.

He stepped out the back door and let the breeze wash over him. It helped only until he remembered Lara had said the light wind had made her nipples tight.

Oh, yeah, she'd been right, too. Her nipples had been hard little nubs, and all he could think about was what they would feel like if he scraped his tongue across them. He closed his eyes, picturing sweeping her into his arms and carrying her to the bedroom, laying her on the bed.

No, no, no.

Dammit, he wasn't a companion unit that could perform at the drop of a hat. When they made love, he wanted her to know exactly who she was having sex with.

He drew in a sharp breath as soon as he realized he was going to make love to her before she went back to Nerak. Gut instinct? Yeah, he was always pretty good at sensing what was going to happen before it happened. It'd kept him and Nick alive more times than he could count.

Besides, a woman who didn't mind walking around naked wouldn't be easy to resist. She might be an alien, but he was only human. Yeah, making love to Lara was pretty much of a gimme.

He'd been having fantasies since he'd watched the holo-gram in Nick and Kia's apartment. Every damned night since then, he'd dreamed about her.

Yeah, he'd gone out on dates with other women since then, but it hadn't worked out. No other woman came close, and it seemed as if he was always comparing them to Lara.

Then he'd met the real Lara, and that had blown his ideal-istic fantasy all to hell. He'd put himself through misery fanta-sizing about someone who thought she was superior to someone from Earth. If it wasn't so sad, he'd laugh.

He turned when he heard a noise behind him.

"The floors are clean, but I don't know what to do to clean myself. Do you have more cloths for that?" Lara asked as she stepped outside and joined him on the back porch.

"I have a shower in the bathroom."

"What's a shower?"

"A thing where you stand under water and get clean." How the hell did one describe taking a shower?

"Show me."

There she went again with the attitude. *That,* he could live without.

"You're frowning," she said.

"I don't doubt it."

"And so you shouldn't. I never lie. Now, show me this de-vice called a shower."

She never lied, she never did any work, she snapped her fingers when she wanted sex . . . . Could he drown someone in a shower? Probably not.

Okay, he'd show her.

For a moment, he pictured himself lathering a washcloth and rubbing it over her high-pointed breasts, her abdomen, slipping down . . . down between her legs . . .

Her skin would have bubble trails, and when he took the nozzle down and sprayed them away . . .

"You have moisture on your face."

He jerked his thoughts back to the present. "I have a feeling I'll sweat a lot while I'm around you," he mumbled. "Come on, and I'll show you how to work the shower." But that's all he'd be showing her.

His bathroom had shrunk considerably. It was difficult to keep from bumping against her. She felt all soft and womanly, and it seemed like a real long time since he'd had a female snuggled next to him.

He cleared his mind, or at least attempted to, and turned on the faucet, tested the water, then hit the shower button. Water streamed from the showerhead.

"Oh, this looks like more fun than our beams of light." She quickly sobered. "Not that it would tempt me to stay on Earth."

"Of course not. Nerak is so much superior," he said with dry sarcasm.

"Yes, exactly!"

"And that's why everyone is leaving."

She pursed her lips. "They'll realize their mistake and return."

"I wouldn't hold my breath if I were you."

Her frown deepened, but he didn't think she looked all that fierce. No, he pretty much had her number. She was all hot air. But cute. And sexy. And he'd better get the hell out of here fast.

"The washcloths are in here, and the towels—drying off cloths—are below. This is soap." He handed her a bottle of body wash.

"I know soap."

"Yeah, I figured that one out fast enough when I returned from fishing. It goes on *you,* not the countertops."

He certainly didn't want to try to explain how she should put some on the cloth and rub it all over her body. Hell, he didn't even want to think about it. "Don't get water on the floor. Make sure you close the curtain."

He hurried out of the room, shutting the door behind him. He stood just outside, catching his breath. Yeah, he was sweating. And he had a killer hard-on. The reason he knew it was a killer—was because he was dying a slow death.

He heard the shower curtain open, then close. Her musical laughter followed. He pictured the water cascading over her luscious body.

He drew in a ragged breath.

No one should get this damn much enjoyment from taking a blasted shower.

Yeah, he was sweating a hell of a lot.

Lara raised her hands upward, laughing when the water washed over her body. This was a good temptation. She poured a good-sized dollop of soap on the cloth and rubbed her face.

And screamed.

Burn!

Pain!

"Owwwww . . ."

The door slammed open, then the shower curtain was shoved back.

"What's the matter?" Sam asked.

"I'm blind! Your soap has made me unable to see!" She wailed. "It's your fault. How can I heal someone if I cannot see?" The pain was unbearable.

"I'm sorry. I forgot to tell you not to get it in your eyes. I'm going to spray water in your face. Close your mouth, and hold your breath."

His words barely penetrated past the burning in her eyes. Would Sam stop the pain? How could he? He wasn't a healer, and his race was inferior. She was doomed.

Water hit her in the face.

And now he was torturing her with what she loved! The cruelty was unbearable.

"Open your eyes."

She shook her head. "Hurts."

"I have to get the soap out of your eyes."

Okay, maybe that did make sense, somewhat. She forced herself to open her eyes. Sam sprayed them. The pain eased, but her eyes still burned.

"Ouch."

He sprayed her off, then wrapped a towel around her hair and one around her body before lifting her in his arms and carrying her to the other room. She sniffed as she rested her head against his chest.

This part was nice. She liked inhaling his scent. And she liked how it felt when he held her close.

He sat in a chair that moved back and forth and spoke in a soothing voice. She didn't know all the words, but she didn't care. She liked the sound of his voice and the way he held her. No one had ever held her like this.

"Feeling better?"

She nodded. "You're not supposed to touch a healer." She sniffed again.

"Want me to stop?"

She shook her head. "Maybe it's not so very wrong to touch a healer. This feels nice."

"Didn't anyone ever rock you when you were little?"

"No."

"What about your mother?"

"We don't have mothers on Nerak."

"You don't come from a test tube already grown." His laugh was shaky. "Do you?"

"Each Nerakian is created in the laboratory, yes. We go to a special place where we are taken care of until we can go to a family unit that has the same DNA. Before that time, we grow and begin instructions on what we will do on Nerak. After we have learned the basics, we go to our family units where we grow into adulthood.

"In our structure, we have Elders who rule, and those before us with our DNA, we call grandmother. If one should pass, then the oldest living is grandmother. My sister is now grandmother."

"I'm sorry."

She moved until she could look into his eyes. "But why? This is a very efficient way to attain adulthood. Each Nerakian is well taken care of. We don't have the wars that Earth has, or disease, or overpopulation. Our society is pure."

"And yet you've never been held like this."

She laid her head against his chest once again, heard the steady rhythm of his heart. It was a soothing sound.

"No. Nerakians are not demonstrative. We bond in other ways. It's different here?"

"In my family, we hugged a lot. Still do."

She closed her eyes and tried to imagine what it would've been like to hug Kia. No, she couldn't see it. Kia was a code enforcer, a warrior. Kia wouldn't have liked hugging. Although she hadn't seemed to mind Nick hugging her.

But Kia would never hug a healer. It just wasn't natural . . . and would upset the balance of everything. And yet, here she was letting Sam hold her.

Now that she thought about it, her whole equilibrium did feel out of sync. No wonder her emotions warred inside her. She'd let this human who was so much inferior get inside her head.

Temptation.

This was exactly what the Elders had warned her about. Already she'd enjoyed the water and a man's kiss. And now this. What other traps would she have to overcome?

"Feeling better?" Sam asked.

She scooted out of his arms and stood. "Yes . . . thank you."

He smiled, and she knew it was because she'd remembered to thank him.

"You're welcome," he said.

She arched an eyebrow. "Knowing some of your phrases might be useful. I'm only adapting while I'm here so I don't bring attention to myself."

His heated gaze slowly moved over her, leaving her body tingling with pleasure. Apparently, being naked or partially naked wasn't appropriate since he looked at her with heat in his eyes. Nakedness on Nerak wasn't that important. You wore clothes, or you didn't. It was as easy as that, and no one thought anything about one's choice.

Sam must be horny again.

"I'll dress now." She went to the room she had chosen and closed the door, then leaned against it. Her body tingled from head to foot. She would meditate and restore the balance within herself.

She opened the carrier that Sam had brought in earlier. Her mind needed to be cleansed to rid herself of the . . . the . . . horniness *she* felt.

She placed her meditation rug on the floor, then donned her white robe. Already, she felt better. The shimmering transparency whispered around her. Next, she pulled out a scenting stick from her special packet.

The sweet aroma from the stick drifted up to her. She inhaled. This was nice. The aroma reminded her of the air that was here at Sam's cabin when she was outside—fresh and clean.

She snapped it in two and laid it on either side of the rug, then sat with legs crossed.

Calmness stole over her as she began to softly hum to herself. This was much better. She hadn't meditated all day. A good healer meditated at least four to five times a day. Her mind, body, and spirit grew stronger as they converged. Her sense of completeness strengthened.

She floated above the rug as her spirit began to separate from her body. She saw Sam still sitting in the rocker in the other room, but she didn't linger. She needed spiritual cleansing.

She rose above the cabin, above the trees. If only she could travel as far as Nerak, but that wasn't possible. Instead, she looked down upon the trees, passed over a half-circle of buildings that were not far from the cabin. She rose to the sky, felt the warmth from Earth's sun.

Peace enveloped her, and with it came the strength to resist.

Her mission was to find the plant that would cure the Elder. She would not forget her quest. She was beyond the temptation of the flesh.

She was Lara.

A healer.

She was superior.

Chapter 5

Sam wondered what Lara could be doing in her room. He glanced at the clock. Hell, she'd been in there for three hours, and he hadn't heard a peep out of her. Just humming every once in a while.

He'd never thought to ask Kia about Nerakian rituals. He hoped like hell she hadn't made a doll of him and was sticking pins in it. He rolled his right shoulder in a circle. Come to think about it, he did have kind of a twinge.

Nah, she wouldn't do anything like that. He was almost positive. It was time to find out just what she was doing, though. Dinner was ready. Not much. Just sandwiches, chips, and the last of the sodas. He'd brought lunchmeat and the other stuff in his ice chest.

He looked toward the guest room again. Maybe he should check on her. Make sure she was okay. Not that he thought she could get into a lot of trouble in the guest room.

He tapped lightly on the door.

Nothing.

He tapped again.

Silence.

This was ridiculous. She could've tripped or something. Hit her head, maybe. He wouldn't put anything past her. After all, she was from Nerak.

He turned the knob and eased the door open. It smelled

good inside. She must've sprayed some kind of perfume. It was kind of sweet like . . .

Ah, crap.

He closed his eyes, counted to three, then opened them.

She was floating. There wasn't a damn thing holding her up that he could see. He was tempted to wave a broom handle under her just to see if she was putting one over on him. He had a feeling she wasn't.

Okay, he knew Mala could read emotions and Kia could zap something and make it disappear, but this was . . . was . . .

Take a deep breath. Inhale, exhale.

It didn't help. Her eyes were closed, and she was sitting with her legs crossed, and she was still about a foot off the floor.

Man, when she meditated, she meditated.

It was unnerving as hell.

Okay, get over it. She wasn't human; she was an alien. He'd known that from the start. She would never be like women on Earth.

There was something strange about looking at a woman who floated above the floor. She must be in a really deep trance. He noticed how still she was. Like a statue.

Was she breathing?

His gaze moved over her. She wore a white, gauzy robe thing that sparkled and shimmered. And it was transparent. Real transparent. He could see her rosy-tipped breasts, and looking at her started an ache deep down inside him.

But yeah, she was breathing. At least he knew she was alive.

He had two choices. Either he could close the door, or he could stand there and stare until she came out of her trance. Right now, staring looked like a pretty good choice.

He was beyond pathetic. Ahh, but what a fantastic view. He had a feeling she wouldn't appreciate his ogling her, though. His stomach growled, reminding him it had been a long time since lunch, and he made up his mind. He figured she was probably hungry, too. He didn't want to disturb her, though.

"Are you ready to eat?" he whispered.

She landed on the floor with a thud. Her eyes flew open. She seemed startled. Then she saw him.

He smiled. "I thought you might be hungry."

"You disturbed my transcendental meditation." She glared at him.

"That's what you call . . ." He waved his arm. "Floating in the air and everything."

"No, that's called floating in the air. Transcendental meditation is when I leave my body."

"You were outside your body? Where did you go?" He'd heard of stuff like that and wondered if people could really do that sort of thing. The possibilities would be endless. No more standing in line to get tickets for the football game. He could hover right above the field. "Can you teach me?"

She arched a mocking eyebrow. Man, aliens could get really testy. He'd only asked a simple question.

"Apparently, you wanted something since you disturbed me," she said, changing the subject.

"Dinner is ready."

"Dinner?"

"Yeah, you know—food."

She closed her eyes. "I don't eat."

"You're pulling my leg." Everyone ate. Even aliens had to eat. Kia ate.

"I take food capsules, and I assure you, I didn't pull your leg."

"Figure of speech," he explained. "You mean to tell me you don't eat anything? Not even a cracker now and then?"

"No."

"Well, if you change your mind, there's a sandwich with your name on it in the kitchen." He closed the door as he left.

Lara thought her planet was so much better than Earth, but they didn't hug, they didn't eat, they didn't even have water. Sex was with a robot. He didn't see anything so damn perfect about it. Sounded weird to him.

He went back to the kitchen and sat at the table. He'd finished half his sandwich when he heard Lara moving about. She went to the bathroom, the water came on, then off. When she entered the kitchen, she wore her green robe again.

A shame. He liked the transparent white one better.

"Change your mind?" he asked.

"No. I was curious to see what food looked like." She sat across from him and picked up the slice of bread, looking under it, then looked at his half-eaten sandwich before curling her lip in distaste. "It doesn't smell good. What is it?"

She was sexy as hell, vulnerable at times, and curious. He could handle all that. It was the damn condescension that drove him crazy. Right now, she was being very condescending.

"It's mayo, ham, and cheese between two slices of bread."

"And this will sustain life?"

"Yeah, if it doesn't clog your arteries and kill you, but I figure everyone's gotta die sometime or other."

She picked up a chip and turned it over, then put it back down.

"What's ham?"

"It comes from pigs."

"Which are?"

"Small animals."

Her eyes widened. "Like the ones at Kia's?"

"No." Damn, what did she take him for? "Those are puppies. We don't eat dogs."

She cocked an eyebrow. "Only other small animals."

"Do you know that you can take something really simple and make it complicated?"

She crossed her arms in front of her. "I'm only trying to understand."

"Your sister likes food well enough."

"She has given in to temptation. I'm stronger."

"You seemed to like water well enough."

Her mouth opened, then snapped closed. Yeah, he figured that would shut her up.

"I have to succumb to some of Earth's temptations. My survival depends on it, and it's imperative that I keep my body free from germs. I'm a healer."

"So you've told me." He was thoughtful for a moment. "Kia never mentioned hospitals or anything like that on Nerak. Just how many people have you healed anyway?"

"None. Nerak is perfect. People don't get sick."

"A doctor without patients. That must be a hard pill to swallow. Makes your job all but obsolete."

She twined her fingers in her lap. "I'm very knowledgeable about healing."

He'd hit a soft spot. And now he felt guilty. Why the hell did he take jabs at her anyway? "But now you have an Elder to heal."

She visibly relaxed. "Yes, I do have that."

He glanced out the window. "Tomorrow, I'll show you some of the plants."

Her gaze followed his. The color drained from her face. "Darkness is descending. We're going to die!" Lara jumped from her seat and ran to the window.

Now what the hell was going on? "No, the sun is only going down." He joined her. "The sun will rise in the morning. Doesn't it get dark on Nerak?"

She shook her head. "We have two suns which rotate opposite each other. The light never goes out." She looked up at him. "Are you sure it will return?"

"Positive."

She nodded, then reached into the voluminous folds of her robe and brought out a packet. He noticed the slight tremble in her hands.

"I thought you didn't eat."

"It's a relaxation smoothie."

"You just do drugs." If he lived on Nerak, he'd probably do drugs, too.

She gave him a confused look. "You have something I can mix it in?"

"Sure." He reached into the cabinet and gave her a glass. "Knock yourself out."

"I don't think I'd want to knock myself out." She frowned. "Is that another figure of speech?"

"Yeah." He leaned a hip against the counter and watched her as she stirred liquid from another packet into the powder. She had pretty hands with long, slender fingers.

He should go back to the table, sit on the porch, or something, but his feet might as well have been glued to the spot because they weren't moving.

She took a drink of her smoothie, closing her eyes. From the look of pure enjoyment on her face, it must taste pretty good. Damn, she was so beautiful.

Man, he was wading in deep water here. Maybe he *should* go sit on the porch. "Is there anything else you need?" he asked before he left.

She sighed. "I'm horny."

He laughed and choked at the same time. She handed him her smoothie, and he automatically took a big gulp.

"Better?" she asked.

"Yeah." He cleared his throat and reminded himself he'd have to watch the words he used. Kia would kill him. Then again, he was almost sure he'd heard her use some pretty colorful language. Nick was certainly no saint.

"Aren't you horny, too?" she asked.

Her voice suddenly seemed to come from a long way off. He tried to clear his head, but he couldn't. Heat traveled through his veins, warming every inch of his body. Ah, crap, the smoothie was probably spiked with Nerakian drugs. But he'd only taken a drink, a big one, but only one, for Pete's sake.

He looked at her. She acted as if she was waiting for him to say something. Oh, yeah, she'd asked if he was horny. Sex would be good. He'd been horny since he saw her in the hologram months ago.

What the hell was he thinking? She was an alien. Not human. Anything could happen if he had sex with an alien. Ah, man, she was really hot, though. Apparently, sex with Kia hadn't hurt Nick. As far as he knew, nothing had fallen off. Still, it paid to be cautious.

"We just met," he finally said, feeling as if he was doing some kind of role reversal.

She sighed. "You have strange customs on Earth." She untied her robe and parted it. "Don't you want to touch me?"

Ah, Lord, there was that luscious body again. He swallowed past the lump in his throat. "I thought I wasn't supposed to touch a healer?" he croaked.

"I think we would both benefit. I'm curious to see how a human has sex."

"I'm not a research subject that you can test."

What the hell was she trying to do to him? Drive him insane? Maybe he'd already lost his mind. The walls of the cabin had taken on a deep purple color swirled with pinks and reds.

What had happened to the knotty pine?

Amazing. He felt as if he was at one of those laser light shows. He reached out to touch the walls. The colors floated toward him. They were warm, too.

His gaze moved back to Lara as she slipped off her robe and walked toward the guest room.

"I was hoping you would want to copulate." Her sigh was long and deep.

He shook his head to try to clear it. Didn't work. "Hey," he called, trailing after her.

She stopped in the living room and turned to face him. "Yes."

He couldn't speak. Not one damn word. Nope, he could only stare. She was perfect. At least, as close to perfect as he'd ever seen. High-pointed breasts, gently rounded hips, flat stomach, a thatch of blond curls . . . he'd never seen a true blond. He was fascinated, staring at those curls. He wanted to run his fingers through them and see if they were as soft as they looked.

"Did you change your mind about having sex?"

It took a minute for her words to register. When they did, he could only nod. Hell, he was human. Right now, he didn't give a damn what she was.

"Good." Her smile brightened the room.

She walked the rest of the way to the bedroom, then turned again at the doorway.

"Are you coming?"

Not yet, but he planned to.

He obediently followed. *You alien, me slave.*

"Don't think," his dick said.

No, his dick couldn't talk. Could it?

Hell, after the smoothie, he wasn't sure about anything anymore. His brain had definitely quit functioning.

He watched as she pulled the covers back on the bed and moved to the middle of the mattress, where she lay back and spread her legs.

"I'm ready to experience intercourse with a human."

He laughed.

She frowned.

Oh, God, he'd probably just blown his chance for hot sex.

Chapter 6

Whatever the hell was in that smoothie, it was doing a number on his head. Maybe this was all some weird dream or something.

He closed his eyes, took a deep breath, then opened them again.

Lara sat up in bed. "Have you changed your mind again?" She was clearly exasperated.

"Oh, honey, I haven't changed my mind. But haven't you ever heard of foreplay?"

"I don't know what you're referring to."

"Well, you're about to find out." He unbuttoned his shirt and tossed it, except instead of dropping to the floor, it just sort of hung in the air for a few seconds before drifting downward. Oh, God, that was so cool.

His gaze moved back to her. She didn't even seem to notice the neat trick with his shirt. Her attention was all on him. Okay, that was pretty cool, too. She watched without embarrassment as he stripped. She seemed curious and not the least bit embarrassed. Not that he thought she would be.

"You did say you've had sex before, didn't you?"

Hadn't she mentioned her own personal companion unit? It cracked him up just thinking about them.

He hoped she told him she had one. If not, he was going to

be in a world of hurt. He wouldn't have to just take a cold shower—hell, he'd have to spend the night in one.

"We have companion units," she told him. "If we find the need to relax, then we have sex with them."

He toed off his boots, then unfastened his pants and pushed them downward.

"They perform quite adequately."

He just bet they did. As long as she didn't try to rate his performance against that of a machine, he'd be okay. He shoved his briefs down.

"Oh, you aren't built quite the same as my companion unit. You're quite large."

A thrill went through him. Okay, he was pathetic, and he knew it. But hell, it was kind of nice to know he was appreciated.

"Do you vibrate?"

"Do I . . ." Ah, crap, there went his short ego trip. "No, I don't vibrate." He moved to the bed. He'd bet the companion unit did, though.

"I won't hold that against you. After all, you're only human."

That was a challenge if ever he heard one, and a Texan never backed away when the gloves were thrown down. He didn't care that the bedroom had turned purple all of a sudden. He wasn't too drugged that he couldn't make love to a beautiful woman.

She lay back and closed her eyes, spreading her legs again. "I'm ready."

He grinned as he moved next to her. "You think so?"

She opened her eyes. "Are you not ready? Is there some ritual that you must perform before you can have sex?"

"You could say that." He leaned forward and brushed his lips against hers. "You taste sweet."

"Your lips are . . . warm. I rather liked the touching of lips earlier and when you stuck your tongue in my mouth. Can we do that again?"

"That and a whole lot more." He brushed his lips across hers again, then dragged his tongue over them before delving inside and more fully tasting what she offered.

Her hands wrapped around his neck and pulled him closer. Nerakian women weren't so different from Earth women, after all. It would seem they both had the same basic instincts, and when she began to massage the back of his neck, waves of delicious heat washed over him.

Man, she tasted hot. And the lights were still swirling even when he closed his eyes. Sweet, so damned sweet. He stroked her tongue with his, cupped the side of her face, then twined his fingers in her hair.

When he finally ended the kiss, she moaned in protest.

"Please don't stop. I enjoyed your tongue inside my mouth very much."

"It's called kissing."

"Then kiss me again."

"Okay." But rather than kissing her mouth, he dropped a kiss on one tight little nipple. She immediately arched her back with a gasp of pleasure.

"And do you like when I kiss you there?"

"Yes," she moaned. "Don't stop."

"Oh, baby, I don't plan to." He lowered his head again, sucking her breast inside his mouth, scraping his tongue across her nipple, then moved to the other side.

"My companion unit never did this," she managed to say. "My body feels as if it's on fire—but a good kind of heat. It doesn't burn."

"Just wait. I'll make you burn for me, baby."

She moaned, her eyes closing.

Oh, yeah, he'd make her burn.

It was difficult to maintain his control. Her body begged for satisfaction. All he wanted was to fit himself between her legs and plunge into the heat of her body again and again.

But he didn't want to stop exploring. He liked the little

panting sounds she made. And maybe he wanted her to see what a real man could do.

He slipped his hand downward and tangled his fingers in her curls. He was right—they felt just as soft and silky as they looked.

"Sam," she whimpered.

"What?" he whispered as he moved to his knees between her legs. Damn, she was beautiful as she lay spreadeagled before him. His gaze worked its way downward. Past the dark areolas of her full breasts, the hard nipples.

He leaned forward, tugging the nipples between his thumbs and forefingers, rolling them between his fingers before cupping them in his hands and massaging. "Do you like that?"

She nodded. "Yes." That one breathy word almost made him come. It was the way she'd said it. The way he knew she'd never experienced what he was giving her. But he wanted more from her.

"I want to hear you say it. Tell me you don't want me to stop."

"Don't . . . stop."

"But I have to."

"No . . . please."

"There's much more of you that I want to touch, to kiss, to taste."

"I need you inside me . . . now. My body aches for you. Please, Sam."

"Just a minute more." He brushed his fingers back and forth through her curls.

She moaned her despair until he flicked his finger across the fleshy part of her sex. She fisted her hands in the bedsheet.

"A woman is never as sexy as she is in the throes of passion," he murmured as he lowered his head and placed a kiss on her mound before running his tongue over her clit. "You taste sweet." He sucked her inside his mouth, sliding his hands beneath her bottom and bringing her closer to him.

She began to whimper, then tremble as she climaxed against his mouth.

He eased her to the bed, noting the lights flashing above his head. That smoothie was something else.

He quickly slid a condom on, then slowly entered her. Ah, man, she was so friggin' tight. As he slid deeper, moist heat enveloped him. He closed his eyes, letting out his breath as he lost himself in exquisite pleasure.

"I'm not hurting you, am I?"

"No, Sam, this is good. More. I want more."

"It's only going to get better." He thrust deeper, then pulled back, then dipped inside again only to pull back out. Her legs wrapped around his waist, and he sank further inside the tightness of her body.

This was sweet. Damn, it was so sweet.

She clenched her inner muscles, and he almost came. No, not yet. Sweat broke out on his forehead. His breathing became ragged as he fought to hold back. Pain and pleasure ripped through him at the same time.

"Now, Sam, now!"

That was what he was waiting for. What he needed to hear. He plunged faster and faster. Her body trembled; she stiffened and cried out.

He couldn't hold back any longer. He growled when the first wave of his orgasm crashed over him. His body shook with the force of his release.

Lights swirled around them, the heat washing over them, settling on them, momentarily binding them together. And then he was collapsing and rolling to the side, taking her with him.

He felt her tears land on him. He swallowed past the sudden lump in his throat. Damn, he hadn't meant to be so rough.

"Did I hurt you?"

She fiercely shook her head. "No. It's just that this has never happened before. I didn't know it could be like this. It will be difficult to leave this behind when I return to Nerak."

He brushed his lips across her forehead. "But you don't have to leave tomorrow."

She was quiet for a moment. "No, I think we'll have sex many times before I leave."

Chapter 7

Aasera stood outside staring up at the night, a worried
frown marring her features as she looked toward the
west. She'd seen the light. A swirling of bright colors. What
was worse—she was pretty sure what it meant.

Why now? It had been thirty years since she'd had any
contact with Nerak.

A rustle of leaves startled her. She whirled around.

"Sorry. I should've made my presence known sooner,"
Lyraka said. "You usually know when someone is approaching."

And she would've known this time if she hadn't been so
shocked by what she'd seen. "Did you see the lights?" she
asked.

Lyraka nodded. "That's why I came outside." She hesitated.

Aasera knew what she was thinking but waited for Lyraka
to speak her thoughts.

"Nerakian? I remember you telling me about the pretty
lights that swirled above when a Nerakian felt intense pleasure."

"Maybe." She drew in a deep breath. "I hope not."

"Do you think whoever it is knows you're here? An Elder
possibly?"

"No, they've let me be as long as I didn't bring notice to

myself. Besides, too many years have passed. I'm old. I'm not a threat."

Something close to regret filled her as she thought about all that had been left behind. Her home, her people. Being constantly drenched in the warmth from the sun. Never feeling the cold seeping into her body.

She quickly got hold of the emotion. No regrets. That's what she'd said when her decision was made, and she hadn't regretted it, not really.

But sometimes she longed for her home, her people. The ones she'd given up.

A tender smile lifted Lyraka's mouth. "You're not old. You're only fifty-one by Earth's years. Your hair is still the same soft brown color I remember as a child, and you don't even have wrinkles. I see other women look at you with envy." She glanced toward where the lights had been. "Surely it isn't an Elder."

Aasera looked at the blanket of stars in the night sky. "I angered them so much." Pain washed over her as she remembered the fear and the disgrace. She'd been so full of herself back then—invincible. Nothing could touch her; nothing could bring her down. She was an interplanetary traveler, and there were so few of them. The elite.

No, she'd been above falling for the temptations of other planets. She'd thought as long as she had the freedom to explore, she would always return to her roots. Her ego had been bigger than Nerak. When she fell, she'd fallen hard.

"The colony isn't in danger, is it?" Lyraka asked, clasping her arms around her middle as she looked in the direction where the lights had been.

"I don't know."

She'd begun the colony years earlier. There were almost forty people living here: psychics, mediums, spiritualists, healers, painters, sculptors, and writers. And her. She blended well with them. No one suspected she was from another planet. Lyraka was the only one who knew everything.

They were quiet, unassuming. No one bothered them here in their little part of the world. She'd made sure the people in the colony stayed just active enough in the surrounding communities that no one thought that much about them.

She knew all the neighbors. It paid to be cautious even after the passing of so many years. Ranches bordered each side of the colony. Except for one small piece of property.

The owner rarely visited the lone cabin. She'd already guessed it was a vacation home. The man had never been trouble. Other than fishing, he left the animals alone, which was good. She would've hated to see harm come to the deer and smaller creatures.

He hadn't worried her—until now.

"Tomorrow, I'll see what's going on," Lyraka suggested.

A moment of panic washed over her. No, it wasn't Lyraka's responsibility to protect. Aasera had created the crisis when she chose to stay on Earth. It was up to her to fix any problems that arose.

"I'll be careful," Lyraka promised.

"No, I can't place you in danger."

"You're not. No one suspects I'm anything other than what I appear to be." Lyraka smiled. "I'm always careful. You've taught me well, Mother."

She was right, of course. Her daughter was born of two worlds. Nerak and Earth. She had a little of both inside her. The black hair and luminous shade of pale blue eyes of her Earthling father. Aasera still remembered how she'd been drawn to his eyes. She'd been caught in a trap by those eyes. The eyes of a father who refused to accept a child.

But Lyraka had gotten some of her attributes as well. A need to explore every chance she got. Having an adventurous daughter was not always a good thing.

And the gifts. She'd gotten those as well.

The mixing of DNA should have weakened her Nerakian strengths, but it hadn't. No, it had made them stronger.

Much stronger.

"Keep your distance until we know for sure," Aasera finally said, giving her permission. "Don't make contact. Not yet."

Aasera's worried gaze traveled once more toward the fading lights. Fear coursed through her veins. That, and excitement. It had been a long, long time since she'd been around her people, much too long.

Chapter 8

Lara yawned and stretched as she came awake. A warm, fuzzy feeling enveloped her. She had never slept as soundly as she had last night. A smile curved her lips. Who knew sex could be so good? She rolled to her side and rose on one elbow, staring at the man beside her.

Sam's breathing was even as he continued to sleep. He was a handsome Earthman. She studied his face, noting the growth of hair that wasn't there yesterday. It gave him a different look: rough and very male. She thought she rather liked this look on him as well.

What would it feel like? She brushed her hand lightly across the hairs. He wiggled his nose and rubbed his face. She jerked her hand away.

Sam continued to sleep.

Her gaze moved down his body. Hair grew on his chest as well. He had a nice chest, too, broad and muscular. It rose and fell with each respiration.

The sheet covered the lower half of his body. She glanced at his face. He continued to sleep. Purely research, she told herself as she carefully raised the cover and moved it downward.

He'd shrunk!

Not fair!

Disappointment filled her.

She eased to her knees and stared at his genitals. He wasn't small like her companion unit. Still, Sam looked . . . limp and all shriveled up.

Had she damaged him last night? It would be such a shame if she had.

Maybe there was a button he pushed to make it grow. That's what she did with her companion unit. One to make it grow and another to make it vibrate. Her unit hadn't grown nearly as large as Sam had, though.

She lightly touched it, and his penis jerked.

It was alive!

Did it have a brain all its own? Surely it did, otherwise how could it get larger when Sam was clearly still asleep?

She sat back on her heels and stared as Sam's penis began to get larger.

He groaned and pulled the cover up to his neck, then rolled away from her.

It would seem her research was at an end. She sighed. She had wanted to examine him a little longer, but she didn't think he'd appreciate her disturbing his sleep.

Another time then. She eased out of bed and went to the bathing room, pulling on another green robe after she'd finished with her daily ablutions.

At least Sam hadn't been damaged last night by the intensity of their sexual intercourse. Little bumps formed on her arms. She glanced at them. How odd. Was it an anticipatory response? Maybe. She did want to experience sex with Sam again.

For a moment, she leaned against the bathing room door and closed her eyes. Her nipples grew hard as she remembered the way Sam had squeezed them between his fingers, then lightly tugged on them. She grew damp just thinking about his tongue on her sex, his tongue caressing her, sucking her inside his mouth.

When she pushed away from the door and left the bathing room, her body trembled. There were some things about this planet that were good, she admitted. Companion units only performed as they were programmed, and there was no one left from the time when there were members of the male species on Nerak. The Elders who were now in charge could only rely on what was written in the ancient books.

Apparently, there had been nothing written about sex.

What a shame.

She went through the cabin, giving the kitchen a cursory glance as she went out the back door. She stopped on what Sam referred to as a porch. For a moment, she could only stare at the magnificence before her. Earth's sun was rising above the horizon with a burst of orange and gold.

Her breath caught in her throat as she sat on the top step. She would never admit to anyone that she'd been more than a little nervous as she'd traveled with Sam to his cabin.

Kia had assured her that Sam was a good man. He was still a man, though. She thought she now knew why the Elders had warned her to keep her distance.

But it wasn't just that she was with a man. The landscape was so different here, and as they had been driving through what Kia had called Dallas, she'd noticed there were so many people moving along the walkways. It would be easy to get lost, to become insignificant.

But as she watched the sun rise in the sky, she knew it might be worth it if you could wake up each day with this magnificent view.

Sam woke up feeling better than he had in a long time. He slowly opened his eyes. He was at the cabin. That was why he felt relaxed. No, there was more than just being here that had him feeling so fantastic.

His memory returned in a flash of naked skin, Lara's killer body, and the explosive sex they'd shared. He flung the covers back and sat on the side of the bed. He should feel guilty as hell, but he didn't. He felt satisfied. Very satisfied.

Lara said it would be hard for her to leave—hell, it'd be

just as difficult watching her go. Not only was she starting to grow on him, but he'd never had mindblowing sex like this before.

Must've been that smoothie. Why else would he see flashing lights?

This was just great. It probably had some kind of hallucinogenic added in. And probably illegal as hell. Now he was harboring a criminal. The hole just got deeper and deeper.

He was going to kill Nick when he saw him. Sam had known Lara would only be trouble.

But the sex had been excellent. Man, he got hard just thinking about it. He wasn't about to pack her up and take her back to Kia's. It wasn't as if she could cause too much mischief stuck way out here in the middle of nowhere . . . he hoped.

Speaking of trouble, where was she?

He pulled on jeans and a T-shirt and padded barefoot through the house, making a pit stop at the bathroom. He finished and picked up the search again, frowning when he didn't find her in the living room. She wasn't in the kitchen, either.

He went to the back door and glanced out.

Not many things in life affected him. He'd seen enough working the streets of Dallas as an undercover cop that there wasn't a lot that unnerved him—he supposed he would be considered hardened—but seeing the enthrallment on Lara's face, so much enjoyment reflected in that one expression as she watched the sun rise in the east, really got to him.

Had she never seen a sunrise? Probably—she said they had two suns on Nerak. But he'd bet his last dollar she'd never seen one like this.

As if sensing he was there, she looked over her shoulder, met his gaze, and smiled. "Another temptation," she grudgingly admitted.

One corner of his mouth lifted—he'd like to think he was another one.

"I love the sunsets and sunrises here. The peace and quiet is so different from the city."

She sighed. "It's beautiful."

"Sorry I disturbed you, but I needed coffee."

"What's coffee?"

"A drink. It wakes me up."

Her eyes widened. "Are you still asleep?"

He laughed. "No. It makes me more alert."

"We have smoothies for that."

He frowned. "Now that you mention it, what was in that one I drank last night?"

She shrugged. "I could explain, but you don't know our chemicals so you wouldn't understand." She stood. "I'll sit with you while you have your coffee, then we'll look for plants. I must start testing them so that I can find a cure."

A cure, and she would leave; then maybe his life would get back to normal. He had a feeling his life would never be normal again.

"I enjoyed sex with you very much last night. I'd like to taste you the next time we copulate, though," she said conversationally as she walked past him, then opened the screen and walked inside.

His body jerked in response. She really had a way with words.

"Aren't you going to have coffee?" she asked from the kitchen.

"Yeah, I'll be in there in a minute." Deep breaths. Slow and easy. He cleared his mind of the image that shot through his brain. Complete control.

Okay, he could do this. How hard would it be to act as if he didn't want to scoop her up and carry her to the bedroom where they would make mad, passionate love for the rest of the day? The lady already had a superiority complex, and he damn sure didn't want to add to it.

He went inside and pulled filters and coffee down from the

cabinet. His gaze met hers. How could she look so innocent yet . . . he mentally shook his head to clear it. "Are all Nerakians this casual about sex?"

"Is there a reason we should deny ourselves pleasure? Or not talk about the pleasures we experience?"

"You give new meaning to locker room discussions." He shrugged. "We just don't talk about it that much here."

"Why not?"

He added water to the coffeemaker and turned to face her as he waited for that first cup. Man, he really needed a lot of caffeine so he could get awake.

"I guess some people might. It happened last night, and this is a new day, I guess."

She nodded. "I can understand this. But I really liked when you touched me and kissed me. Even now, I want to have sex."

It was all he could do to breathe. His body reacted immediately to her words.

"Oh, good, you aren't broken. When I looked at you this morning, I thought you might be. It was quite flaccid." Her eyebrows drew together. "Although you started to stiffen when I touched you."

He coughed. "You what?"

"I looked beneath the covers. I've never seen a naked human, and I wanted a closer look. Last night, I was too excited to take the time to examine you. And later, I was quite worn out from the orgasms I had."

He had to keep reminding himself that she wasn't from Earth. Sex didn't mean the same thing.

"But we can't have sex now," she continued. "I must find a cure, and that's where my duty lies."

All he could think about was untying the sash and stripping her robe from her body and having sex again.

"You don't mind that I studied you, do you?" she asked.

God, he needed coffee bad, but it was still dripping into the carafe.

"People don't examine other people when they're . . . when they're vulnerable." He didn't like the thought of what else she might do when he was asleep. A whole different kind of ache started down low. He almost reached down to make sure everything was still intact.

"I'll examine you when you're awake then. Tonight, we'll have sex again after I've studied your plants."

It wasn't a question. It was more of a command. He started to tell her they *might* make love or they *might not,* but he knew damn well he'd be lucky if he lasted until nightfall. It was going to be a very long day.

"I'm ready," Lara said as she came out of the bedroom still wearing her green robe.

"I thought you were changing," Sam told her. What the hell had she been doing in there for the last hour?

"I meditated so that my mind and body would be in sync. It's better if I'm in complete harmony. And I also asked the ones who've passed before me to guide me in this journey of healing."

He raised an eyebrow. "Did they speak back?" He glanced around the room. The last thing he wanted was a bunch of ghosts popping out of the woodwork.

"Of course they didn't." She looked at him like he had the brain of a bug.

"Well, you can't wear that into the woods. All you'll find are a lot of brambles and sticks stuck in the hem of your robe. Didn't Kia send a suitcase of clothes?"

"My robes are a symbol of who I am. All healers wear green robes, or white if they're meditating. Sometimes other colors because we can, but mostly green."

"Or nothing at all if you want."

"Yes, of course. I often go naked. The temperature on our planet is quite pleasant."

Why the hell had he mentioned her going naked? Now he

had a vision of her traipsing through the woods without a stitch of clothes. And worse, he wasn't that far behind her. Adam and Evil.

No, it was his thoughts that were evil, not Lara. He was discovering how open and honest she was. Not something he was used to.

His gaze moved over her. "If you don't want to ruin your clothes or scratch your legs, then I'd suggest you wear what Kia sent."

She looked as if she wanted to argue but apparently decided against it. "I'll change."

Sam didn't think she looked too happy, but it was for her own good. He went to the front door and looked out. It was going to be a nice day.

If he'd been here alone, he would already be fishing or just taking a morning walk through the woods. Deer were plentiful in the area. There used to be a ten-point buck that hung around. A beautiful animal.

"Okay. I'm ready," Lara said.

He went back inside, then had to bite the insides of his cheeks to keep from laughing. He probably should've laid her out some clothes.

"Is this good for the woods? It's quite pretty."

She wore a long gown of shimmering gold. He had a feeling Kia had never packed for the woods. Hell, she probably had no idea what the woods were.

"You look beautiful, but no, that won't do, either." When she looked crestfallen, he continued. "Come on. I'll help you find something."

They went back to the guest room, and he dug around in the suitcase until he finally came up with a pair of jeans, tennis shoes, and a T-shirt. Kia had packed thongs—oh, God, thongs—but no bras—oh, God, no bras. He swallowed past the lump in his throat.

Okay, he could handle this. Lara didn't have to wear a bra.

Hell, it was just the two of them in the middle of nowhere anyway.

He handed her the clothes, explained what went on first, then went back to the other room. If he stayed in there very much longer, they wouldn't be looking for plants until this afternoon.

She was frowning when she rejoined him. "This isn't comfortable. The pants are binding."

He turned around. Oh, man, he probably should've let her wear the robe. The jeans fit her like a second skin, and the T-shirt didn't even meet the waistband. There was a nice expanse of creamy skin and a cute little belly button showing. And the shirt fit snugly. There was just a little bit of a bounce when she moved, and her nipples poked against the material.

"Oh, you're horny again," she commented.

Kia was going to kill him for teaching her some of Earth's more colorful language.

He cleared his throat. "Sit, and I'll tie your tennis shoes."

"Have I mentioned how very pleased I am to see you weren't damaged last night?"

"Yes. Do you think we could talk about something else?"

"Why?"

"Because if we don't change the subject, I might just pick you up and carry you to the bedroom."

"But I'm not tired."

He shook his head. "Baby, we wouldn't be sleeping."

Dawning shined in her eyes. "I think I'm horny, too." She bit her bottom lip as if she was worrying over a big problem. "I need to start researching plants so that I can find a cure, though."

"Then we'd better get started."

She nodded but glanced regretfully one last time toward the bedroom.

The quicker he walked off his horniness, the better. He grabbed a bag to put samples in, and they left the cabin.

They hadn't walked far when Lara pointed toward some flowering ground cover. "What's that?"

"I don't know very many of the plants by name, but I think that's called phlox."

She pulled some and ran a scanner of sorts over it, then handed it to him so he could put it in the bag.

"What are you doing?"

"I'm checking to see if it might be compatible with the chemicals I brought with me. Our chemicals will cause a reaction. From that, I can produce a remedy."

"But don't you need a certain kind of plant? Like foxglove is a plant that works on the heart—if you know what you're doing. It's also very dangerous."

She shook her head. "No, the chemical reactions will tell me if it's safe or not. You forget, we're far more advanced."

There she went again, but he chose to ignore her words.

As they walked deeper into the woods, her gaze roamed the area. She collected and dropped samples inside the bag until it was full.

A couple of hours had passed when the hairs on the back of his neck began to tingle. A couple of times, he'd caught a flash of something moving. Deer? No, gut instinct told him someone followed them, but whoever it was, the guy was good. So far, all he'd seen was a brief flash of movement.

His gun was locked in a box at the cabin. Hell, he hadn't thought he would need it. They were only looking for plants. The bad guys were back in the city. The cabin was his refuge. But right now, it didn't feel like one.

"That should be enough for now," Lara said.

"What?" He looked at her, then realized what she'd just said. "Sorry. I wasn't paying attention."

"No, you were trying to discover who watched us."

"You saw him?"

"I suspect no more than what you witnessed. Maybe not as much. The person was very careful not to be seen."

"You think it was a human?"

She shrugged. "I don't know the animals on your planet. I know what some are called, but I'm not sure what they look like. It might have been an animal."

"Maybe."

"But you don't think so."

Had she learned to read him that easily?

"Your forehead is wrinkled, and you've been frowning for quite some time. Also, you've been scanning the area as if you were looking for something." She smiled. "I can't read minds, if that's what you were thinking."

He relaxed somewhat. "That's a relief."

"And what have you been thinking that you're afraid I would learn?"

His gaze met hers. "I'll show you later."

"I've had no doubts that you wouldn't."

"And you were that certain?"

She nodded, then looked pointedly below his waist.

Okay, so he couldn't hide how he felt, but she should learn to expect it as long as she was around him. How could he not want her?

"How long will it take you to study the plants we gathered?"

Disappointment shone on her face. "Not as quickly as I'd like."

He had been afraid she was going to say something like that. They started back toward the cabin with the bagged plants. He stayed alert, watching for a flash of movement, but he had a feeling whoever had been watching had already left.

A hunter? Some of them got so caught up in what they were doing they didn't think anything about crossing a fence. The next time Lara wanted to come out, he'd make sure he brought a gun.

Just in case.

Chapter 9

Lyraka peeked around the tree. She could hear them talking. It hadn't been hard with her hypersensitive hearing. Her mother called it a gift.

As far as Lyraka was concerned, it was more a pain in the butt, especially when she tried to sleep. Ah, the sounds of nature. Most city dwellers longed for the peace and quiet. It wasn't all it was cracked up to be. If she had to choose, it was still better than the blast of horns and the constant construction that she'd encountered the few times she'd gone to town with Aasera.

Right now, her hearing did her little good in trying to figure out who the woman was. They hadn't said anything that even hinted the woman might be from another planet. At least, not since she'd been watching them.

The man was a different matter. She'd seen him before. Tall, nice-looking, and deliciously tanned to perfection. She'd even had a few fantasies about him. Who wouldn't? Lyraka figured he wasn't much older than her.

The woman with him looked younger by a few years.

Her age, maybe.

Was she Nerakian? Maybe. It was hard to tell, which was why her mother blended in so well with the people on Earth.

When the two began to make their way back toward the cabin, she followed closely, moving from tree to tree with a speed that would make anyone watching wonder if they'd actually seen movement or if it had only been a trick of the light.

She froze when the man stopped and looked around. He was good—for an Earthman. But she was better.

When he continued on, she studied the female again. The woman certainly didn't dress like someone from Nerak. She wore the typical clothes of anyone on Earth, which didn't mean a thing. Clothes did not make the person.

The man and woman walked into the clearing. She didn't venture further than the trees, staying instead in the shadows where she easily blended in.

At the door, the woman turned and seemed to look straight at her. Lyraka held her breath until she went inside.

Had she only imagined the woman had seen past the camouflage? Another Nerakian might have been able to, but only if she had strong powers. A warrior would. The woman hadn't looked like a warrior, though. A healer? She would be sensitive to her surroundings and might have sensed a presence. She wasn't sure.

Lyraka stepped farther into the dense woods before turning and going back the way she'd come.

The woman had been gathering plants. What reason would she have to come to Earth unless something was terribly wrong on Nerak?

There were still too many unanswered questions. Aasera was not going to like the lack of information she'd gathered.

She stopped at the fence, then sat on the ground and rested her head upon her drawn-up knees. She knew her mother still felt the pull of her old home. Sometimes, she blamed herself for her mother's fall from grace. If Aasera hadn't been pregnant, she would've returned to Nerak.

What had her mother gone through, being all alone in a strange land and pregnant?

Anger swept through her. Her father hadn't cared enough to stick around. Not after Aasera told him she was going to have a baby. He'd wanted no part of fatherhood. Lyraka had suspected there was more to it, but Aasera had refused to talk about him.

She took a deep breath, raising her head. Aasera had given up everything for her. She'd faced the wrath of the Coalition of Elders and refused to eliminate her child.

As Lyraka stood, she knew she would do anything for her mother. She could give back no less.

She crossed the fence, then looked back.

Something tugged inside her. But sometimes, she wanted more. She wanted to be free to explore and see what else was out there.

She was caught in a web as much as her mother. Caught between Nerak and Earth, even though she'd never been to her mother's home.

Nerak held her in its tightfisted grip and refused to release her.

Chapter 10

Sam had given her part of the kitchen so she could do her research. He'd even fixed shelves so she could place the small glass plates all in a row and have plenty of room.

Just a couple of long boards against one wall with cans to hold them up. Not as nice as what she would have had on Nerak, but it would do for now.

It was a nice gesture. He might not be so bad, Lara thought as she placed the plant stem on a glass disk, then added the chemical that would tell her if she might have the right combination for a cure.

Actually, Sam wasn't bad at all. He was quite good at copulating. No, he'd called it making love. And he was right—there had been a difference.

She looked at the specimen plate. The chemical would need to merge before she could take a reading. That wouldn't happen until the next day.

As she straightened, there was a pain in her back, as if a Hypotrond was sitting on it. She groaned, reaching behind her and pressing, but the ache didn't ease.

"What's the matter?"

"My back feels as if it's breaking in two," she told him. The pain was almost unbearable.

"You've been working all afternoon," he said. "It's no wonder you're hurting."

"I have never had discomfort in my life. I don't think I like it."

He raised an eyebrow. "Never?"

She shook her head.

"What about exercising? Aren't you sore afterward?" he asked.

"What's exercising?" She didn't recognize this word.

"Exerting yourself physically," he explained.

Exerting herself. On purpose. "Why would I do that?"

"You know, to feel good."

He was talking in circles again. "Why should I feel good about pain?"

"It's hard to explain."

She frowned. "I'm discovering there are a lot of things that are hard to explain on Earth. It's as I told you—Nerak is far superior."

"Yeah, kind of like living in a coffin," he muttered.

"What's a coffin?"

"Never mind. Here, let me see if I can make it better." He moved behind her, kneading the overworked muscles, pressing with his thumbs and moving them in a circular fashion.

She closed her eyes, liking the way he massaged. He was almost as good as a healer. His hands didn't produce the heat that hers did, but still, it was nice.

"Feeling better?"

She nodded. "You're almost as good as I am."

His hands stilled. She sighed. He was just beginning to ease the ache. She opened her eyes and glanced over her shoulder. And now, his mouth was set in a grim line, and there were many wrinkles on his forehead.

"Almost as good as you?" he asked.

No, he wasn't happy at all. She didn't see what the problem was. "I'm a healer. I've been trained. Of course I'm better than you."

"You've been trained in giving massages? I thought you were some kind of doctor."

"There are many facets to a healer. That's why we hold a high position in our society. The body is very complex. A healer learns much by touch."

"Like what?"

She shrugged. "I can feel something as simple as tension or more serious like an illness."

"I didn't think you had illness on Nerak. I thought it was perfect."

"True, it is. But if someone should need my services, I'm highly trained."

"And you're better at this than me?" His expression said he didn't believe her.

"Yes."

He snorted.

Earthmen were very stubborn. She stood and motioned for him to sit. No one snorted when she offered a healing massage. That was very rude. She was a healer and should be given the proper respect.

She continued to stare.

"Okay, I'll let you show me how much better you are," he finally said, giving in.

She'd known she would win. Hers was the superior race, after all. But he was more intelligent than she'd first thought. When he started to sit, she shook her head. "No, turn the chair around and straddle it," she said.

He complied with her request. "Okay, do your worst."

Worst? Oh, no, she didn't think so. Sam Jones was about to grovel. "Take off your shirt."

Their gazes locked as he slowly began to unbutton his shirt. Her body began to awaken and respond to his heated look. The ache inside her began to build. If she wasn't careful, he would have her groveling.

He slipped his arms out of the shirt and tossed it onto the back of one of the other chairs. Her mouth went dry as she stared at all the naked male flesh. Sinewy muscles that flexed when he moved. Very nice.

She drew in a ragged breath and met his gaze again, seeing the knowing look in his eyes. He knew exactly what he was doing to her.

Amazing.

She was that obvious? Apparently. She had a feeling he was just as horny as she was, but the way he sat, it was difficult to tell.

It might be worth exploring later, but right now, she wanted to prove she was right. "Put your hands on the back of the chair and rest your head on them."

When she had him in the position she wanted, she began to rub her hands together. The heat started to build. When her fingers tingled, she knew she was ready.

"I hate to tell you this, but I don't feel a thing," he mumbled against his arms.

"Shh, don't talk."

He sucked in a breath when she first laid hands on him.

"They're warm."

"I'm a healer. Shh. Don't talk. Close your eyes and feel. Think of what you'd like to be doing right now."

She worked from his neck, feeling the tension leave his body as she moved downward. Touching Sam was an experience in itself. His arms were well muscled, his back firm. Tingles of pleasure shot down her body.

She manipulated his flesh, letting her thoughts join with his. The pictures in his mind were fuzzy at first, but when they began to clear, she sucked in a deep breath, her body exploding with desire. She wasn't as good at connecting with the emotions as her cousin Mala, but Sam's desire was strong enough that the visions came easily.

Her hands moved without her having to think about what she was doing as her eyes drifted closed and she lost herself in his sensuous thoughts.

She stood before him without clothes between them. Her gaze moved over him: the wide expanse of his chest, past the sprinkling of hairs, then over his abdomen, and down to his erection.

She stepped closer, brushing her fingers over the tip, sliding her hands down its length. He jerked, sucking in a deep breath.

"You like this?"

"Yes."

She continued to massage his back, but she knew their thoughts had melded and he felt her touch in other places. She knew healers could do this, but she'd never had a chance to explore this side of her training. Something about a complication that went along with deep meditative massages. She just couldn't remember what.

And right now, she didn't care.

This was good. Very good.

She slid the foreskin down, excited that she could explore him at will. The tip was soft, pliable. She cupped his heavy sacks, lightly kneading. His muscles clenched. A surge of energy shot through her.

For the first time in her life, she was giving someone pleasure. She studied his face and knew it was true. He did get enjoyment from her touch. Would he get the same amount from her mouth as she had from his?

She leaned forward, running her tongue over the tip of his erection. He grasped the back of her head lightly and began to massage. Encouraged, she sucked him inside her mouth. He tasted salty, and not unpleasant.

Her body reacted to his gratification at her touch. Her nipples tightened, and she became damp between her legs.

As if he sensed her need for his touch, he reached beneath her arms and pulled her up. His eyes were glassy and full of desire.

"What are you doing?" he groaned. "It's like you're inside my head."

"Does it matter?"

"No." He lowered his head and captured a nipple, sucking it into his mouth. She gasped, arching her back for more.

He massaged the other breast, tweaking the nipple between his thumb and finger, rolling it around. He moved back, massaging with both his hands.

"Do you like this?" he asked.

She nodded. "Yes," she moaned. He was making her body feel things it had never felt before. The heat. The incredible heat that burned through her body, threatening to engulf her in flames.

She braced her hands on his chest. Naked, raw strength. She touched and caressed. Leaned forward and flicked her tongue across first one nipple, then the other. His hands moved to her back, pressing her closer.

"Am I dreaming?" he asked, his breath whispering across her bare skin.

"We're sharing thoughts and images." She scraped her fingernails lightly down his back. He trembled in the wake of her touch.

"I want you," he said. "I want to bury myself inside you."

He lifted her. She wrapped her legs around his waist as he sank inside her moist heat.

"Ah, God, this is so damn good."

He sank deeper; she moved to his rhythm. Each thrust seemed to go a little deeper, brought her a little closer. She gritted her teeth, leaning back. He lowered his head, running his tongue down her neck, sucking on first one breast, then the other.

She held tightly to his arms, letting the sensation wash over her in waves. Faster and faster, he increased his moves. Her orgasm hit her so hard she let go of him, could feel herself start to fall, then he was catching her, bringing her back to him, his lips meeting hers in a searing kiss as his body jerked.

Sam gasped, fighting for air. He sucked in deep gulps like a baby taking its first breath.

What the hell had just happened? He was still sitting in the chair, his head resting on his arms.

He dragged his gaze to the floor. Lara was in an exhausted heap beside his chair, her breathing just as ragged as his.

"Okay," he finally managed to get out. "You win hands down at massages."

"I've never done that before."

"Done what?" He was still confused about what the hell had happened. A mindblowing wet dream? Nah, he'd never had a wet dream that good. He'd actually touched her, felt Lara's mouth on him. Man, talk about safe sex.

"I've never gone that deeply into anyone's thoughts." She lay on the floor, rolling to her back. "I didn't realize it would take so much out of me. I feel as if I've been running for a very long time."

He came to his feet, grabbing the table to catch his balance. Man, he felt as if he'd run a marathon himself. Sweat covered his body. Lara looked a little worse for wear, too. He stuck his hand out, and she let him help her to her feet.

"I need a shower."

"Me, too," she said.

"You first." He was afraid to take a shower with her. Damn, he wondered if too much sex would make him go blind. His vision seemed a little blurred. He needed food. Sustenance to regain his strength.

She went to the bathroom and closed the door while he made his way to the kitchen. He turned on the water and stuck his head beneath it. When he came up for air, he slung water across the room, but he didn't care as he grabbed a towel and dried his head.

Damn, he'd never felt this alive. Making love with Lara was like a jolt of electricity going through him. As soon as the initial shock wore off, there was this incredible surge of energy.

He reached into the cabinet and grabbed a bag of chocolate bars.

Maybe this was why Nick had begged him to take Lara to the cabin. He had known what his friend would experience.

He shook his head as he unwrapped a candy and took a bite. This was good. He hadn't realized how hungry he was. He tossed the bag to the table and walked outside, inhaling the aroma of pine trees.

Lara had turned his world upside down. Not good. She wouldn't hang around like Kia and Mala. She'd leave as soon as she found her cure.

A win-win situation. Right? No commitments. No recriminations.

The shower stopped. A few minutes later, he heard the door open and close. He went inside and made his way to the bathroom.

Man, he'd miss the massages though. She'd definitely beat his idea of working the kinks out.

Chapter 11

"They were gathering plants," Lyraka said.

Aasera moved to the kitchen counter and poured another cup of coffee. Awful stuff. She'd almost gagged the first time she drank it. She didn't mind it so much if she added plenty of cream and sugar. The caffeine kick was good.

Temptations. Just as the Elders had warned.

She slowly stirred, then set the spoon in the sink.

"Could she be a chemist? A chemist might gather plants." She went to the table, sitting in the chair across from her daughter.

Lyraka shrugged. "She has long blond hair—more like you described healers. She wore clothes like someone from this planet, but there's something different about her."

"How so?" She took a drink, then closed her eyes, savoring the taste. Funny how she'd adapted to the ways of Earth over the years, easily accepted all they had to offer.

"It's nothing that I can put my finger on. Everything about her says she's lived here all her life. But I sense there's more to her than meets the eye."

"And the man she's with? Is it the same one who comes every year?"

"His name is Sam."

"I know."

Lyraka let out an exasperated sigh. "He's not my father. Not all men are like him."

Aasera knew this was the only real contention between them—the male species. On that, she thought the Elders were right—men were destructive. Sex was good, she'd admit to that, but the explosive anger, the fights. It wasn't worth it. Nothing was.

The tenseness suddenly eased. There was one good thing about the man she'd coupled with—the child he'd given her.

She reached across the table and squeezed Lyraka's hand. Never in her life would she have thought she could feel this much love for another person. If anyone ever harmed her child, she would make sure he regretted it for the rest of his life.

"You haven't been around that many men," she said. Lyraka didn't know what they were capable of doing.

She snorted. "That many? I haven't been around any. The only ones you allow at the colony are ones you know I wouldn't be remotely interested in."

So Lyraka had caught on to that. She'd known she would sooner or later. There had been one man, though. She didn't know how far the relationship had gone before she'd discovered Lyraka was sneaking out at night to meet him. She'd given him money, and he'd left. It was as she had thought. Men were all the same.

"It was for your own good that I kept the men away from the colony. I didn't want you to be hurt."

"But they've been nice, and that just proves not all men are bad."

"They wear masks. You don't know what they're capable of until you let them get too close."

Lyraka looked as if she wanted to say more, but she only sighed deeply as she stood, taking her cup to the sink.

"You're right, of course," her daughter said.

But when she turned, there was sadness in her smile. Guilt washed over Aasera. Sometimes, she felt much like the Elders. They were only trying to protect their people, but in turn, they were suffocating them.

"Don't worry, Mother. It will all work out as it's supposed to."

"I hope you're right."

"What are you going to do about the woman?" Lyraka asked, changing the subject.

"There's only one thing to do. I'm going to see for myself."

Now she'd shocked her daughter. It was rare that she left the safety of the colony. Maybe this was Fate. Or maybe it was the beginning of the end.

A shiver of fear swept over her.

"Today?" Lyraka watched, waiting for an answer.

Her daughter knew her so well. "Not today. Maybe tomorrow. They're causing no harm for now."

Even she heard the lack of excitement in her voice. Where had it gone? It used to consume her. There'd been a time when she couldn't wait to climb inside her craft and set off for the unknown. Her laughter had rung true. She'd been invincible.

Somewhere along the way, she'd stopped living.

Chapter 12

"Your plants are inferior!" Lara jumped to her feet, her chair scooting halfway across the floor behind her. "How can I be expected to find a cure for the Elder if the plants are no good?"

Sam turned from the sink. Now she was pissed because of Earth's plants? "How do you know they're inferior if Nerak doesn't have any?"

She shoved her hair behind her ears and began to pace back and forth. "This isn't good. If I don't find a cure, the Elder's lifecycle might end. It will be my fault."

He leaned a hip against the counter. "You're only human . . ."

She arched an eyebrow.

Sometimes, it was hard to remember she was an alien. "You're only a Nerakian," he amended. "It's not your decision who lives or dies."

"You don't understand. I was born a healer. My DNA was manipulated so that I'd have all the qualities of healers before me. If I can't save the Elder, then what is my purpose? I might as well have not been created."

And that's why she was angry. Now he could see why she must be feeling frustrated. "There was a reason for you to be . . . uh . . . created. Maybe it wasn't so you could heal someone. We don't always know what our purpose in life is. Maybe you're supposed to help someone in a different way, and you just don't know what it is yet."

Man, he really sounded lame. Hell, he wasn't a philosophical person. But he didn't think telling her to just have fun with life would make her feel better.

"You don't understand. Everyone has a purpose. On Nerak, each one of us knows what our function is in life. Some are code enforcers or therapists or rulers. Don't you see—everyone has specific duties to fulfill? If I can't make the Elder well, then I've failed in mine."

"You can't save everyone all the time."

"But I've never saved anyone!" She waved her arms. "That's the problem. I'm worthless."

She turned from him, walked out the back door, and stood on the porch. He followed, and when she stopped, he wrapped his arms around her, enveloping her in his embrace.

She stiffened before finally relaxing and leaning against him.

He'd never seen her lose control like this, except when they made love. What he was seeing now worried him. He had a feeling it scared her, too. What was happening to her? Something in the air, maybe.

"I never get upset," she admitted, breaking the silence. "Earth has a strange effect on me. I'm not sure it's good."

"What did you do on Nerak?"

"I'm not sure I understand your question."

"You know, during the day. How did you spend your time? Your daily routine."

"I'd get up and take my food capsule, then my companion unit would assist with my grooming. I meditated most of the day. Sometimes, I would admit a guest, and we would visit. In the evenings, there are concerts where art is performed. It's quite a rewarding life—very calming—"

Now he knew why she was reacting so emotionally, but did she? And would she accept his explanation, or would it scare her more?

"—Until now. I don't know what's happening to me," she continued. "My life is no longer calm."

"This is what we call living, and with it comes pain and sorrow, laughter and joy. It's a package deal. You can't pick and choose."

She tilted her head until she could look at him. "And you've felt this pain and sorrow?"

Tightness gripped his chest. "Yeah. I've felt it." Memories flooded his mind. "My grandfather was special. He had a small place in Louisiana, and I'd spend a couple of weeks with him every summer. We'd walk down to the river to fish and just talk. But then he died. His heart just stopped beating."

"His lifecycle ended."

"Yeah."

"And that's why you fish. To feel close to him again."

He'd never really thought about it. Whenever he needed to think, he'd go fishing or just get out his rod and reel to check the line or clean out his tackle box until the solution would come to him.

"I guess I do."

She nodded. "The holograms are good, but I wish I had known my grandmother. She had so much courage. She would travel from planet to planet exploring what each had to offer."

"There're others out there? I mean, inhabiting other planets?" This was getting a little weird.

"Of course, there is much out there still left to discover."

"So your grandmother was like our early explorers. A modern day Christopher Columbus."

"She was very brave." Her body tensed.

"What?"

"Fear filled me when I had to travel to earth. I'm a coward," she admitted.

He shook his head. "A coward? No, a coward wouldn't have attempted the journey. It's okay to be afraid. You faced your fears and pushed past them."

She was quiet as she digested his words.

"Yes, you're right. I'm not a coward."

He smiled. Lara was something else. Since he'd met her, he'd wanted to kiss her, comfort her . . . and kill her.

His life certainly wouldn't be the same when she left. Maybe hers wouldn't be the same, either. Maybe it would be better.

"And your purpose in life? What is it that you do?"

"I'm a cop." He realized she wouldn't know what he meant, so he explained. "A warrior like Kia."

"You have wars here?"

"Not in the United States. At least not recently, but we have bad guys. I catch the bad guys."

"And your friend, Nick. Is he a warrior, too?"

"He's a cop, too. We're partners."

"This is why Kia won't ever return to Nerak." The sadness was evident in her voice. "She's finally getting to be a warrior."

"That, and she loves Nick."

She nodded. "I saw it in her eyes when she looked at him. When she thought I was there to take her home. I'll miss her very much."

There was a movement in the trees. He held his breath, holding Lara a little tighter.

The person from the other day? One of the bad guys? If he eased back, he could slip inside and grab his gun, but that would put Lara in more danger.

He didn't have to make the choice—it was made for him.

The buck cautiously stepped into the clearing, looked around, then came out a little further. His coat was reddish brown, his lines pure and sleek.

Lara drew in a deep breath. As if sensing she needed to be still so as not to scare the animal away, she didn't make a sound.

So hunters hadn't gotten him. That was good. Man, he was a magnificent creature. He stood in the clearing looking as if he owned the world.

The buck turned and looked at them. It was almost as if he

were saying, *Welcome back, I'm still here. They haven't gotten me yet.* Then he snorted and leapt back into the shadows.

They exhaled at the same time.

"What was it?" Lara asked with awe.

"A deer—a buck. Beautiful, wasn't he?"

"I've never seen anything like him. I think I'm beginning to learn why you love your cabin so much. It's not the structure, it's the place."

"Exactly."

"Nerak has many wonders, too," she said as if to reaffirm her loyalty. "We have beautiful light from our suns. When it touches our buildings, they sparkle like great stones. We have no bad guys."

"But if you don't have bad guys, then how can you have heroes?"

They couldn't. It was plain and simple. They lived their life from day to day. Nothing bad happened, but nothing exciting, either.

Where were these thoughts coming from? She was beginning to compare Nerak to Earth. Nerak was starting to lose.

"I need to run more tests on the plants we gathered." She left his arms and went back inside.

Temptation. Maybe she wasn't as strong as she'd thought. Earth was a very complicated place. Nerak was simple. There was good about both places.

But Nerak didn't have deer.

Or sex. At least, not the kind she'd experienced with Sam.

She carefully pulled out one of the glass specimen plates from the tray. The chemical she'd added had liquefied the plant and made a small puddle. She held her breath as she inserted the probe that would tell her if this plant would cure the Elder.

No reaction.

She closed her eyes, forcing the frustration away. She couldn't help the Elder if she let her emotions overwhelm her. When she opened her eyes, she was once again in control.

A cure *would* be found. It just might take a little longer than she'd hoped. She stood and walked to the door and saw Sam walking toward the woods. Was something bothering him? He had his fishing equipment with him.

He was a strange man. She'd seen his kindness when he offered to bring her to his cabin so she could search for a cure. She frowned. And she'd seen his frustration with her, but he'd controlled his anger. That was a good sign.

And she'd seen his passion. A smile touched her lips. Making love with Sam had been good. Much better than a companion unit. And he'd also been right—there was a difference between making love and just having sex.

The mental connection they'd shared worried her a little, though. Her lack of knowledge could cause a problem later. Maybe nothing would come from it other than feeling closer to Sam than she had before.

When she turned away from the door, her gaze landed on a package. Curious, she sauntered over and read what was written on it.

Chocolate!

She jumped back, stumbling into the counter and bringing up her arms to ward off any dangerous rays the bars might give off. The Elders had warned her about chocolate. She was going to disintegrate, she was sure of it.

She drew in a painful breath. It was getting hard to breathe. And the light had all but extinguished . . .

Wait. She moved her arm from in front of her face and opened her eyes, then frowned. Now she could breathe . . . and see. The light hadn't grown dimmer.

And the chocolate wasn't giving off harmful waves of radiation. Now that she thought about it, the Elders had said humans consumed chocolate as part of their nourishment.

It appeared quite innocuous inside the plastic bag. She stepped closer, thinking it didn't look that appealing either. The shiny part of the package was pretty, but still, these bars didn't entice her to leave her home and stay here so she could enjoy looking at them.

She picked up one corner of the package with two fingers, and the chocolate bars spilled onto the table. There they were in front of her, and she didn't have any desire to do anything with them.

Resisting temptation wasn't so very difficult.

She touched one. It was hard. Was this what had seduced her cousin and sister to give up their home, their people? That, and probably sex. Sex with Sam was very good. That would make leaving more complicated, but leave she would.

The little bar looked quite harmless. She brought one to her nose and inhaled. It smelled nice. She glanced out the door before tearing off the wrapper. Sam wouldn't have to know about her curiosity. He would probably laugh at her.

The chocolate bar was dark in color and scored into sections. She broke one section off. A taste wouldn't hurt, and she could dispose of the rest. She wanted to know what power this chocolate had over Nerakians. One bite only.

She placed the chocolate on her tongue.

Nothing.

It was as she suspected. Healers had better control of emotions.

The chocolate began to melt inside her mouth. She ran her tongue over the bar, then closed her eyes, savoring the taste.

Not fair! It had snuck up on her.

Oh, but it was so good. She chewed, swallowed, and it was gone.

No, she wanted more. She grabbed the rest of the bar and shoved it into her mouth. Yes, this was better. Lights began to swirl around her—warm, colorful lights.

Taking the bag, she went to the other room and curled up on the lounging sofa.

This was almost better than sex with Sam. At the very least, it was just as good. She opened another one, leaning against the lounging sofa's pillows, and took another bite, then another.

"Umm, yes, this is so-o-o good." Her body tingled from head to toe.

She could see how it would be a great temptation. But she wouldn't think about it. Not right now. There would be plenty of time later. For now, she only wanted to savor the exquisite taste.

All too soon, that bar was gone. She reached inside and got another one, slowly unwrapping it, delaying the moment of consumption. And there it was, in front of her, waiting for her to take that first bite.

But rather than bite into it, she ran her tongue over the bar once, then again, releasing the flavor. She needed gratification and couldn't wait a second longer. She bit into the bar and slowly chewed.

"Oh, Great One, no one warned me it would taste this exquisite. Please forgive me."

One more chocolate bar, and she'd stop.

Chapter 13

For some crazy reason, Sam was experiencing an enormous amount of pleasure. His whole body tingled. He frowned. Well, it damn sure wasn't from catching anything because the fish weren't biting. What else was new?

He'd thought if he gave Lara a little space and left the cabin, she would be able to work better.

Damn, he missed her.

He leaned against the rock as visions of her filled his mind. It was funny now when he thought about her sprinkling the detergent all over the cabin and staring at the powder crystals as if they were actually supposed to do something.

He laughed, knowing if there happened to be a fish in the area, he'd probably just scared it away. Not that he really cared.

But just as suddenly as his laughter started, it stopped when he remembered how she'd looked when she took off her clothes to finish cleaning.

Sweet. Really sweet.

High, pointed breasts, curvy hips, a thatch of blond curls at the vee of her legs. Oh, yeah, that was a good vision. He swallowed past the lump in his throat.

Okay, enough fishing. Time to head back. He quickly reeled in his line and packed up his stuff. When he realized he was practically panting, he stopped and slowed his breathing to a more normal rate. He wasn't *that* horny.

And then again . . .

He grabbed the handle of his tackle box and headed back toward the cabin. So what if he was anxious to see what Lara was doing, to see if she was still working on her research? She'd been absorbed in her work when he'd left. He didn't even think she'd heard him tell her he was leaving. She could be looking for *him*.

As he stepped from the woods, he glanced up. There was a haze of lights swirling above the cabin. Lights like the other night. What the hell was happening? Something electrical in the air?

Was Lara okay? He picked up his pace, dropping his stuff on the back porch as he hurried inside. As worried as he was, his body still tingled with pleasure. It was probably linked to the lights in some way. Lord, he hoped more aliens hadn't landed. He could barely handle the one already here.

"Lara?"

Was that a whimper from the living room? Why the hell had he left her by herself? Stupid! Maybe it hadn't been the deer the other day but an escaped felon or something.

His blood ran cold as he cautiously made his way to the other room, sliding his gun out of his ankle holster. It was just a .22, but it was enough to make someone think twice about what they were doing. He crept to the doorway of the living room, then peeked around the corner.

Huh?

Lara was curled up on the sofa, covered in candy wrappers. He must've made a noise because she turned to look at him, her mouth smeared with chocolate.

"Temptation," she mumbled. "I was only going to take a small taste. I'm a healer, so it was my right," she said, jutting her chin out and frowning at him.

"It's fine with me if you want to eat chocolate," he said.

"But it was so good that I ate a little more, and then more, until there was none left. I'm as weak as my sister and cousin."

He chuckled but quickly covered it with a cough when she cast a glare in his direction.

"It's your fault. You left the chocolate on the table so I would be tempted." Her defiance drained, and her bottom lip trembled.

He holstered his gun, then went to the sofa and sat down, gathering her in his arms, liking the way she snuggled against him.

"It's okay," he told her.

"No, it isn't, but I don't expect you to understand."

"Because I'm inferior. Yeah, I know." He noticed she didn't push out of his arms, though. "Hey, I thought I saw lights swirling above the cabin. Do you know anything about that?"

She shook her head. "Only the lights inside."

The living room light was on. He started to explain but changed his mind. Maybe it was the light hitting the antennae. He'd been walking from the shadow of the trees into the sun's glare. God, he hoped it wasn't a smoothie flashback. How would he explain that to the captain?

Sorry, sir, but I have to go into rehab for smoothie hallucinations?

She sniffed. "I thought I would be stronger, but I wanted to see what it would taste like, and then I couldn't stop, and even now I want more . . ."

"Shh, it's okay. Chocolate is hard to resist. I won't leave any more temptations lying out."

"Yes, it's your fault I succumbed."

He laughed.

"It's not funny. I can't take chocolate back to Nerak. It might topple our whole structure and cause irreparable damage." She sniffed. "But then, I can't have any more, either. That's not fair."

"No, it isn't." He sobered.

"And now that I've given in to this temptation, how easy

will it be for me to taste other foods? To try other things that Earth has to offer?" She drew in a deep breath and looked at him. "Is there something out there better than chocolate?" Her face had grown a shade paler.

"I don't think so." He wouldn't mention ice cream drizzled with chocolate sauce or coconut cream pie or jelly-filled dough-nuts.

Man, he hated seeing her this dejected. It *was* his fault, but he hadn't really thought she would eat any of the candy bars. She'd acted so damned superior when she said she didn't eat anything nor did she care to eat anything Earth had to offer.

Now he had to make everything better.

"What if you tried different things and showed these won-ders to the Elders," he began, saying the first thing that came to mind. "Maybe they'd want to incorporate some of these . . . uh . . . wonders into your world. What if they no longer had to be temptations?"

She was quiet as if she was actually taking his words seri-ously. In a way, he'd meant what he said. He thought it sounded good—sort of.

"You're right," she finally said.

He breathed a sigh of relief. "Yeah, you'd be like your grandmother, charting new territories, except you'd be intro-ducing new things to Nerak. Start an export and import busi-ness or something."

She sat up, moving out of his arms. "If I brought some of Earth's treasures to Nerak, then no one would want to leave, and that would make the Elders happy."

"Yes!" Great, now she wouldn't feel so bad. And she could take a bag of chocolate back with her to Nerak. A win–win situation. Sometimes, he amazed himself.

"You will show me more temptations."

His grin was slow.

"No, not that," she told him as she stood. "I want to know everything that Earth has to offer."

His hopes deflated, and that wasn't all.

"I'll try other foods." She jumped to her feet. "And there are more animals to see. I could take back deer. We can have everything!"

My God, he'd created a monster.

"You'll tell me more."

Like what? Man, this was supposed to be his vacation. All he'd wanted to do was fish a little, drink a little beer, and do a lot of relaxing. Why'd he have to be the good guy?

Now what the hell was he supposed to do? Lara looked at him as if he'd have all the answers.

His gaze fell on the TV. That should keep her entertained. He grabbed the remote control and clicked it on.

"This is television. If you put a satellite in outer space, you might get some of Earth's channels."

He could only get a few. He had an old antenna perched on top of the cabin. It wasn't the most high-tech equipment, but at least when he stayed here, he could catch the news.

"Television." She moved closer, sitting on the floor in front of it.

Dr. Phil was on.

"I need more chocolate," she said without looking at him.

He cocked an eyebrow and didn't move. She glanced over her shoulder.

"Thank you?"

He softened. "Please is the word you're looking for."

"You'll get me more chocolate . . . please."

It still sounded like a demand.

"There's none left. You ate it all."

She faced him, her eyes as big as saucers. "None?"

He shook his head.

"If we had chocolate on Nerak, we'd make sure there was plenty, and that we didn't run out. But then, we're superior, so I can understand why you had not stocked sufficient supplies. Do you have something else worthy to eat?"

"Yeah, meat and veggies. I bet you'll just love steamed broccoli." There were ways to get revenge.

"Good. You can bring me some."

"I'd love to."

He turned on his heel and went to the kitchen, careful not to disturb her experiments. He only hoped they weren't radioactive. If he started glowing in the dark, he'd definitely kill Nick.

He grabbed the steamer from a cabinet and a couple of steaks out of the refrigerator. After he had everything cooking, he took a quick shower. Lara was still enthralled with TV and didn't notice him as he went back to the kitchen.

After they ate, he might even show her how much fun it was to play in bubbles while washing dishes. Maybe she wouldn't be quite so superior if he put her to work again.

Somehow, the thought of her surrounded in bubbles didn't make him feel better. No, now he felt worse.

He put the food on the table before going back to the living room. "You ready to eat?"

She dragged her glassy-eyed gaze away from the screen. "Food?"

She caught on real quick. He nodded. She glanced one more time at the TV, but apparently, eating was a bigger enticement. She came to her feet and followed him back into the kitchen.

Her nose wrinkled. "It doesn't smell as good as chocolate."

"No, but it's healthier."

When a puzzled expression appeared on her face, he decided this was part of the package deal he'd told her about earlier. The good with the bad.

"If you're going to eat Earth food, then you need to know what's good for you and what you should avoid."

"And chocolate is a food I should avoid?"

"Yes."

"Why?"

"It has no health benefits."

"It makes me feel good."

He shook his head. "Doesn't count. You have to eat your meat and veggies."

"Then I can have chocolate?"

She looked hopeful. How could he say no? "Yeah, we'll make a chocolate run after we eat."

She relaxed and pulled out the chair across from him and sat down. Sam didn't think she looked at all enthused by what he'd cooked.

"Just try it," he said.

"It looks like a little tree." She moved the broccoli around on her plate before taking a bite. Her expression quickly changed to a grimace. She chewed as if she was in horrible pain, then visibly swallowed.

"You don't like broccoli?"

She shook her head. "This does not tempt me."

"Try the steak."

"What is it?"

"Meat. You'll like it better."

She took a small bite.

"Better?" he asked. He cooked a mean steak. It was all in the seasoning.

"It's hard to chew. I think chocolate is much better."

First, his cabin, then his food. "You can't live on chocolate."

She arched one eyebrow and glared at him. Here it comes again. The I'm-superior-and-will-do-what-I-want look. He really hated that look.

It didn't stop him from getting up and making her a PB&J sandwich, though. Maybe her palate wasn't ready for steak. He cut the sandwich in half and put it on a plate, setting it in front of her.

"You'll like this better."

She gingerly lifted one corner and looked under it, then sniffed. "It has a nice aroma." She took a cautious bite and chewed. When she looked at him again, she was smiling. "This is better. Not as good as chocolate, but I like it more than the small trees and meat."

"I thought you might."

"What's a casino?" she asked out of the blue.

He cut into his steak, watching the juice run out. How could anyone pass up one of his steaks?

"Where'd you hear about casinos?"

"From your box. It said *The Golden Eagle* was a place for fun and games. Try your luck, and you can get rich."

"A commercial. They were talking about the casino in Bossier City. They have several. You can gamble."

"And you've done this?"

"A few times," he said, concentrating more on his steak, which was cooked to perfection, no matter what Lara thought. He cut a bite and forked it, bringing it to his mouth, then savoring the taste. He loved nothing more than a good cut of meat.

"Will you take me to the casino?"

He swallowed and choked, then gulped down enough water to move the bite of steak down his throat.

"No," he said, the word raspy.

"Why?"

"It's a temptation you don't want to fall prey to. Trust me on this one."

She laid her sandwich on the plate and squared her shoulders. She might have pulled off her haughty demeanor, except she had peanut butter on the side of her mouth.

"You will take me. How can I bring these things to Nerak if I don't experience them first?"

Kia was going to kill him. In one swoop, he was polluting Nerak by offering up every kind of vice. From simple chocolate, to TV, to sex—okay, he didn't consider sex to be a vice, actually. But gambling—he wasn't even going there.

"Please."

Yeah, right. The way she said please, it came out more like an order. He shook his head.

She arched an eyebrow. "I want to go."

"No."

She came to her feet. "Then I'll take myself. It shouldn't be hard to get someone to give me a ride."

He leaned back in his chair, grinning. If she thought she could tell him what to do, then she'd better think again. The front door slammed. His grin turned down.

His cell rang. He brought it out of his pocket and flipped it open. "Yeah."

"I'm using the telephone again." Kia's voice came over the line.

Why couldn't Lara be more like her sister? His forehead wrinkled. Of course, Kia had also started a barroom brawl.

"You're still there?"

He brought himself back to the present. "Yeah. Did you need something?"

"I wanted to ask Lara how she was doing and if she'd found a cure for the Elder."

How the hell would he explain Lara had just walked out the door, especially with the sun starting to set?

"Uh, she's in the shower." Damn, he'd never been good at lying.

Kia laughed. "Water is good. Nick and I had sex in the shower. We enjoyed it very much. Have you and Lara had sex yet?"

"Uh . . ."

"I think I'd better talk to Sam," Nick said in the background. "Nothing like being direct, huh?" Nick said after he got on the phone, but there was laughter in his voice.

"You're dead meat," Sam told him.

"You're having that much fun?"

"No."

"Then everything is going okay? Good."

"No." Sam was starting to wonder if Nick had lost his hearing. Then it dawned on him what Nick was doing. "You're doing this for Kia's benefit, aren't you?"

"You've got that right."

"That's even low for you. So just keep talking, but I'm hanging up. I have to find Lara, who just walked out the front door because I won't take her gambling."

Nick snorted.

"Laugh all you want. This shit isn't funny." He clicked his phone shut, hoping it had been loud enough to bust Nick's eardrums.

Now what the hell was he supposed to do? Go after her? Yeah, right. That's exactly what she wanted him to do. She was probably sitting on the front porch, just waiting for him to come outside so she could give him an I-knew-you'd-come-after-me look. That wasn't going to happen.

He slipped into the living room and sneaked a look out the door. She wasn't on the porch. He opened the screen door, and stepped out, his gaze scanning the area.

Nothing.

Not a creature was stirring . . . Yeah, he was definitely going to kill Nick.

No, what he was going to do was throw Lara over his shoulder and bring her back to the cabin. He was damned if he'd let her get the best of him!

Chapter 14

"How much farther to the casino?" Lara asked.

Did he just growl at her? Lara frowned. What had she done? Was it so bad that she'd asked how much longer before they arrived? He was the one who'd suggested she research some of the things Earth had to offer so she might take them back to her planet.

"We're five minutes closer than we were the last time you asked," he said.

"I have to use the . . ." What had he called it? Oh, she remembered. "The bathroom." Her memory was actually quite good, but then, she was of superior intelligence so remembering what things were called on Earth would not be so very difficult. It was quite easy, actually.

"We're almost there."

"I don't think you're happy about going to the casino. You were the one who suggested I discover more things. I really do want to know more about Earth, and if I can bring back some of the pleasures, it might please the Elders."

"Or really piss them off," he muttered. "They don't zap people, do they?"

"Zap?"

"Yeah, you know, vaporize people."

She laughed. "Of course not."

"Good."

"They haven't done that in . . . years."

"Great. Now I feel a lot better."

"Nerakians aren't violent. We believe in the purity of the mind, body, and soul. Violence would have no place in our lives."

She was sure she'd mentioned that before. His memory wasn't nearly as good as hers. He was better at sex, though—that she would give him. She would improve with practice, of course.

"As I mentioned before, we are a superior race."

Why were his knuckles turning white as he gripped his steering device? Was that another sign he wanted to have sex? There'd be enough room in his pickup—maybe. She didn't think it would be as comfortable as the bed, though.

No, his facial expression didn't look happy. Besides, it might not be a good thing for her to think about sex. She didn't want to get horny until after she'd seen the machines. They would have sex later.

"Tell me about these slot machines," she asked.

He shrugged. "They're games of chance. You put money in, push a button to spin the reels, and if you get something that pays, you win."

"And what do people win?"

"More money."

"And money is good?"

He quickly explained the monetary system in his country. How people worked to earn money and the different amounts that it came in. It was a very simple system. Of course, Nerak's was much easier.

"What do you do with this money?" she asked when he finished.

"You can buy clothes, pay your bills, buy food. But it doesn't grow on trees, so you have to be careful how you spend it."

It sounded very simple, but where was the source of the

money? If one could find out, then they would have a lot of power. "Where does money come from?"

"How is it made?" he asked, looking across the seat at her.

She nodded.

"Pulp." He shrugged. "From trees."

She frowned. "But yet it doesn't grow on trees."

"Not exactly."

Very confusing if you asked her, but when lights began to appear on the horizon, she lost interest in money. The bright lights were almost as pretty as the ones on Nerak, and the closer they got, the brighter they were.

Sam pulled off the highway and drove toward a tall building with clusters of lights and a fountain. Would they let her play in it? The water shooting at different angles looked like it would be fun.

"What's that?" She pointed toward large statues that sat on either side of the entrance.

"Eagles . . . birds that fly in the sky."

She didn't think it would be very easy for them to fly in the sky, but she wouldn't question Sam. Maybe they broke out of their stone cage and flew at certain times.

He pulled under the brightly lit awning and got out. A man dressed all in black opened her door—without complaining—and she got out. As least this male knew how to show her the proper respect due her status.

Not that he could possibly know. She wasn't even wearing the robes of a healer. Sam had said he was putting his foot down on that one. She'd wanted to tell him that both his feet looked to be firmly on the floor, but she didn't.

The black pants weren't as uncomfortable as the jeans she'd worn, and the red top fit rather loosely. Sam said loose was better since she wasn't wearing a bra. For some reason, talking about her lack of a bra made him stutter, and the bulge appeared again.

He certainly got horny a lot.

Inside, the ceilings were high and very brightly lit. There were tall columns, and one wall had something similar to their walls with pictures of people. These were wearing white cloths and holding jars.

"Are these the ones who have passed before you?" she asked.

"What?"

She pointed to the wall. "Are these your ancestors immortalized in the pictures?"

He didn't look quite as tense as he had. She wondered what she'd said that had caused just the whisper of a smile on his face.

"No, it's just a picture someone painted."

"Well, it's nice anyway." Her gaze drank in all the sights. Everything sparkled, much like the promise stones on Nerak. And there was a vehicle in the middle of the floor on a pedestal, turning around and around. It was much prettier than Sam's pickup.

"What's that for, Sam?"

"They're giving it away."

"You should get one. Your vehicle is very uncomfortable. This one might ride better."

"They don't just give it away."

"But you said . . ."

"You put your name in, and if they draw it out, then you win the car," he said, scraping his fingers through his hair.

Was he getting agitated? No matter.

"Then you should put your name in."

"I like my pickup."

He frowned. He was doing that a lot, too.

"Listen, we're here to look around. That's all."

"Of course. And to play the slots."

"No."

"On the commercial, they said they were a lot of fun. I

would think you had to play them, as the man said, to experience the fun."

"They also cost money. Money I don't have to throw away."

"Please."

"No."

He could be very obstinate, and after she'd said please, too. She didn't have to say please—she was a healer. She didn't think it would hurt to play one of the slot machines.

"Remember, look but don't touch."

She would touch it if she wanted. He was not her ruler, and since he wasn't an Elder, she didn't have to do as he commanded.

Sounds began to intrude. Lots of clanking noises. Fun sounds. Her heart began to beat faster as a rush of adrenaline shot through her.

They walked around a corner. Lights flashed, and bells were going off. People laughed and talked. The atmosphere was very festive.

Oh, the commercial was right. This was going to be fun.

"Look, don't touch," Sam warned.

He seemed worried. She wondered why. They were machines, like companion units, except they provided a different kind of pleasure. Surely, no harm would come if she touched one of them. She saw the other people hadn't been vaporized or anything.

As she walked past one, she lightly ran the tips of her fingers over the surface, making sure Sam didn't catch her. Nothing happened. She hadn't thought anything would. She was a healer and could sense these sorts of things.

A woman sat in front of one of the machines. Lara stopped and watched. The woman pressed a button. Reels spun. Three bars on the first spin, three on the second, and three on the third.

The woman jumped up and clapped her hands, screaming, "I won!" Bells rang.

The slots looked like fun. Other people were hitting the button and winning. Why couldn't she play, too? She looked at Sam, afraid she might have to say please again.

Sam didn't like the look in Lara's eyes. They were starting to glass over as she stared at the woman who'd just hit triple bars.

"Just one, Sam. How can I tell the Elders about slot machines if I don't try one?"

"Believe me, you don't want to tell them about slot machines." They were going to zap him for sure. Sodom, Gomorrah . . . and Nerak. Damn.

He looked out over the sea of slot machines, but his gaze came right back to Lara like a magnet. She waited patiently for him to cave. He could see it in her eyes. She wouldn't stop until he gave in.

Why the hell had he told Lara the gambling boats were within driving distance? He could've just as easily lied. But he hadn't, and now he was stuck.

"Okay, but only one machine. I said I would show you a casino, and I have. You can play one slot machine, but as soon as you lose the money, then we're going back to the cabin. Deal?" His eyes narrowed.

"Yes."

Too easy. "Do you know what deal means?"

She shook her head.

Ha! Just as he thought. "It means that you agree to play one slot machine, then we leave."

"I agree."

He didn't trust her. One machine, and if she didn't leave, he *would* throw her over his shoulder and carry her out. He refused to let her get the best of him.

Yeah, just like he'd refused to bring her to the cabin and refused to take her to the casino. He was such a sucker. He squared his shoulders. No, this time, he'd be firm.

"Which machine do you want to play?"

She grabbed his hand. "I don't know. Let's go further inside."

He didn't think he wanted to mention she wasn't acting at all like a healer, especially the way she clutched his hand.

Her hand was small compared to his, and it was warm, like when she'd given him a massage. He liked the tingles that shot up his arm when she held his hand. He could actually feel her excitement. But then, it was hard not to—it was written all over her face.

"This one," she proclaimed, stopping in front of an empty machine.

It was a wild cherry quarter machine. He'd carefully steered her away from the dollar machines.

He pulled a twenty out of his wallet. "When this is gone, we leave—agreed?"

She nodded and sat on the stool. It was a weeknight, so the casino wasn't filled to overflowing. He inserted the money and sat at the next machine to watch.

"Now what do I do?"

"You push the button and see what happens."

She pushed the button. The reels spun before clicking into place one at a time.

"What did I win?" she asked, practically squirming on her seat.

"Nothing."

She frowned. "I don't think I like slot machines."

"Good. Let's go back to the cabin."

"I'll try again."

She pushed the button.

The reels stopped. Again, nothing.

Her lips pursed. He had a feeling it might've been better if she'd won. The look on her face said she wasn't leaving until she hit something.

"The odds are in the favor of the casino," he told her.

"That's not fair."

"They couldn't stay open if it was fair," he explained.

She spun again, and this time, hit a cherry. She laughed and clapped her hands.

"I won!"

"Not exactly."

She frowned again, and he tried not to laugh.

He pointed to her credits. "See, you only got back the amount of your play. It's like getting a free spin. You're not winning, though."

"I'm not sure I like your slot machines."

"They're not mine." He cleared his throat. "I have to make a bathroom run. Will you be all right and stay right here?"

She nodded, already pushing the button again as if he wasn't even there. He glanced at his watch as he headed toward the men's room. Fifteen more minutes, and the money would be gone, and they could leave.

He was corrupting her. He didn't think this was what he was supposed to do. Seeing the deer was a good thing. That's the kind of sights he wanted her to take back. Certainly not a smoke-filled casino.

He exited the bathroom a few minutes later, looking around as he did. His hands were tingling, and he realized he was sweating. When he looked at the machines, he had an almost uncontrollable desire to play one.

Crazy. He never gambled. Maybe a few times, but he'd never felt any kind of pull until now. He ignored the desire to play and walked back toward where he'd left Lara.

It seemed there were more people in the casino. His eyes narrowed. Maybe not more people, just a concentration of them where Lara should be.

His heart skipped a beat.

A hazy swirling of colors flickered above the small crowd. Just like what had been above the cabin earlier today and when they'd had sex. What the hell was with all the colors?

He had a feeling this wasn't a flashback from the smoothie, either. And it damn sure wasn't a laser light show. No, he had a feeling it was Lara.

Damn.

The closer he got, the worse it looked. This was bad. What if she'd gotten mad at the machine and zapped it or something. He elbowed his way through the crowd.

"You've got a hot machine, honey." An older, heavyset woman with blond highlights streaked through her dark red hair stood beside Lara. The woman rubbed the side of Lara's machine. "Come on, jackpot. Mama needs a new pair of shoes." Her mixed drink sloshed over the side of her glass, spilling onto the floor.

"Come on, jackpot!" Lara yelled. "Mama needs shoes!"

"That's right, sweetie, you gotta talk to the machine."

"Like companion units?"

The woman's brow creased. "Whatever the hell they are." Her eyes widened. "Oh, gotcha, honey." She winked. "I've got one of those in my bedside drawer. Best friend I've had since Billy Ray kicked the bucket."

The reels spun, clicked one, two, three. Triple bars.

"Yes!" Lara clapped her hands, then hugged the woman.

For a healer who didn't touch, she was touching a hell of a lot lately. He eased up to her. "Lara, what are you doing?" He spoke as quietly as he could over the noise.

She looked up, eyes glassy, cheeks flushed. "Winning!"

Oh, God. He glanced at her credits. She'd turned the twenty into two hundred dollars. He'd have to pry her loose from the machine. Not good with the crowd standing around. He'd have to wait until they dispersed before he could get her safely away without causing a scene.

She spun the reels and lost the next five times. The crowd began to thin, as did the flashing lights above them.

"Come on, baby. I need shoes." She didn't sound nearly as confident as she had a few minutes ago.

"Honey, looks like the machine has gone cold. Take the advice of a slot machine junkie and find another one." The woman tossed back the last of her drink, then left.

"Another machine, yes, that's what I need to do. Find another machine."

"Now, Lara, you were only going to play this one, remember?"

She turned on him, eyes narrowed, teeth bared.

Evil alien! If her head started spinning, he was out of there.

He took a step back, came close to crossing himself, and he wasn't even Catholic. Right now, it seemed a good thing to do.

"I want to play another machine," she said between gritted teeth.

What happened when a Nerakian got angry? He didn't think he wanted to find out.

He hit the cash button and waited until the white paper spit out of the slot. "You can put the paper in another slot machine, and it'll give you credits, but remember, when this is gone, that's it."

She softened, smiling. "Of course." She immediately began to look around. He might as well have left the building for all she seemed to care.

She'd caught the gambling fever. There was only one thing to do—let it run its course and hope the losing streak stayed with her.

"This one," she said, reaching her hands out and closing her eyes. "I can feel its power."

"Can you really?" he whispered, glancing around.

No, don't even go there, he thought to himself. He was already harboring an alien, the smoothie could very well have been a hallucinogenic, and now, he was looking at illegal gaming practices.

"Gertie said that's what I needed to do."

"Who's Gertie?" He glanced around to make sure Lara

wasn't calling too much attention to herself. Yeah, right, they had cameras everywhere in these places.

"The woman who told me how to play the machine. Gertie said I had to talk to it in order to win."

"And what did she say about picking one?"

"That I had to feel its essence." She turned back to the machine. "I feel this machine's essence."

"Whatever." He took the paper from her and fed it into the slot, then sat on the next stool over.

She sat down and began to hum.

"You aren't going to start levitating or anything, are you? Management isn't going to like it if you start floating in the air."

"Shh, I'm becoming one with the machine."

She sat there for a few seconds, then opened her eyes and hit the spin button. The reels spun around, then stopped. Nothing, nothing, cherry.

"I knew this was a lucky machine." She smiled when she looked at him. "I'm a healer. I have the power of sensing these sorts of things."

He ran a weary hand through his hair, afraid this might be a long and emotional night.

Chapter 15

Lara couldn't understand it. She'd felt the machine. It had practically called her name. Why was she not winning? It wasn't fair. Not fair at all.

"You only have ten dollars left," Sam told her.

She whirled around on her stool and faced him. "Yes, I can see that."

The odds were in her favor. She had pushed the spin button exactly forty-nine times and hadn't hit. Of course, the bars would line up or maybe she would even hit the jackpot.

"My race is far superior. I've put one hundred and forty-seven dollars in this machine. It'll start winning any moment now."

"That's not always true."

"I felt this machine. I'm a healer. I'm sensitive to this kind of stuff. I'm never wrong." And she *had* felt it. The machine had practically called out to her.

He mumbled something she couldn't understand. Not that it mattered. The machine, that's what she had to focus on. She closed her eyes, concentrating on her next spin. She only had to think about her objective. Yes, she could picture the reels spinning. "Come on, baby, mama needs a new pair of shoes." She rubbed the side of the machine, then hit the button.

The reels clicked into place. One, two, three.

Nothing. Not even a stupid cherry. Gertie was wrong. It was her fault. She didn't even need new shoes.

She closed her eyes and hummed. This time she would win. "Okay, mama needs some chocolate." There, that was at least something she actually needed. She rubbed the side of the machine before hitting the spin button.

Click. Click. Click.

Nothing.

She spun again and again.

Nothing.

She glared at the machine and slammed her hand down on the button. Nothing happened. The reels didn't spin. "It's as I thought. This is a defective machine. That's why it didn't win."

"No, you've run out of money," Sam said.

Her gaze flew to her credits. Zero. Sam was right. She looked at him. He was gloating. How dare he gloat!

She squared her shoulders. "That's not fair. I didn't know that was my last spin. You'll give me more money." She sat in front of the machine patiently waiting for him to put in more money. When he continued to sit on the other stool, she crossed her arms in front of her. Had he suddenly gone deaf? "I'm waiting."

"We had a deal."

She opened her mouth, then snapped it shut. Anger would get her nowhere. She'd already discovered this fact. Two deep breaths, and she looked at him again. "But, Sam, I don't want to leave . . . please." There, she'd asked nicely.

"No."

Nice wasn't working. She clamped her lips together. He would give in, just like the other time. She just had to sit and wait.

"I know what your game is, and the answer is still no." He casually crossed his arms in front of him.

She knew he was waiting for her to give up. Time passed slowly. Anger rose inside her. It wasn't fair. He shouldn't have let her run out of credits.

From the corner of her eye, she saw he hadn't moved. Just sat there, waiting patiently. She had a feeling she wouldn't win this time.

"Okay, I'll leave then." She jumped off the stool and strode toward the entrance, not even waiting to see if he followed. As she neared the exit, she saw the restroom sign. "I will use the facilities before I leave."

He didn't say a word.

She flounced inside and went into one of the stalls. This wasn't good. She wanted to play the machines.

She could feel the color suddenly drain from her face as a horrible thought occurred. What if someone played on her machine while she was away from it? They might win all her money. That wouldn't be fair at all. She'd put the money into the machine. It was hers.

She quickly finished and went to the basin.

"You okay, honey?" a woman asked. She looked very sympathetic. "My name's Janice."

"I'm called Lara, and no, everything isn't all right. Sam won't give me any money. I cannot play without money. I know if I could've played just a little more, I would've won. But he said we had to leave."

Janice frowned. "They're bastards. Every one of them. Hell, we work, too. Why can't we have a little fun? My old man's the same way. Tightfisted bastard."

"Yes, that's what they are." Not that she knew exactly what a bastard was, but it felt good to talk about her anger. She should've known a woman would understand much better than a man. It was as she suspected—women knew more than men.

A woman wearing a crisp black dress came over and handed her a small drying cloth. She took it and began drying her hands. The woman in the black dress held out her hand.

"She wants a tip," Janice whispered.

She had many to give her, but she would settle for one.

"Don't play the slot machines here." She handed her back the towel. Janice chuckled as they left the bathroom together. She didn't know what was funny, and the way she felt, it didn't matter.

Janice glowered at Sam and winked at her, then quickly lost herself in the sea of people and machines. Sam didn't look happy.

"I'm ready."

"Good."

He could've offered to let her play a little more. She wouldn't lower herself to ask again, and she certainly wouldn't beg.

They left the machine area, her feet dragging. She didn't want to leave. She kept glancing Sam's way, but he looked straight ahead, his strides purposeful.

She'd made a deal, and from Sam's explanation, she was almost certain that was the same as a promise. Never in her life had she broken one.

But that didn't mean she had to like it.

She didn't speak to him even after they were on the road that led to the cabin. But when they were almost there, he stopped in front of a building with fuel pumps, but he didn't pull his pickup next to them.

"Why are we stopping?" Hope flared inside her. "Do they have slot machines here?"

"Not even one, darlin'. I just need to pick up a couple of things. Do you want to come inside with me?"

"No." She turned her gaze out the window, refusing to look at him. Actually, she'd have loved to see what was inside the building, but she didn't want to be around Sam right now.

He was mean.

And she was mad.

Mad was good. Her body felt very energized. As if she could bend metal. She reached out and gripped the door handle, twisting it as hard as she could. Nothing happened. Maybe she couldn't change the shape, but it felt good to try.

It would probably feel better to throw something. She glanced around the seat. Sam's pickup was very clean. She didn't see anything to throw.

A short time later, Sam came out of the store carrying a bag. Maybe she would throw that out the window when they started down the road again. It would serve him right because he wouldn't let her play more machines.

He climbed back inside the pickup, setting the bag between them.

"Still mad?"

He'd guessed her emotion, but that still didn't make him smarter than her. She raised her chin and refused to look at him.

"Healers don't get mad," she told him. Now she could add lying to her growing list of bad habits.

"I bought you something that might make you feel a little better."

"I don't want it." She sniffed.

"Okay, then I'll eat it myself."

"Eat?" She glanced across the seat at him. "What is it?"

"Just a chocolate bar." He unwrapped the candy.

"I don't think you're playing fair."

He grinned. "Probably because I'm not." He sobered, drawing in a deep breath. "Slot machines are fun, but you have to know your limits. They can be very addictive."

She drew in a deep breath and glared at him. "I am a healer and therefore, above such temptations. I was only doing research. I do not need them . . ." She raked her gaze over him. "Nor do I need chocolate."

"Okay, fine." He started the pickup and backed away from the store.

His jaw clenched, and his lips were clamped shut. Her gaze strayed to the sack. There were more things inside. She wondered what else was there, but quickly dismissed her curiosity. That's all it was.

Her nose twitched. Chocolate. She closed her eyes and inhaled. It smelled so good. She could almost taste it. Almost, but not quite. Why had she told Sam she could live without it? She bit her bottom lip. As soon as she got to the cabin, she would meditate. She was a healer and just as she'd told Sam, above earth's enticements.

But could she get away with sneaking her hand inside the sack? He must've bought more than one candy bar. She lightly bumped the bag with her arm. It rattled. Sam glanced her way, but she kept her gaze straight ahead, surreptitiously watching from the corner of her eye.

Taking one from the bag was not an option. He would see her and then know he'd won, and she wasn't about to let that happen.

"This is really good chocolate," he broke the silence. "It's different from what I had at the cabin. This is milk chocolate. What you had was dark. This kind is creamier, sweeter, and it has a soft center so when you bite into it, there's a burst of raspberry. Do you know what a raspberry is?"

"No, nor do I care to know."

"Raspberry is a small fruit," he continued as if she hadn't said a word. "They're a little tart. It gives the chocolate that extra zing. You'd absolutely love it."

Her mouth watered. She could almost taste this raspberry flavor just from the fruity aroma that filled Sam's vehicle.

He reached in the bag, pulled out another bar, and slowly unwrapped it. "There's just something about chocolate. They say when you eat it, endorphins are released that'll improve . . . mood and generally make you feel better. Sure you don't want to try some?"

"No."

"The mood you're in, you need to eat a bunch," he mumbled.

"My hearing is quite good, and I heard what you just said."

"Then admit you got carried away at the casino."

"Research."

"You were totally out of control."

"Research."

"Obsessed."

She gritted her teeth. "Research."

"Fanatical."

"Research! Research! Research!"

"Do all healers have tempers like yours?"

She snapped her mouth shut and turned toward the window. "Nerakians are a superior race. I will resist from now on."

Sam knew he should feel at least a little guilty for picking on her. Why was he pushing her buttons?

Easy. Because she'd pissed him off. But dammit, she had to take responsibility for her actions. Research his foot. She'd been like a crazy woman. Eyes all glassy. Hell, there for a minute, he'd thought she might attack him.

The candy bar had probably been pushing it a little. He'd meant for it to be a peace offering, but he'd taunted her with it. Now he felt bad. Sort of.

Hell, she was pushing a few of his buttons, too. Even Nick hadn't been able to do that. Nick was always telling him that he was the most passive person he'd ever seen.

Well, he hadn't been passive since Lara came into his life.

He turned off the highway and down the dirt road. They'd be at the cabin in a few minutes. Maybe a good night's sleep would help them both. He glanced at the clock. Nearly midnight. No wonder they were on edge.

When he stopped in front of the cabin, Lara didn't waste any time getting out of the pickup and going up the steps. He stared. Man, she really could fill out a pair of jeans, and even though he'd made sure the shirt was loose fitting, he could tell she wasn't wearing a bra.

He might've been the only one who could tell. It was the fact that he positively knew she wasn't wearing one. All he could think about was caressing her naked breasts.

"Hot, hot, hot," he murmured. He also had a feeling looking was all he'd be doing until she was over her mad spell.

Another twenty wouldn't have mattered that much, right?

Yeah, one more twenty would've led to another and another until there was nothing left. It was going to be the pillow he snuggled tonight.

He grabbed the bag off the seat. Maybe by tomorrow night she would have mellowed. He'd bought a pizza. Kia loved pizza, so he figured Lara would, too.

For added measure, he'd grabbed a bottle of wine. Briefly, he'd wondered if a Nerakian could have wine. Probably. He didn't see what a glass of wine would hurt. It was just a bunch of mashed grapes.

The cabin was dark except for a sliver of light under the door of the guest room. He listened and heard humming. She must be meditating to rid her mind of Earth's temptations.

He frowned. Did that include him?

"You can meditate all you want, but Earth is still better than Nerak."

Thump.

A second later, her door swung open. His gaze slowly traveled over her. She wore the white robe again, and the way the light came in from behind her, nothing was left to the imagination.

Definitely hot.

"You cannot disturb me when I'm in a trance." She planted her hands on her hips, her feet apart as she glared at him. "In this, you will give me the respect due a healer."

Her eyes shot angry sparks as she apparently waited for him to answer, but the only thing on his mind was the way her breasts were thrust forward, the dark areolas and tight nipples beckoning him to touch, to taste.

"Are you listening to me?"

He shook his head. "How can I listen when you stomp out of your room wearing practically nothing? The only thing on my mind is making love to you."

She opened her mouth, then closed it. "I . . . I must meditate." She whirled around and escaped to her room.

The last thing he saw was a glimpse of two very sweet cheeks. But the door quickly shut behind her with a solid thud.

"I guess making love is out of the question," he said, but the room was empty. Man, he was in pain. If she'd wanted to get even, she had. Won hands down.

He hobbled to the kitchen and put the groceries away. He'd take a cold shower, but it was kind of like giving a drunk coffee—all you got was a wide-awake drunk.

Did Nick have this much trouble with Lara's sister? And what about her cousin Mala? She seemed to blend right in. No, he was almost certain they weren't nearly as much trouble as Lara. Probably because she was a healer and therefore exalted—yeah, right.

He wasn't about to bow down to anyone.

Grabbing a semicold beer, he went out the back door and sat on the top step. After twisting off the cap, he took a long pull, then leaned back on his elbows.

His grin was slow in coming, but it eventually showed up. He had to admit, she hadn't acted much like a healer tonight. No, she'd acted like a normal person with her first taste of gambling fever. It was kind of nice to know she wasn't that different from everyone else.

He finished off the beer and stood. It was a beautiful night. He headed for his room, tempted to pound on the wall that was between them. Her ass would slap the floor again, serving her right.

But that only brought another vision to his mind, and it was purely sexual. Just great. Damned great. He humped over as he shut the door and shuffled the rest of the way to his bed.

Did women hurt as much as men? He hoped so.

Chapter 16

The next morning, Sam dragged his eyelids open and stared at the ceiling. Not a good night. He'd dreamed of Lara. But his dreams hadn't been filled with images of him making slow, sensuous love to her.

No, it was more like he was a dog panting after her, and she was a snotty cat, tail in the air, as she waltzed away chanting, you can't have any.

He rolled over and sat up on the side of the bed.

"Damned chocolate." It had kept him up most of the night. He'd forgotten about the caffeine in it. Speaking of which, he needed some.

He grabbed his pants off the floor and tugged them on, then pulled a T-shirt out of the drawer, and stumbled barefoot to the bathroom.

One look at his face, and he knew it was an image that could give kids nightmares. He settled for washing it and brushing his teeth.

Lara was in the kitchen working with her research plants. She didn't even look up when he walked into the room. As he fixed the coffee pot, he stole glances at her.

She looked as if *she'd* had a good night's sleep. Had she even thought about making love? Probably not. After all, *she'd* meditated.

Oh, God, why'd he have to think about that? The white

transparent robe. Tight nipples, dusky areolas. The thatch of curls between her legs.

He did a quick retreat, going back to the bathroom. After stripping out of his clothes, he turned on the shower and stepped beneath the spray, sucking in air when the icy cold water hit him.

He was one large goose bump when he shivered out and grabbed a towel. But he wasn't hard as a rock. Mission accomplished. The ache was still there, though.

He knotted the towel at his hip and headed for his room. Too bad if she caught a glimpse of his near nakedness. He was only returning the favor.

Except for some reason, he had a feeling she wouldn't suffer nearly as much as he had last night.

Lara happened to look up just as she was putting a drop of chemical on another plant, so she saw Sam making his way back to his bedroom. Her mouth dropped open.

All that beautiful, naked male flesh. Sinewy muscles, tapered hips, firm legs. The drying cloth barely covered him. She tried to swallow and couldn't. "Oh . . . my," was all she could mutter.

She squeezed the stopper, then jumped, immediately realizing what she'd done. "No," she mumbled with disgust. Now she'd ruined this specimen. One drop only, not the stopper-full of chemical.

It was Sam's fault.

She frowned.

No, it wasn't. Just as last night hadn't been his fault, either. He'd been right. Her face grew warm as she remembered how dreadful she'd been. How could she even call herself a healer?

The Elders would've been so ashamed. She was so ashamed.

Sam came into the kitchen. He wore the pants he called jeans, and he'd pulled a black shirt on. His dark hair was damp and fell to the side of his face. She drew in a ragged breath. He looked good even wearing clothes.

He went to the cabinet and got the coffee down without speaking a word. She bit her bottom lip. The silence wasn't good. It made her feel as if her stomach was tied in knots.

When the coffee began to drip into the glass receptacle, she knew she couldn't go on any longer. This wasn't going to be easy. Healers never had to say they were wrong—because they never were.

She stood, bowing slightly. "Forgive me." When he didn't say anything, she raised her head and looked at him. He didn't appear angry, more as if he was trying to decide what to say. She waited patiently.

"It's okay to mess up occasionally," he finally told her.

His words made her feel better, but he still didn't understand. "Thank you for exonerating me of my deplorable behavior."

"But?"

"More is expected from a healer where I come from. No one is closer to the royal family than a healer. We are set above everyone for a reason. We never make mistakes. We're very close to perfection. Do you understand?"

"No."

She raised an eyebrow.

"Okay, maybe I do. Just because you're supposed to be higher than everyone else and better than everyone else at what you do doesn't mean you can't experience life."

"It's complicated."

"But you had fun."

She ducked her head, not wanting him to see the truth of his words reflected in her eyes. It caused her deep sadness to know she'd broken away from what was expected of her.

Before he could say more, there was a noise out front that sounded like a car.

Sam heard it, too, and looked at her, then at the plants on

the glass dishes. "Damn, it looks like a drug lab in here," he muttered as he went to the door.

She followed, curious to see who might be outside.

"Stay here," Sam said as he went to the porch.

A red car had parked beside his pickup. The woman getting out of the driver's side looked the same amount of years as herself. She had black hair and delicate features, and she wore the casual dress of most Earthlings: dark slacks and a short-sleeved white top.

The passenger door opened, and an older woman got out. Lara tensed as she took in the Nerakian clothes. She was vaguely familiar. Lara studied her.

The woman wore the clothes of an interplanetary explorer: deep blue vest coat that reached to the top of her thighs and gold pants. Her hair was a soft brown, swept away from her face.

Her eyes grew wide as the woman came closer, and Lara could see her clear gray eyes.

"I am Aasera," the older woman said. "This is my daughter, Lyraka.

Lara pushed open the screen door and stepped out, glad she'd worn her robes today so she wouldn't bring shame upon herself and all healers. She looked at first one woman, then the other.

Sam groaned. "You were supposed to stay inside," he whispered.

Aasera drew in a sharp breath before bowing. "Welcome, Healer."

Sam looked between them. "Oh, Lord, more aliens."

The younger woman followed her mother's example, murmuring her words of greeting.

Lara stepped further out on the porch. "No, it is I who welcome you, Grandmother and . . . daughter."

"Grandmother?" Aasera's head jerked up. "You are of my DNA?"

Lara nodded, a smile forming on her face as she walked

down the steps. "I have holograms of you. I've visited with you often. Your memory is strong within me."

"What did they tell you . . ." Aasera stopped and looked away.

But she didn't have to finish—Lara knew what Aasera was asking. "That you had passed while on a mission. They told how very courageous you were."

Lara's gaze moved to the younger woman. There was something familiar about her. Then she knew. "You were the one who watched."

"Forgive me for not identifying myself. I needed to know if you were Nerakian. You must be very powerful. No one has ever been able to detect my presence."

Lara nodded her head, accepting the girl's words for what they were—acknowledgement of Lara's superior abilities. Not that detecting people was a strong gift for her.

"You were very good, but you wore a particular fragrance. If not for that, I wouldn't have known anyone was there," she conceded, then reached beside her and took Sam's hand, drawing him forward. "This is Sam."

Aasera raised her eyebrows. "You touch him, Healer?"

Sam grew tense as he stood beside Lara. And so he should. Her grandmother had just insulted them when she forgot her place. Maybe she should remind her grandmother where they stood.

She squared her shoulders. "He has given me shelter so that I might test Earth's plants."

"Forgive me." Aasera bowed her head.

"I have coffee," Sam said, apparently deciding that was a good enough apology. "That is, if you drink it."

Aasera stiffened slightly. No one else seemed to notice. Lara found herself curious to know what had happened to her grandmother. Why she seemed to dislike Sam, or was it because he was a man? In time, she would have answers.

They went inside to the living room.

"I'm sure you have a lot of catching up to do. I'll get the coffee."

As soon as Sam had left the room, Lara took a seat, knowing they wouldn't sit until she did. It was the way of her people, and she acknowledged their deference with a nod of her head.

They sat on the lounging sofa.

"You had a child," Lara said, studying Lyraka.

Aasera clasped her hands tightly in front of her and raised her chin. "I refused to eliminate her. She was born from my body."

"Amazing." She had suspected Nerakians could have children if the circumstances were favorable, but she hadn't been sure. It had been so very long since a woman from her planet had borne a child. "Did you suffer greatly?"

"It was not as bad as the Elders had warned us."

"You question their wisdom?"

Aasera bowed her head. "No, Healer."

"My mother did what she had to do," Lyraka spoke up, then continued. "My father was of this planet."

Lyraka showed a fierce protection toward the woman who'd borne her. She had much of her mother's courage. This was good. But the admission that her father was from Earth intrigued her. She wanted to know what effect it had on her.

"You have gifts?" She already knew Lyraka could move about undetected.

Before she could answer, Sam brought in the coffee and set it on the small table, then looked toward her. "You'll be okay?"

She nodded.

"I'll be out back if you need me."

"Thank you."

Maybe Sam had gifts also. He knew she needed to be alone with Aasera and Lyraka.

When he left, she waved her hand, giving permission for them to serve their drink. Aasera hesitated before filling two cups and adding cream and sugar. After she took a drink, Lyraka followed suit.

"Tell me about these gifts. Did they dilute with the mixing of DNA?"

Lyraka glanced at her mother. It was good that Aasera's daughter would ask permission first. She had given her daughter excellent qualities to live by. When Aasera nodded, Lyraka began to speak.

"My gifts increased with the mixing of Nerakian and an Earthman's DNA. I have speed and hypersensitive hearing."

"Do others know?" This could be dangerous for Aasera's daughter.

"We have been cautious," Aasera spoke up.

"You are wise."

She could see that Aasera wanted to say more. She waited patiently while the grandmother assembled her thoughts.

"Are they exploring again? The Elders told me just before they . . . exiled me that because I had fallen prey to temptation, they wouldn't be taking any more chances and they were stopping interplanetary travel."

Lara could see the hopefulness in her eyes. "My cousin came to Earth after viewing some of your documentation. When her craft returned, there were Earthlings on board. One of them became ill and infected an Elder. I was sent here to find a cure."

Aasera's face drained of color. "An Elder ill! Which one?"

Hearing which Elder was ill would not be easy. Torcara had lived long and was the strongest and most supreme of all the rulers. Everyone looked to her for guidance.

"Torcara," she said as gently as she could, but the blow was visible.

Aasera drew in a sharp breath. "You can heal her?"

"I don't know. I'll try."

Aasera looked toward the back of the cabin, the direction Sam had gone, then faced Lara again. "I have room for you. After I was exiled, I started a place where artists and others can work on their craft in perfect harmony. We have writers and painters, sculptors and poets. You would blend in and be safe."

"I'm safe here."

"He is a young male. They are dangerous to be around. You will think they care, but they don't."

"I cannot disturb my research at this time." She knew there were other reasons, but she refused to voice them.

"We are close if you should have need."

Lara could see it upset Aasera that she wouldn't go with her, but she bowed to her authority. "I'll take your advice under consideration."

They spent the next hour talking about Nerak and the changes that had occurred since Aasera had been gone, and the whole time, Lara could see the longing to return in her eyes.

At one time, the interplanetary travelers had been revered because of the stories they brought back with them. Interplanetary travel stopped about the time Lara was created, but she had a feeling she'd have loved to hear them. The stories had been replaced with artistic dancing and viewings the hologram makers created.

It might not be as exciting as it once had been, but the performances were very . . . beautiful.

The conversation soon began to lag. There was research that needed to be completed. She looked at Aasera and gave an imperceptible nod indicating that their time had come to an end.

"We will leave you to your work." Aasera stood; Lyraka also came to her feet. They bowed at the same time.

Lara stood at the door, watching the dust swirl as the car went down the road. It was good that the grandmother lived. She would like to have time to make the connection with her more complete before she went back to Nerak.

And also with Lyraka. There was something very unusual about her. Her eyes were a luminous shade of blue and very pale. And her hair was very short and dark. She sighed, sensing Lyraka didn't quite know where she belonged.

"They left?" Sam asked as he came back inside.

She nodded.

"I was afraid you'd go with them."

She turned. "My research."

"Is that the only reason?"

She shook her head.

"Good. I kind of like having you around." His smile only lifted one side of his mouth. It was very engaging and made her horny. And his eyes told her he knew what she felt for him. The man was much too full of himself.

She arched an eyebrow. "I was afraid they wouldn't have chocolate." She swept past him.

His laughter followed her to the kitchen. She smiled, not caring that he saw through her façade.

She was starting to see why Mala and Kia couldn't leave. Men were very addictive. But she didn't have the luxury of staying as they had. An Elder's life depended on her finding a cure and bringing it back to Nerak.

No matter how much she would like to stay, it was not an option. But she would make many memories to hold close when she was home once more.

They would be enough to sustain her. They would have to be.

Chapter 17

Lyraka pulled into the small parking area at the colony. Her mother had done a good job pulling everything together here. There was one main building flanked by rows of smaller cabins. Some visitors had one night reserved as they passed through, and others had been here for months.

A bubbling fountain sat in the center of the grounds, surrounded by flowers in an array of bright colors. Tall pines encircled the area like guards watching over everyone. Each day, much like today, there were people standing or sitting in front of their easels as they tried to recreate the woodsy setting on canvas. And then others sat on blankets and meditated as they communed with nature.

Benches were scattered throughout the trees, and though you might not see the person, you would hear the light tones of a flute.

The setting was serene and peaceful, as she often heard people say who visited—a delight to the senses. They couldn't seem to get enough of the colony.

Lyraka lived with her mother in a larger cabin set slightly away from the others. It was much like the size of Sam's cabin, but with a sunroom. Her mother worshiped the sun and seemed to need it. She would often sit there for hours and meditate.

It was a place that had been started for quiet reflection, where one could explore their creative side, but after twenty-nine years, Lyraka had reflected on everything until she felt as if she would start screaming if she had to reflect one more minute.

Maybe because Rick had shown her something more. One brief affair with a guest who'd stayed for a week, then drifted out of her life much like he'd drifted in. One day, he was there, and one day, he wasn't.

But she couldn't leave. It would kill her mother, and she'd never hurt her mother.

She glanced across the seat as she put the car into park and switched the engine off. Aasera had been quiet on the ride back. She worried about her mother's silence.

What emotions had gone through her when she discovered the woman was a healer from Nerak? Not only that, a relative—at least as much as anyone from Nerak could claim a blood relation. It had been a little strange for her to even think of Lara as her aunt when she knew they were about the same age.

Her mother had shown very little reaction. It was the Nerakian way. She might have thought it hadn't affected her mother so very much except the sadness that always lurked somewhere in her mother had come to the forefront. That was evident when Lara had said the people of Nerak were told Aasera's lifecycle had ended.

The Elders had almost been right. Her soul had died when she went into exile.

"Will you be okay?" Lyraka asked.

Aasera smiled, but even that looked sad. "It was good to see the healer. I'm worried about Torcara. We were once very close."

Anger flared inside her. Though they'd never really spoken about the Elders, she had her own opinion, and it didn't coincide with that of her mother's.

This time, she wouldn't hold back. "Torcara told everyone you were dead."

Aasera squared her shoulders. "She did what she had to do to protect Nerak, as she has always done."

It wouldn't do any good to argue with her. She'd already learned that from experience, so she let the matter drop.

They got out of the car but before Aasera had taken more than a step, Lyraka asked, "Do you ever regret your decision? If you'd aborted the . . . pregnancy, no one would've known, and you could've carried on as if nothing had ever happened. You wouldn't have even had to tell the Elders."

Aasera turned and looked at her with a soft smile. "I would've known, and it was unacceptable to me." She shook her head. "I've never regretted the choice I made."

"But you miss Nerak."

She hesitated. "Yes. I miss it." She turned and walked to the cabin.

Aasera would meditate for hours. Go to that special place in her mind. The place that Lyraka had never seen and probably never would. Her mother probably didn't realize it, but she was also shutting out her daughter.

She steeled herself against the pain, told herself it didn't matter. Aasera had given up a lot so that she would have a chance at life. She deserved her mind travels.

Over the years, she'd reminded herself that Nerakians didn't have moments of intense emotions. To do so was rare. Unless, of course, one traveled to Earth. She didn't have to guess what the healer and Sam had been doing.

Lyraka wasn't just Nerakian, though; she was also a part of Earth, and she had emotions. It was getting harder and harder to hold them in check.

The sound of heavy footsteps alerted her that someone approached. She cocked her head to the side and listened. Had someone overheard her conversation with Aasera? No, she would've heard them before now.

She relaxed when Mr. Beacon walked around the side of the building. If she could've picked her father, it would be this man. He always seemed to sense when she needed some-one to talk to.

She smiled. "Hello, Mr. Beacon."

"I can't believe you actually talked your mother into going outside the colony."

Everything about him was thin, from his hair to his frame. He came and went from the colony. Sometimes, she thought he just wanted to be in the company of artists. As hard as he tried, he just didn't have an artistic bone in his body.

"We took a drive in the country," she lied. "I think it did her good." Mr. Beacon had taught her how to drive a few years ago after she'd pleaded with her mother for a solid month. Aasera had finally given in.

"And did it do you good to be away?"

As much as she enjoyed Mr. Beacon's company, she knew she had to be careful what she said. Always, she had to watch her words.

"You know me, I love adventure."

He studied her. "Yet you never leave except to walk in the woods." His forehead knit in concentration. "You were homeschooled, too, weren't you?"

"Aasera wanted my artistic side to develop. She said it would be stifled in public school."

His questions were getting too personal, making her feel uncomfortable. Oh, she knew he offered her no harm. If he did, his true character would've been revealed before now. No, he was only a lonely man seeking company.

He nodded. "Of course she would." He looked toward their cabin. "Aasera is a remarkable woman. I hope whoever hurt her gets his just reward." He tugged on his cap before walking toward the main building.

Could he have a crush on her mother? Was that the real reason he came back so often? Her mother wasn't that old, and she was still a very nice-looking woman.

Not that it would do poor Mr. Beacon a bit of good. Her

mother never accepted any attentions from the men who drifted into the colony. It was rare she even let them stay, and only with impeccable references.

So why did she let Mr. Beacon come back?

She'd watch them interact the next time they were together. If her mother fell in love, wouldn't she loosen her hold a little?

Hope sprang inside her, chased by a quick flash of guilt. She was such an ungrateful child.

"Oh, by the way," Mr. Beacon said, turning around.

"Yes?"

"Did you see the lights?"

Her blood ran cold. She'd hoped no one else had seen them.

"Lights?" she asked as innocently as possible.

"Over in that direction. Very odd, bright flashing lights."

"No, I haven't noticed anything."

"I know what it is."

She began to tremble. "Wh . . . what?"

"It's time to get new glasses." He grinned. "I should've gone back to the doctor last year, but I've been putting it off. You think that might be the reason I can't paint worth a darn? No, don't answer that."

She relaxed and laughed as he turned and started walking away from her again.

That had been a close call. She walked toward the woods, losing herself in the thick trees. This is where she felt the most peace, and she really needed some in her life right now.

The further she went, the more her skin took on the color of her surroundings. She hadn't told the healer everything. No, it wasn't good to reveal all one's secrets.

Once, she had told Aasera about her speed and hearing abilities, but when she saw the fear and worry in her mother's eyes, she immediately stopped. She wouldn't hurt her mother for anything. So she'd quit telling her about each gift that had been revealed over the passing years, and Aasera hadn't asked, assuming her speed and hypersensitive hearing were all the powers her daughter had been given.

She sat beneath one of the trees, leaned back, and closed her eyes. After a few minutes, a squirrel scurried up her chest, stopped, and looked around as if it sensed a presence but wasn't sure where the intruder was.

She was careful not to move, to barely breathe. Once she had laughed when a squirrel ran up and stopped on her. The poor thing keeled over dead.

Her life was filled with guilt, it would seem.

Chapter 18

Deep in transcendental meditation, Lara floated over the buildings again, but this time, she knew them to be Aasera's. She paused and found the grandmother also meditating. Her emotions enveloped Lara in a cloud of sadness and longing to return just once more to Nerak.

Aasera's thoughts were her own. She shouldn't intrude. The cool breezes called to her to explore. Earth was a remarkable place with its tall trees and animals. It felt as if she could travel forever. She wanted to learn as much as possible before she left.

But maybe today was not the day.

Much like she had connected with Sam, she joined Aasera's thoughts.

"Healer, I can feel you with me," Aasera communicated through her own thoughts. "Why?"

"I sensed your longing," she told her.

"Nerak was my home," she defended herself. "It doesn't mean I want to return."

"Doesn't it?"

"I wouldn't leave Lyraka, even if I could return. She wouldn't be accepted by the Elders, and I fear for her safety if I were to leave her."

"But I can take you there. I have many images of Nerak. Let me take you home."

She sensed Aasera's acquiescence, and together they went to Nerak. It was much like the holograms, and they both knew it wasn't as good as actually being there.

Aero units passed by them, gliding between the buildings. There was no grass, no trees like she'd found on Earth. No animals.

But there were skyways where people were transported from one place to another, and bright, shining light that was so pure and magnificent. Earth's sun didn't compare with the glory of Nerak's two.

"The Elders meet here with the people," Lara said, taking her into the new building with golden walls and floating seats. The ceiling reached almost higher than she could see. The artists had created intricate images on the walls depicting great Nerakians: Elders who had passed before them, explorers, and inventors. She showed Aasera the image that had been made of her.

Then she closed her eyes, breathing deeply several times. When she opened them, the room was filled to capacity.

"Oh, the Elders. Torcara," Aasera whispered, her deep emotion washing over Lara. "I'm sorry. It's too much. I must go back."

In an instant, Lara had her back in her windowed room.

"Thank you, Healer, for giving this to me."

"Do not despair. There is a reason for everything. You may yet go home before your lifecycle ends."

She left Aasera's thoughts and moved on, flying high, relishing the freedom. The sun lowered in the sky, creating a palette of deep oranges and dusky blues. It was truly magnificent.

A stream of water ran between the trees. What would it feel like to jump in? She went higher and higher, listening to the sounds around her. She heard the songs from the small winged creatures that flew alongside her. She heard . . . She heard . . .

Tap, tap, tap.

She landed on the floor with a jarring thud.

"Are you meditating? I have dinner ready if you're hungry. I know you said you were resisting, but you might as well eat while you're here."

She heard Sam.

She opened her eyes and glared at him. "I told you not to disturb me when I was meditating." Were men unable to retain anything?

"I whispered." He leaned against the doorframe and grinned, crossing his arms in front of him. "Besides, cold pizza tastes terrible."

Why did he have to look so tempting—more so than this pizza he spoke about?

No, she would be strong and resist. She didn't want his pizza or . . .

A wonderful smell drifted into her room from the open door, very faint but very enticing. Her stomach rumbled. She slapped a hand over it.

"See, I knew you'd be hungry."

The rumbling continued. It felt very . . . strange. "My stomach is making noises."

"That means you're hungry."

He was right. She'd forgotten to swallow a food capsule today. It would take a while for a pill to take effect. She didn't like feeling as if her stomach would cave in at any second.

She raised an eyebrow. "I will eat the food you have prepared."

"Yeah, I know."

"No, you did not know this . . ." Unless. "Can you read minds?" She hadn't thought about people from Earth having gifts. This was quite awkward.

"I know you're worried right now." He looked very self-assured.

"I don't think it's fair you haven't shared your ability to read thoughts."

"Why, Princess? Have you been thinking naughty things?

Things you want to do?" He made a clicking noise with his tongue. "Shame on you," he spoke softly, seductively.

His words were lazy as they drifted over her, causing heat to flare inside her. When his gaze dropped lower, she knew he could see how her body reacted to his words. Her nipples were hard and pressed against the thin robe she wore.

She suddenly realized that nothing was hidden from his heated gaze. The diaphanous material of her white robes left little unseen. She would wear her green robes the next time she meditated.

Her gaze dropped past his face. Yes, she could see he was quite horny. Her thoughts immediately filled with the two of them making love. Her body tingled to awareness as her anger disappeared. Sam had a way of taking it away and replacing it with other, more delicious ideas. She wet her lips.

"Sometimes, anticipation makes everything all the sweeter." His gaze raked over her. "I like what you're wearing. Leave it on and come to the table," he said before he casually turned and left, leaving her feeling quite disappointed.

Desire quickly changed to anger. He'd given her an order. She only took orders from the Elders or one of the princesses. She did not take orders from . . . from . . .

But if she wore her white robe, it would almost guarantee they would have sex after they ate the food he'd prepared. Her body trembled in eagerness.

Another thought occurred. Did he have chocolate? She inhaled. She couldn't smell any, but still, the aromas coming from the kitchen were wonderful.

Sex and food . . . or pride? She weighed the two.

Nerakians were the superior race and highly intelligent. There was only one logical response.

She jumped to her feet and hurried toward the kitchen. When she entered, he was standing at the sink. He turned and looked at her. His smile was almost conceited as his gaze traveled over her. But there was such heat in his look that she didn't really care.

His passion-filled eyes also told her he was glad she hadn't changed. So maybe the victory was part hers. Why should either one of them deny what they wanted? She drew in a deep breath, and suddenly, food wasn't as important. Maybe they could eat later.

"It'll be ready in a few minutes."

What? It was as if he was telling her that sex wasn't as important, that he could wait. But she wanted to have sex, and she didn't want to wait. Then it dawned on her—she knew what he was doing.

Did he think she couldn't resist him? She was a healer, and if she wanted, she could last longer. His reaction to her was quite visible.

She raised an eyebrow. A silent challenge passed between them.

We will see, her thoughts told him.

His look taunted, so we will, she could almost hear him telling her. Before she could study him longer, he turned and continued with the food preparation.

Maybe he *could* read minds. She didn't understand. She was almost certain he couldn't when first she'd met him. No, of course, he couldn't. He was only guessing. Yes, that's all it was.

But she wasn't quite so sure. He did seem different since when they'd first met. As if he was more in tune to what she felt. No, of course, he didn't have special abilities.

She turned her attention elsewhere. Sam had transformed the room. There were small flickering flames on long white sticks set in the center of the table.

"What are those?" she asked, her curiosity getting the better of her.

He glanced over his shoulder. "Candles," he told her. "And those are some flowers that grow nearby. I've always liked them, but don't tell Nick."

"About the flowers? Would he take them away from you?"

"No, but he'd probably razz me about it for the rest of my life." He shrugged. "It's a guy thing."

She reached out and touched one. It was soft.

He'd made the room look very warm and inviting. He'd done this for her. She smiled to let him know how much she appreciated everything. "I'm hungry. We shall eat now."

Had she said something wrong? He wanted her to eat, so she'd come to the kitchen. Maybe her tone had been too demanding. "Thank you, please?" When he smiled again, she relaxed.

"That'll do for now."

He pulled out her chair, and she sat down. "One pizza coming up."

He slipped his hands into gloves and opened the big white box he called the stove. The aromas assaulted her senses again. She closed her eyes and inhaled. She hoped it tasted just as good, and not like the meat and little trees he'd fixed. That had not been good at all. The PB&J sandwich had been much better, though.

"I love the smell of pizza," he said as he inhaled, then removed his gloves and rolled a metal disc with a handle over the pizza. "Okay," he said, slipping the gloves on once again. "This is hot, so wait. I'll get you a slice."

"I like the aroma, too."

He set the pizza in the middle of the table and removed his gloves, tossing them onto the counter.

"Wine," he said, holding up a bottle before twisting off the cap and pouring the dark liquid into glasses. "It's not the expensive stuff, but I've always preferred this and never felt the need to put on airs and drink something I didn't care for."

"It's pretty—lights sparkle inside it."

He handed her one of the glasses, their fingers touched, and tingles spread over her body. She quickly set the glass on the table so she wouldn't spill any of the liquid.

"Thank you for not changing. I like looking at you. You're quite beautiful."

"Yes, I know . . ." No, she wasn't supposed to know. She frowned, then looked at him. "Please?"

He chuckled. "Thank you."

She relaxed. "Thank you. Now we'll eat?"

She must've said something funny again because he laughed some more. Then it dawned on her that maybe he laughed at her. She squared her shoulders. "I do not know your customs."

His gaze dropped. "You're doing quite well."

Sam wasn't looking at her. Well, technically he was, but she wanted him to listen to her. Sex would come later. "Sam!"

He raised his gaze to her face. "I'm sorry; that was rude of me. I wasn't laughing at you, though."

He *could* read her mind!

This wasn't good at all. If he knew her thoughts, he would know how much she wanted to copulate with him. He didn't look as if he'd been reading her mind. But then, she'd found he was quite intelligent.

Had this been what Aasera had tried to warn her about? The tricks men used? If so, she was afraid she might be falling for them as well.

Not good. Not good at all.

Chapter 19

"Here, try this." Sam put a slice of pizza on her plate. "Be careful. It's hot. Let me show you." He took the pronged metal, then stabbed the pizza.

She looked at him for a moment, wondering if this was a trick on his part. She looked at the pizza. It had round things on it, a glob of yellow and green stuff. She'd already discovered she didn't like green stuff, except for money. "Does it taste like the little trees?"

He chuckled. "No, now take a bite. Just try it. Kia loves pizza."

She wasn't so sure about this, but took the bite he offered and slowly chewed. Flavors burst inside her mouth. If this was a trick, then it was a very good one. Different from the chocolate, but this was really good, too.

"Oh, this is fantastic." She took the fork and stabbed another bite. Why did Nerak ever create food capsules? That hadn't been a good idea. Not good at all.

"Try some of the wine."

She picked up the glass and brought it to her lips, taking a tentative sip. The sweet drink had an underlying taste that she couldn't quite describe. Not unpleasant but not exciting, either. "It's not as good as the pizza," she finally decided.

"An acquired taste, I guess."

She took another drink. The second taste was a little better than the first. Odd.

They had liquid on Nerak. It was a special blend of water, which was in short supply, and chemicals to increase the volume, and had no real taste until it was mixed with a smoothie. The liquid provided their bodies with adequate hydration since water supplies were limited.

There was a ringing noise. She looked up. Sam reached in his pocket and removed a sleek black object.

"Nick," he said. "I'd better take this."

She stared at the little box as he flipped it open. Nick did not emerge, though. Maybe it was like their communicators. She'd never really handled one—there was no need. The companion units delivered all messages.

"We're eating," Sam spoke into the little box. "Yeah, pizza. Just like Kia." He smiled across the table at her. "And wine."

He was silent, then regarded her with a look that was almost like . . . fear? He began to choke and sputter before grabbing his glass of wine and downing it.

She took another drink also before he reached across the table and grabbed it out of her hand. How rude. She still had at least two more drinks left.

But she began to forget about her thirst as her body started to tingle and burn, but in a very nice way. Yes, she liked the way she was starting to feel. She studied Sam. Did he seem more handsome, more appealing?

"Yeah, but wine doesn't have that much alcohol in it," Sam said. "I mean, it's like what percentage . . ."

What had him looking so worried?

"But . . ." He looked across the table at her. His smile looked wobbly.

Suddenly, she didn't care. If he was upset about something, Lara was certain she could make it better. In fact, she thought she could have him feeling very good in no time at all.

She ran her tongue across her lips as her gaze slowly traveled over him. He'd wanted her to wear her sheer white robe, but he had all his clothes on. She was the superior race. She should command him to remove his clothes so she could admire his body.

He looked startled, as if he'd read her thoughts. She didn't care about that, either. She wanted to copulate. She needed to copulate, have sex, make love. She didn't care which one, possibly all three at least once, maybe twice or more times tonight.

She was really horny.

"I think I'd better call you back," he mumbled.

She could hear laughter coming from the box before Sam snapped it closed.

"Uh . . . Nick said it wasn't good for Nerakians to drink alcohol. It makes you . . ."

"Take off your clothes," she ordered.

He raised an eyebrow. Surely, Nick had only been pulling his leg. No one became a nymphomaniac on just a few sips of wine. She still had at least a half . . . maybe a fourth of a glass left.

Okay, he'd always been in the driver's seat. The seducer, not the seducee. But there was something in the way she looked at him that said she'd taken control.

Damn it, what the hell was happening? He could feel her need. It swirled inside him a lot like the lights he saw whenever she was having intense pleasure.

No, there wasn't anything strange going on with him. Hell, he could see she was horny. That was pretty obvious.

The feeling inside him grew stronger. He couldn't lie to himself any longer. It was like that day when she'd joined their thoughts. They'd made some kind of connection that didn't completely break when she moved out of his head. He'd been sensing what she felt before she voiced her thoughts. Problem was, it was getting stronger.

Just like now. He could feel her burning need.

She stood, walking toward him. Her nipples were hard little nubs poking at the transparent material. Her near nakedness was a hell of a turn-on. He'd barely made it through dinner. All he'd wanted to do was stare at her. He wanted to do more than that now.

He scooted back in his chair, but before he could stand, she straddled him, rubbing against his erection. He grasped her bottom, pulling her closer.

"I need to have sex," she said, then ran her tongue up the side of his neck. "My body is burning."

"It's the wine. Nick said alcohol heightens sexual desire in Nerakians."

"I ache. Down deep."

"I'll make it okay, baby."

She brought his hands up to cover her breasts, moaning when he automatically began to massage them. "Don't talk. Just touch me," she said right before she covered his mouth with hers.

Lara even tasted hot. Her tongue caressed, then stabbed at his. She devoured him with her lust. He ran his hands through her hair, pulling closer as they sparred, her breasts crushed against his chest, her sex rubbing harder against his erection.

When he ended the kiss, they were both breathing hard. "I have to get out of these clothes," he said, words raspy.

She scooted off his lap and stood, then untied her robe and shrugged it off her shoulders so that the silky material caressed her body before it puddled at her feet. Even that faint touch drew a whimper of arousal from her slightly parted lips.

He couldn't move. Damn, she looked like an alien goddess standing on a cloud. A very sensuous alien goddess with her long blond hair draped across one breast. His gaze skimmed over her tiny waist and gently rounded hips to the thatch of blond curls between her legs, then down her long, slender legs.

"Sam?"

That was all it took to break the trance she'd enveloped him in. He ripped off his shirt and let it fall to the floor. Toed off his boots. Socks, jeans, and briefs were off in record time.

"Yes," she breathed.

He shoved the dishes to the end of the table and went to her, picked her up, and set her on the wooden surface. Would he ever get enough of her?

Make love to me.

Had she spoken aloud? He didn't think so, but her thoughts were becoming his.

She flicked her finger over one of his nipples. He sucked in a breath, then she was covering it with her mouth, sucking, teeth scraping across the hard nub. Her hand slipped between his legs, fingernails trailing up his erection, then encircling him and sliding downward.

He sucked in a deep breath, closing his eyes as his body quivered with the restraint it took to keep from pushing her down onto the table, opening her legs, and plunging inside her again and again.

Damn, he'd wanted her since last night. Since the last time they'd made love. It seemed like forever. He only knew he couldn't hold out much longer if she kept this up. He gently nudged her shoulders until she lay back on the table, letting go of him.

A feast for his eyes.

He ran two fingers down the middle of her chest, circling around each nipple, tugging, then taking them into his mouth one at a time and sucking.

She whimpered.

That's what he liked. To hear a woman crying with need. Wanting release as much as he did.

He ran both hands down the sides of her hips, planted his palm against her mound. She cried out, arching, wanting more.

"I need you now, Sam," she whimpered. "I ache so much."

"I know, baby." He quickly slipped on a condom, then stroked between her legs, sliding a finger inside. She was already damp and ready.

He entered her slowly, deeply, then eased out. She brought her feet up, resting her heels on the edge of the table. When he sank inside her again, he went deeper.

The lights swirled around them: deep fiery reds, hot pinks, wild orange . . .

"Ah, damn, this is so friggin' good," he groaned.

"Yes," she breathed. "Very friggin' good."

Oh, hell, he'd just taught her another word he shouldn't be teaching her. Kia was definitely going to kill him. But right now, he didn't friggin' care as he sank into the wet heat of her body. He slid in faster and faster. The lights swirled around him. Their heat intensified until all he saw were flashes of brilliant colors.

Lara cried out, her body tightening as she took all of him. He came at the same time, could feel the intensity as his orgasm hit him like a jolt of electricity.

As his body came back down to Earth, a wave of exhaustion swept over him. He was drenched in sweat. He leaned forward, not wanting to break the connection with her yet, and rested his elbows on either side of her, his head on her stomach.

"That was friggin' good," Lara said.

He laughed. "Yeah, it was pretty damn hot." And this position was getting uncomfortable. "I'll be right back."

Sex with Lara just got better and better. He quickly used the bathroom, then went back to the kitchen. He was starved. Good thing he liked cold pizza.

She was sitting on the table when he returned. The heat building inside her was almost palpable. Nick had said this would happen, that he should prepare himself for an all-nighter, but Sam hadn't really believed him. Nick was always trying to pull something. Of course he'd been lying.

"Sam?"

Or maybe not.

"A cold shower. That'll help," he told her.

Lara didn't think it would. The heat was rapidly building inside her. "Sex will make it better, I'm positive."

"Ah, man, Nick wasn't pulling my leg when he told me about Nerakians and alcohol. Damn," he muttered.

"We can have sex again?" She looked down. "How long before it will rise?"

"Let's try the shower. I swear I can't have sex for at least an hour."

"My body is starting to burn and tingle again." She didn't know how much longer she could last. She didn't think pouring cold water on herself would make her less horny.

They went to the bathroom, and he turned on the water, then pulled back the curtain. She wasn't too sure about his plan. When she stuck her hand beneath the water, she immediately jerked it back.

"I don't think so," she told him, arching one eyebrow. "That's friggin' cold!"

She wanted release, and she wanted it now. She cupped him in her hand. He began to stiffen. She smiled. Her superior intelligence proved Sam wrong. He *could* get hard again.

He groaned. "I swear I'm not up for a marathon of sex, Lara."

She arched an eyebrow. "You look *up* to me." She turned the handle that would make the water warm, then as soon as the spray was a more reasonable temperature, she stepped beneath it, raising her arms above her head, then slowly lowering her palms over her body, lifting her breasts, offering them to him.

"Make love to me, Sam," she said, her words throaty, husky with need. "I want to feel you buried deep inside of me."

"Screw it. If I go blind, I'll always have this to remember," he mumbled. He stepped into the shower with her, grabbing the shower gel. He poured a good bit into the palms of his hands, then began to lather her body. "I fantasized about this once."

He soaped her breasts, massaging, tugging on her nipples, sliding his thumbs to the underside before cupping them.

"Yes, this is what I need," she moaned as sensations flooded her body. She wasn't so lost in her own pleasure that she didn't want to give back. She took the bottle and squirted the gel onto his chest, then ran her fingers through the hairs, creating more bubbles.

"Having fun?" he drawled.

"Yes." She looked into his eyes and saw the heat. She had known she could make him want her again. Her hands slid behind him, cupping his butt, bringing him closer, rubbing herself against him. "This is good." She clasped his shoulders.

"Yeah, it's real good." He reached up and grabbed the nozzle, spraying the soap from her body. "But the shower is getting slippery."

She didn't care as she moved back so he could spray her front. She liked the way he sprayed water against her breasts. But then he lowered the nozzle. She gasped.

"Do you like that?"

She nodded. He brought the nozzle closer until it was against her sex.

Sam didn't want to move. He wanted to stay right here in the shower and watch. He'd never seen anything so erotic as right at this moment, watching Lara in the throes of passion.

He ran the nozzle slowly up and down her sex. Her hands slid up her body, caressing, touching her breasts, massaging them. He leaned forward, sucking a nipple into his mouth. She moaned.

That's when he knew the bedroom was out of the question. He took her hand and guided it down to the nozzle.

"Right like that," he told her, tugging on her earlobe with his teeth. He jumped out of the shower and grabbed a condom from the cabinet, then slid it on. When he looked at her, heat coursed through him. She leaned against the yellow tiles, her leg raised on the edge of the shower stall, the nozzle against her sex, her other hand caressing her breast.

Her eyes slowly opened. "Sam, I need you inside me."

He swallowed past the lump in his throat as he went to the stall and stepped inside. She let go of the nozzle and stepped closer, kissing him just above his right nipple, then dragging her tongue downward and encircling it before sucking on it.

His ass clenched. Oh, yeah, this was good. He took her leg and brought it to his waist. She wrapped her arms around his neck as he braced her against the back of the shower.

She sucked in a breath when he entered her. Hot, wet heat surrounded him. He closed his eyes, letting the rush of fire spread through his body, fill his testicles, and engorge his erection.

He thrust inside her, sliding out, then thrusting deeper. The colors were back again. They caressed his body. He felt her need, felt the lust coursing through her.

Lights swirled over and around him, passing through his body. Hot reds, cool blues rocking his body. She opened her eyes and met his gaze. The connection was complete. He read her thoughts, cupped her ass, and brought her closer to him; she tightened her hold around his neck.

He plunged inside her body. She bit her bottom lip, wanting more.

Now, Sam, now.

He heard her thoughts. Drove deeper, faster inside her.

"Yes," she cried out as her body stiffened.

Fire swept through him. He couldn't see her, only felt her body shudder against him as his orgasm rocked over him, seeming to shake the ground beneath where he stood.

He looked up at the lights above the cabin. It wasn't the first time he'd seen swirls of color like this. He could almost feel the energy coming from them.

There had been many other times, other places.

When he turned and walked back to the cover of the woods, he was thoughtful.

Chapter 20

Sam couldn't move. Hell, it was too much of an effort to drag his eyelids open. Maybe they *were* open. Oh, Lord, he was blind. He slowly forced one open, and a sliver of light broke through.

Okay, he wasn't blind.

Maybe if he just sort of rolled over, he could swing his legs over the side of the bed and onto the floor and make it to the kitchen for a cup of coffee—or seven. Caffeine sounded good right now. A couple of pots might make him feel alive and less like the living dead.

There was a moan beside him. Lara? Had she survived? He reached out. His hand came up against something soft and warm. He ran his hand over it, stopped at the nipple.

Reaction.

Excruciating pain!

Down, boy!

Oh, man, it hadn't fallen off after the sixth or seventh time they'd made love. He'd been almost certain it had.

Nope, it was definitely there. He knew because if it could talk, it would be cursing him, screaming out, are you an idiot or what!

"I want to vaporize you, Sam," Lara murmured beside him.

"I think you already did." Not even one little drop of alcohol would pass her lips as long as he was alive. "No more wine."

"No," she agreed. "No more wine."

He finally managed to sit up on the side of the bed, resting his head in his hands. So this was what death warmed over felt like. He scraped his fingers through his hair, then reached for his jeans.

It even hurt to raise his leg and slide his jeans up. He grimaced as he fastened them. His gaze moved to the bed.

Ah, damn, was she into torture or what? The sheet was draped across her hips, but that was just about all it covered. Her rosy-tipped breasts were just too damn tempting . . . except he was in severe pain. She'd turned on her side and stared at him through bleary eyes.

"Kitchen . . . coffee," he mumbled as he hobbled out of the room before he did something that would hurt both of them. Damn, he could barely walk.

He made a pit stop at the bathroom, then onward to the kitchen. In no time, the coffee was dripping, the rich aroma drifting upward, tickling his senses.

A few minutes later, he heard Lara moving about, and then she walked into the kitchen looking a hell of a lot better than he felt.

"I like this time the best," she said as she went to the screen door, drinking in the morning.

She was so beautiful. How did a guy like him end up with a woman like her? He'd dated some nice-looking women, but Lara was different, special.

She's an alien, idiot. Of course she's different.

Yeah, he needed coffee.

Sam had a feeling that even if she hadn't been from Nerak, she'd be special. She'd traveled to a distant place with very little knowledge about Earth, risking her life to save one of the Elders. She had more courage than most hard-nosed cops that he knew.

Yeah, she'd be special no matter where she was from.

He poured some coffee and raised the cup to his lips. There was something about that first drink. He closed his eyes and savored the taste. This was living.

She turned and smiled.

And now his day was brighter.

"There's some orange juice in the fridge. Do you want some?"

She bit her bottom lip. "It won't make me horny, will it?"

He chuckled as he set his cup on the counter and went to the refrigerator. "Probably not." He got the juice out and poured her a glass.

She took it from him and sniffed, then took a hesitant drink. When she lowered the glass, she was smiling. "It's good. Much like a smoothie."

Just as suddenly, her smile wavered, and he felt her anxiety. "What's the matter?"

She shook her head. "I'm not any closer to finding a cure."

"Do you need to test more plants?"

She shook her head. "I'll check these that I already have. Add more chemicals, and see if there's any reaction at all. Maybe one will be the right plant."

"How sick is the Elder?"

"She seemed very ill before I left. I've never examined someone this sick."

"There's no disease on Nerak? I mean—none?"

"No."

"What about death? People die. The heart has to stop at some point."

"We have ways to ease the passing when it's time so there is no pain."

Okay, enough on that subject. If they said, 'bye, grandma, then zapped them into dust he didn't even want to know about it. He already had an illegal alien and drugged smoothies on his growing list of things he probably shouldn't be mixed up in. He certainly didn't want to add zapping people when their time had come.

Although, zapping might not be a bad idea. He could think of a few people he'd like to zap—at least one, in particular.

His phone rang. He reached for it, flipped it open, and glanced at the number. Speak of the devil.

"I'll leave you alone so you can do your research," he told Lara.

She nodded, already getting started.

As soon as he was alone, he pushed the button so he could talk. "Do you think a warning would've been in order?" Sam said to Nick.

Nick chuckled. "I'd forgotten about it. Kia's never had alcohol."

"Then how did you know?"

"Mason warned me before we left his ranch. Told me he and Mala had been in San Antonio, and she'd wanted to try a margarita."

"It would've been nice if you'd shared that information. Is there anything else you might want to tell me?"

"Your dick will turn purple and fall off."

He could feel the color drain from his face. "You're kidding!"

"Yeah. Gotcha, didn't I?"

He moved the phone away and frowned at it before bringing it back to his ear. "That isn't funny. I could've had a heart attack."

"Other than the alcohol incident, how are things going?"

"No cure yet." His stomach lurched. Damn, he didn't even want to think about Lara leaving. "But something did happen that neither one of us expected."

"What's that?"

"Their grandmother didn't die. She's living practically next door. Lara said she had an artists' colony or something. The reason she didn't leave was because she was pregnant."

"Kia said her cousin had told her there were other Nerakians living on Earth."

"It feels like a damn family reunion here. I don't think the grandmother likes me, or men in general." He cleared his throat. "How's your partner working out?"

"It's my day off. Thanks for ruining it."

"It's nice to know I can get a little revenge."

"Gotta run. Kia is dragging the pups and me walking. Do you know how bad it looks to be dragged around by four girly pups? I'll tell Kia about her grandmother. I've noticed they're funny about family, though. There's not much of a connection. It's almost as if . . ."

"They were created in a laboratory? Not taught how to hug or show real emotion?"

"Yeah, I see what you mean. They learn real fast, though."

They said good-bye, then Sam clicked his phone closed and slipped it into his pocket. He walked to the door and looked out. The trees were thick and tall. A light breeze carried the scent of pine through the house.

A squirrel ran up one of the trees, stopped halfway, looked around, then jumped to a nearby limb.

He thought about his mother and father. They had hugged their kids a lot, praised them, gone to bat for them, and even spanked them when they'd needed it. But all through his growing up years, he'd known he was loved.

Lara had grown up so differently. He sensed curiosity and wonder warring with all she'd been taught. Maybe she could at least change a few things when she got back home.

He looked over his shoulder, knowing he didn't want her to leave any time soon. He grinned, remembering how uppity she could get. It had infuriated him at first, but then he realized she came by it naturally. It was all she'd ever known. He wanted more for her. Before she left Earth, he hoped Lara would have a different outlook on life.

He went to his room and finished dressing before stepping outside, then grabbed his fishing pole and headed for the river. She needed to be able to concentrate on her research, and he wouldn't mind having fish for supper.

But when he got to the edge of the woods, something didn't feel right. Gut instinct told him something was out of place. He scanned the area. He was about to put it down to being a cop way too long when he noticed how the grass was crushed in one area. As if someone had stood there, watching.

A closer inspection revealed a boot print a little further away. Sam straightened. From this angle, he had a perfect view of the cabin. The print was fresh. It was too big for Lyraka or Aasera.

Then who? A hunter? The imprint showed a slick-bottomed shoe. Most hunters wore ridged shoes or boots for better traction. He didn't think this was the print of a hunter. Someone was apparently interested in him . . . or Lara.

Lara checked another plant that had been sitting in the added chemical. Still nothing. She came to her feet, pushing away from the table. All morning, she'd been working. Nothing. What if she didn't find the cure? A shudder swept through her. No, she wouldn't think like that.

A sudden feeling that she wasn't alone swept over her. She whirled toward the screen.

"I'm sorry. I didn't mean to startle you," Lyraka said.

"On Nerak, we let our presence be known," she reprimanded, raising her chin. "You may enter."

Lyraka hesitated for a second, then opened the door and came inside. "My mother doesn't know I'm here."

Lara moved to the area Sam called the living room. She didn't want to disturb her research.

She sat in the chair. Lyraka went to the lounging sofa, sitting on the edge, looking as if she might dart out of the cabin at any second.

"Oh, was I supposed to wait for you to give permission so I could sit?"

"It's no matter. You don't know all our customs."

She stiffened. "But I wouldn't shame or embarrass my mother."

"You aren't." She studied Lyraka. They were about the same age. "Why have you come?"

"I want you to take my mother back with you."

"That would not be permitted. You must know that. It would upset everything on Nerak."

"But I'll stay behind. No one would have to know I exist." She drew in a deep breath. "She's dying here. She misses her people."

"And wouldn't she miss you just as much?"

Lyraka jumped to her feet. Lara didn't tell her that was not permitted; the girl was so clearly agitated that she decided to relax protocol. Besides, Lyraka wasn't from Nerak and didn't know the ways of the people—her people, too.

"Aasera could come back. You know, for a visit or something."

"Interplanetary travel is forbidden."

Lyraka turned, a hard edge in her eyes, in her stance. "I know I would never be permitted to see that part of my ancestry. I'm, after all, only half Nerakian. My blood is tainted."

Lyraka strode to the front door. The screen was the only barrier between inside and out. She stood there without speaking, but she didn't have to. Her frustration, the turmoil inside, rolled off her in waves.

"Maybe you're the best of both worlds?"

Lyraka jerked around to face her. "Yeah, right. I bet they would accept me with open arms on Nerak." Her laugh was bitter. "I would be ostracized, an oddity only. After all, isn't Nerak the perfect planet? That's what my mother has always told me."

Lara's gaze traveled out the door to the tall trees Sam called pines. She inhaled their fragrance, which scented the cabin when both doors were left open. And Earth had chocolate and pizza. They had lots of water.

Aasera had kept the good memories of Nerak, but Lara was discovering it wasn't quite as perfect as she'd thought.

"Maybe we only think it's perfect because it's all most of

us have known." There, she'd admitted aloud what she'd started to feel.

"I thought you were a healer, one of the exalted ones, next to the royal family? Yet you admit Nerak isn't all it's cracked up to be?"

Now Lyraka had confused her. "No, Nerak isn't cracked at all. Our planet is quite stable." Had she given the impression that Nerak was defective?

Lyraka laughed. Lara enjoyed the sound. Deep and throaty and vibrant. She would make a good warrior. Like Kia.

"If you weren't a healer, I think we could be friends."

Friends? She thought about it for a moment. "Why can't we be friends?"

"You're practically royal blood."

"Yes, but it doesn't mean we can't be friends. I'd like someone other than Sam to discuss Earth with—a female's point of view. I'd like to know more about it. Sam has shown me some things. He took me to gamble."

Lyraka raised her eyebrows. "You gambled? At the boats? Why would he take you there?"

"They mentioned it on the television. I wanted to experience fun and excitement like it said. It was quite frustrating, though. The slot machine took all my money. Have you gambled?"

"No. I rarely leave the colony. Aasera worries about my safety, but there are artists and writers who live there. Mostly women. Because of my father, Aasera doesn't trust men. I've enjoyed their company."

"Then you haven't had sex."

Her face took on a rosy hue. "There was a man once." She smiled and hugged herself. "But then he left." She shrugged. "I enjoyed the time I spent with him. Aasera didn't know about him. Or maybe she did, and that's why he left."

Good, she would hate it if Lyraka hadn't enjoyed some of the better things on Earth. "And do you know your purpose in life?"

"I'm not sure I have one." Her shoulders slumped as she went back to the sofa and sat, curling her feet beneath her.

"But you have many gifts that you haven't told Aasera about." When Lyraka looked at her, Lara could see the truth in her eyes. "Why haven't you told her?"

"It would only upset my mother."

"I know loyalty," she said. "I came to Earth for one of the Elders."

"But do you know a love so fierce you would do anything to protect the other person? Even if it meant giving up your own life? I don't mean traveling to Earth. Would you give up everything for the one you loved?"

"But why would anyone do that? It's foolish."

"Then you've never known love."

"If this is what love is, then I don't think I want to know it."

There was a wistful expression on Lyraka's face as if her past, her present, but most important, her future rose up in front of her. "Sometimes, it feels like a slow death." When she looked at Lara, the melancholy was gone, replaced with a smile. "What do you think about Earth so far?"

"I enjoy the sex very much. I'll miss it when I return."

Lyraka laughed. "Ah, yes, there is that."

A knowing look passed between them. Lara had a feeling Lyraka had a passionate nature that was ready to break free. She reminded her of her cousin Mala. Maybe Aasera would realize that her daughter needed her freedom.

It would be interesting to see what happened. But she would be on Nerak by then. Maybe someday, the Elders would allow travel once more—and chocolate.

Chapter 21

Sam stayed at the edge of the woods, watching and waiting, but the only person he'd seen coming or going had been Lyraka. That had been an experience in itself. One minute, no one was around the cabin; he blinked, and there she was standing on the back porch.

He'd heard Aasera, Lyraka, and Lara talking the other day while he'd waited outside. Their words had carried easily on the soft breeze. Lyraka had admitted to some kind of gift—speed or something. He just hadn't known she meant so fast if you blinked, you'd miss her.

Someone had been watching them. He didn't think it was Lyraka. But who?

As soon as Lyraka left, he walked back to the cabin, leaving his pole and tackle box on the front porch. He went in through the front door, then to the kitchen where he stood watching Lara. He was careful not to say anything so she wouldn't jump and mess up something.

She brushed a strand of hair behind her ear and reached for another stopper, extracting liquid from a vial. Each movement was precise. He studied her features as she concentrated on what she was doing. She had a heart-shaped face and delicate features.

He grinned. There wasn't anything delicate about her,

though. She was as tough as nails. He kind of liked that about her. She wouldn't take anything off anyone.

Something must have alerted her that he was there. She looked up and smiled.

"I didn't mean to disturb you."

"You didn't."

"More testing?"

Her forehead creased. "Nothing seems to react. I would've thought one of your plants would have worked by now."

"I saw Lyraka leave."

She raised an eyebrow.

He turned serious, wanting her to know they should be on their guard. "Someone has been watching the cabin. I'm not sure who, but I came across a man's footprint near the edge of the woods. It might be nothing, but better safe than sorry. From now on, don't leave unless I'm with you."

She bowed her head slightly in acquiescence. "Of course. Do you think he offers me harm? That he might suspect I'm Nerakian?"

He could see that she was hiding her fear of this unknown interloper. He would try to reassure her the best he could. "I'm not sure, but don't worry. I'll protect you."

"Yes, you are a warrior." She turned back to her tubes, effectively dismissing him.

He frowned, but she was already lost in her research and didn't notice. She could've at least said thank you, or, you're my hero. She just assumed he would put himself in danger for her.

Maybe he would, and maybe he wouldn't.

Damn, would she ever stop being so uppity? He strode toward his room. By the time he got there, his irritation at her was gone.

Of course, she'd known he would protect her. And he would. He was a cop, a warrior like her sister. It was probably just a trespassing hunter in the woods anyway. No one knew about her, and he didn't have any enemies that even knew about the cabin.

The fact that he probably didn't need to protect her still didn't make her any less uppity, though. But perhaps, uppity in a good way.

And now he was stuck guarding her, just in case. Okay, not so bad a deal. He could take her fishing. She could get out of the cabin for a while. He'd already seen that she had to let the chemical sit for a few hours at least before she could do any testing.

He heard her moving about. Maybe she was finished for a while. He hadn't gotten to go fishing this morning because he had been watching the cabin. What woman wouldn't love dropping a line in the water? He grinned. She wanted to experience what Earth had to offer. This was the perfect solution.

When he went back to the kitchen, she was standing beside the sink with her back to him, fiddling with something. "Need some help?"

She jumped, then looked over her shoulder.

"Sorry, I didn't mean to startle you."

"I was thirsty, but there isn't any more juice. I found this . . ." She grunted. "Got it!" She tossed the cap on the cabinet and turned with a smile on her face. "I found this." She raised the bottle to her lips.

"No!"

She paused, frowning.

"Put . . . the . . . beer . . . on . . . the . . . counter . . . and . . . step . . . slowly . . . away . . . from . . . it."

"Why can't I have a drink?"

He took a deep breath. Sweat broke out on his forehead. "That's alcohol."

Her face lost some of its color. She carefully placed the beer on the counter and stepped back. Her sigh was visible.

"I didn't know."

"I understand completely. I should've warned you." He hurried to her side and took her into his arms. Her body trembled.

"It's not that I don't want to make love with you, but maybe not so frequently."

"It's okay. I know exactly what you mean. We should pour out the beer." She reached for the bottle.

"No!" He grabbed it away from her. "What I meant to say was we shouldn't waste it. I promise to buy you some sodas the next time I make a grocery run."

"Sodas?"

"You'll like them."

"Good. But no beer."

"Right. No beer." That tragedy had been safely averted. "Hey, can you take a break? I thought I'd take you fishing."

"I'd like that. What's fishing?"

"Trust me. You'll love it."

Lara didn't think Sam was correct in his assumption that she'd love fishing. It all seemed rather mundane to her. She reeled the line in—again. Throw it out, reel it in. What was the point in doing this? Could this be the exercise he'd mentioned?

"You've caught on really fast," Sam commented.

"Of course, I'm a superior being."

"No, you're not."

She glanced his way. He cast his line and began to slowly reel it back in.

"You doubt me? I told you, I don't lie."

"I believe you think you're superior, but you're not. In fact, I've come to the conclusion that we're the superior race."

She sputtered, but nothing intelligible came out of her mouth. She cast the line and furiously began to reel it back in. What did he mean Earth people were the superior race? The idea was ludicrous.

"No, you're not," she finally told him in a voice that brooked no argument.

"Yes, we are."

"We have interplanetary travel. You don't."

He shrugged. She didn't like the way he didn't even look at her. As if it was of no consequence that her people could travel from one planet to the next. She was a healer, and he should show her the proper respect.

"We send men to the moon. It's no biggie."

She raised her chin. "We don't have wars."

"Or passion. You had to build robots just to have sex."

True, but she didn't like his implications. "Men killed each other off in their wars. What were we supposed to do?"

He laughed as he tossed his line in the water. "You didn't do anything. That's the problem. You stopped living. You dug a hole and buried yourselves."

"We encourage cerebral thinking, beauty, and peace."

"And what do you do for fun?"

She threw the line out again and slowly reeled it in. They didn't have gambling. That had been a lot of fun, but what they did have on Nerak was very pleasant. "We have holograms that will take us anywhere we want to travel."

"Kind of like your companion units. They're not real, either."

"They're much safer. And we have artists. Dancers that perform each night. It's all meant to be very calming."

"Sounds just dandy."

He was a man. He couldn't understand. Their planet was quiet and serene . . . and she was afraid very boring compared to his. But she wouldn't agree with him.

"We're still superior."

"No, you're not."

She stomped her foot. "Yes, we are."

"Have you always had this temper, Princess?"

"I am not a princess. And I don't have a temper. There was something in my shoe."

"You're not dead, either."

"I'm quite aware of the state of my health." She reeled her line in, except there was a tug that hadn't been there before.

Like it was pulling back. "Your fishing pole is broken," she finally said.

"No, it's not. I just put a new line on it the night before I left Dallas."

"It doesn't want to wind back up."

"You've got a fish!" He dropped his pole on the ground and made a grab for hers, but she moved it away from him.

"You gave it to me. I'm not giving it back."

"But this is the only damn fish that's even nibbled. Don't let it get away."

"Then tell me what to do. As I said, I'm superior. I can do whatever it is I'm supposed to do." She arched an eyebrow. "Did you growl at me again?"

His forehead wrinkled, but he looked as if he was through arguing. "Slowly reel it in," he told her.

She'd won again. Of course, she'd known she would. Besides, he was rather handsome when he became upset. She liked sparring with words, especially with him. It created an energy inside her that was almost sexual in nature and very pleasant. It made her quite horny.

"It doesn't want to come in," she said.

"Let it out a little then. You want to play with the fish. Let him think he's winning."

Ah, much like it was with Sam.

So maybe she would catch this fish just to prove she was superior and could do it. Hmm . . . she wondered what she was supposed to do when she caught it. Or what a fish even looked like.

"Okay, pull back on the rod. That's it. Now, let it drop forward and reel it in as fast as you can until it gets tight again."

"It's tight."

"Let it drop forward."

He came up behind her. She leaned back and for a few seconds forgot she'd felt almost like a warrior as she tried to bring in the fish. His warmth enveloped her in a cocoon when he stood this close to her, and her thoughts were filled with more than catching a fish. No, the fish didn't really matter any more at all.

"Nope, this is your fish," he said, again reading her mind. "I'm just here for moral support."

"I don't believe the fish wants to be caught."

"They never do. You just have to let him know who's boss."

"I don't feel like I'm the boss. What's a boss?"

"Someone who has control."

"I'm not sure I do."

"Think of it this way. I don't think fish have brains, and if they do, then they're pretty small. Are you going to let it outsmart you?"

Her shoulders stiffened. "Of course not." She reared back, loosened the line, and then reeled it in.

"That's it! You've got him!"

He grabbed a net and eased to the edge of the bank, scooping it into the water. When he brought it back up, there was a wiggling creature inside. She stepped closer, bending down to observe it.

"Wow, I didn't think there were any fish left. This one's at least three pounds."

"Now what do we do?"

"I'll scale it, gut it, and fry it up for supper."

She straightened. "You expect me to eat this . . . creature?"

"You better believe it. Best eating you'll ever have. The biggest, most beautiful bass I've seen in a long time." He raised it out of the net with his fingers inside the neck of the fish.

It was still attached to the line. She watched as he wiggled the hook loose. For just a second, the fish looked at her.

"You'll take its life?" she asked.

"Well, yeah." He shrugged. "People eat fish."

"I don't want to eat it. It looks sad. Does it know you're about to murder it?"

"No, see, it's like this . . ."

She raised an eyebrow, not understanding how it could

be anything other than what she'd just said. She waited to see what Sam would do next. She didn't much care to watch the poor creature's demise.

He sighed. "Or we could put it back in the water and let it swim away."

She relaxed. "I think I like that idea much better."

He mumbled something she couldn't understand as he returned the fish to the water.

"Will its mouth hurt from the hook? It looked quite dreadful when you pulled it out. I should've taken a look to see if I could help ease the pain."

"I doubt it hurt." He shook his head, staring into the water. "That was a beautiful fish," he said as he began to gather their things.

"Yes, aren't you glad you returned it to its home?"

"No."

"Sam?"

"I'm glad you're happy."

"That's good enough." She turned and began the trek back to the cabin. "Thank you for taking me fishing. I enjoyed it very much."

"Yeah, yeah," he grumbled.

"Sam, I'm hungry. Do you have any chocolate?"

"Nope."

"What will we eat?"

"I can tell you what we won't be eating."

"What's that?"

"Fish. Beautiful fish filets, tartar sauce, fries, hush puppies . . ."

"But you let something live."

"You bet." He didn't sound as if he were at all happy with his decision. But she was. Maybe after she left, Sam would have a different feeling for the lives of fish. She'd almost bet he wouldn't take the life of another one.

Maybe this was part of her purpose. To save Sam from murdering fish.

Chapter 22

If Nick ever found out Sam had let a fish go, he would never hear the last of it. Man, that had been a sweet fish. Lara just didn't understand about some things. Fishing was a part of men as much as breathing.

"I'm ready," she said.

He'd laid out some clothes for her to wear. It would be fun taking her out to eat, seeing what she thought of a real restaurant.

He should order her fish, then tell her later. Nice thought, but he wouldn't do that to her. It had been a sweet-looking bass, though.

He turned from the door where he'd been staring out at the night. There just seemed to be more stars in the East Texas sky than in the city.

But when he turned, he saw something that shone even brighter and threatened to take his breath away. All he could do was stare. Had there ever been a more beautiful woman than the one standing in front of him? He didn't think so.

Lara had brushed her hair until it shone. It fell to her waist in soft golden curls. The dress Kia had packed fit her like a glove—a slinky black glove showing every curve, every indentation to perfection as it fell in soft folds down to her knees. Man, she had killer legs.

It was cut low in the front, baring the curves of her

breasts. In the center was a red stone on a chain. It looked like a ruby, but one as big as his thumbnail? It was big enough to buy twenty cabins.

He remembered Kia's promise stones. Okay, it probably was genuine. It looked real enough the way it sparkled when the light hit it. Big enough that most people would probably think it was a fake, a nice fake but still a fake. That should keep them safe from a mugger.

The stone still couldn't compare to the fire that radiated from Lara, though.

"You look beautiful," he told her.

She raised her chin in a way that would've made the Queen of England proud. "Yes, I know, even if I'm not supposed to. There's a mirror in the bedroom."

"Yeah, I guess it would be pretty foolish to deny it." She was funny. He liked that even if she didn't realize she was being funny. There was a lot about her he liked. Trouble with a capital T. At least for him. He knew she wanted to find the cure so she could get it back to Nerak. Yeah, he'd miss her a lot.

She was quiet on the way to the restaurant as she stared out the window.

"What are you thinking?" he asked.

"That I like your night. The stars sparkle like our promise stones. There is a peacefulness about the darkness. We can dim our lights, but it isn't the same."

"Do you think you'll ever get to return to Earth?" he finally asked the question that he already knew the answer to. Maybe he wanted her to make it final.

She shook her head. "No. Even if interplanetary travel was permitted, I wouldn't be allowed to travel. It's not in my DNA to explore. I'm a healer."

"But you're here now. Maybe you can come back to test other plants."

"We have others who do that. I would only work with

them when they returned. I'm only here to remove a step in the process. It won't be necessary in the future."

"Then we'll never see each other again."

"I'll have regrets, too," she admitted after a few seconds passed. "I'm not like Kia and Mala. My home is Nerak. My loyalty is to the Elders."

"Yeah, I kind of figured as much." He could feel her sadness at the thought of leaving. Maybe he just sensed it. That gut instinct thing again.

He wasn't in love with Lara or anything. It was just that he liked being around her. There was something about her that tugged at his heart. He'd miss her a lot.

"I'll miss you, too."

His head jerked around. "Are you sure you can't read minds?"

"Sometimes, I think I can hear your thoughts."

"Me, too. Yours, that is. Odd, isn't it?"

"We make connections with people who mean . . . who mean more to us than others, I think."

"Do I mean something more to you?"

"For an Earthling, yes."

He chuckled. "Go ahead, you can admit it. I mean more to you than you want to say."

She sighed. "Yes, Sam Jones, you mean a lot to me."

"Is it my good looks, my prowess in bed, or my great sense of humor?" He liked teasing her.

"No, none of that. It's the fact that you didn't kill the fish today that has endeared you to me."

Okay, now that wasn't a bit funny. "Is that the only reason?"

She laughed. "And no one thinks healers have a sense of humor."

"I think you've been talking to Nick."

They arrived at the restaurant. He hurried to her side as she was opening her door. "Here, let me."

"I'm capable of opening a door now that I know how. I learned very quickly what is expected of me while I'm on Earth."

"Sometimes, a man likes to do it."

"Why?"

"Because they just do."

"I accept your gesture." She bowed her head slightly in acknowledgement.

He couldn't resist. When she raised her head, he kissed her. Just a light brushing of his lips across hers, but it sent fire through his blood. Her pupils dilated, telling him she felt the power of that one touch just as much as he did. It was nice to know that he made her want him.

"Come on." He took her elbow, but then let go. He wanted this night to be special.

"You may touch me."

She had her nose up in the air, but he noticed it wasn't as high as it used to be. And again, he could almost sense her thoughts. "I think you want me to."

"Maybe you'd be right," she said without missing a step.

He grinned when he took her arm again. They walked in the restaurant. It was dimly lit, the atmosphere romantic with candles flickering on the tables.

"Welcome to Land's End," an older, gray-haired woman said. "Are there only two in your party?"

"Yes," he said, but his gaze was on Lara as she looked around, her eyes as big as they were the other night at the casino.

"This way."

They followed her to a small table in the corner. It didn't take Sam long to notice the way everyone in the room watched Lara. She was a strikingly beautiful woman. He couldn't blame them for staring.

"Your waiter will be with you in a moment. Enjoy your meal."

"Thank you." Sam held the chair out for Lara. She sat down, then he went to his.

A waiter came over, looking very starched and formal in his black pants, crisp white shirt, and black jacket. "Welcome to Land's End. Would you like to start off with a glass of wine?"

"No!" they spoke at the same time.

Startled, the waiter stepped back.

"We're allergic to wine. Both of us," Sam quickly told him.

"That's not exactly true," Lara told the man. "It makes me horny, and we have sex many times before I feel satisfied, and Sam gets very sore."

"Uh . . ." The waiter looked between them, his face turning a bright red. He cleared his throat. "I'll just get some water then." He hurried away as if the restaurant was on fire and he was the only one who knew where to find the extinguisher.

"He seemed nice." Lara smiled.

It was all Sam could do to keep a straight face. Damn, he really liked this restaurant a lot. Too bad he wouldn't be able to set foot in here again.

"Yes, he seemed nice."

She frowned. "Did I do something wrong?"

"He's only dazzled by your beauty."

"Of course."

The waiter returned to the table with a bottle of water and poured them each a glass before he handed them menus. "May I suggest the grilled salmon with a lemon dill sauce? It's a specialty of the chef."

"What's salmon?" Lara asked.

"No, uh, she has allergies," Sam quickly said. "How about the rice and vegetables and baked potatoes, and I'll have the same but add a nice juicy steak."

"Very good, sir."

"Are they going to murder another animal so you can eat it, Sam?"

How could she look so damned innocent when she asked him that? He drew in a breath. This was her night. He glanced at the waiter, who was looking very snitty if you asked him.

"Just bring me what she's having."

He raised an eyebrow. "No steak, sir?"

Okay, he was getting real tired of all the condescending people in the world—or any other world, for that matter. "You want a tip or not?" he countered.

The waiter scooped up the menus and quickly departed.

"I don't suppose they have a peanut butter and jelly sandwich?"

"I think you'll like this."

"It'll be hard going back to food capsules."

"Maybe you can talk to the Elders about introducing real food."

"Maybe."

"What if you don't find a cure?"

"I'll still return. The Elders set a time limit. If the specified time has completed and I still don't have a cure, then I'll leave."

He went still. "You didn't say anything about having to leave at a certain time."

"I didn't think it mattered. After all, if I found a cure, I would've left anyway."

"When?"

"In three of your Earth days."

He drew in a shaky breath, not realizing her leaving would affect him this much. He'd just assumed they'd have a lot longer. "That soon?"

"You're upset."

He shook his head. "No, just surprised."

He leaned back in his chair, but he couldn't relax. A band had assembled on stage, and they began to play a slow song. He stood, reaching out with his hand. "Come on, let's dance." He needed to hold her, to feel her head against his shoulders.

"But I'm not a dancer. It's not in my DNA. I . . . I can't."

"It doesn't have to be a part of your DNA or anything. If you want to do it, Lara, just do it. Come on, I'll show you. You'll have fun."

She hesitated, then stood, taking his hand. He led her to the dance floor, then turned and took her in his arms. Her skin felt warm to the touch, and she smelled so damn sweet. And she trembled.

"Just move with me. That's all you have to do. It isn't a big deal."

"People are watching," she whispered. "Do they expect us to perform?"

He smiled. "No, they just like looking at a beautiful woman, and you're very beautiful." He held her close, breathing in her essence, knowing it would have to hold him for a lifetime. Three days? Man, it wasn't nearly long enough.

Ah, damn, when had he started to care? He knew the answer—the minute he'd seen her. But she couldn't stay. He really had rotten luck sometimes.

The song ended all too soon. He stepped back. "You dance beautifully, even if it isn't part of your DNA."

She was smiling, her eyes sparkling with excitement. "I enjoyed that very much. This would be fun to introduce also." Just as quickly, her smile was gone. "I don't think it will be the same, dancing with our companion units."

He didn't much care to think about Lara dancing with her companion unit, even if he was a damned robot. Now that he thought about it, he didn't much care for her companion unit at all.

The food arrived as they sat back down. Two steaming plates of vegetables on a bed of wild rice with a stuffed baked potato on the side.

"It looks good," Lara said as she sniffed. "And it smells good, too."

He looked at his plate. What he wouldn't give for a steak right now! He glanced across the table at Lara and realized some things were just worth giving up.

"It isn't a dead animal, is it?" She moved a carrot around on the plate.

"No animals were injured, maimed, or killed during the preparation of this plate of food."

She sighed with relief. "Good."

He watched as she took a bite and chewed. For a moment, she closed her eyes as she savored the taste, a look of rapt enjoyment on her face. She opened her eyes and smiled.

"This is better than the little trees you served the other night."

"I never claimed to be a good cook, only a decent one," he said.

"That's true." She dug into the baked potato. "What's the orange stuff on top?"

"Cheese."

"I like cheese best of all, and the stuff that's melting is very good also."

"Butter."

He noticed the lights flickered as she ate. They did that a lot when she experienced pleasure. He would need to be careful so she didn't draw attention to herself.

The waiter removed the dishes. "Would you care for dessert?"

"The check, please." Sam reached in his back pocket for his wallet.

"Dessert?"

Great. They didn't need a light show in here.

"Yes, ma'am. Tonight we have bread pudding with a raisin and rum sauce, pecan pie, or death by chocolate cake with fudge sauce."

"Chocolate? Yes, I want that."

"To go," Sam quickly spoke up.

"Yes, sir." The waiter bowed slightly and left.

"You'll enjoy it a lot more at the cabin."

"And soda."

Now she'd confused him. "Soda?"

"You said you would buy soda for me to drink."

Ah, he'd forgotten that. "We'll stop on the way home."

He paid the check and took the box the waiter handed them, noticing Lara eyed the white Styrofoam as if it contained the crown jewels. He didn't know how she'd last on Nerak without her beloved chocolate. He had a feeling she'd survive missing him a lot easier.

"I can have the death by chocolate now?" she asked when they were in the pickup.

"Not long. There's a store right down the road, and I'll grab some sodas."

"It smells very good."

He turned a corner and parked in front of the store. He started to get out but thought better of leaving her alone with the chocolate dessert.

"Come with me. Someone from Nerak should see at least one store while she's here on earth."

She looked longingly at the white box before getting out. It was just a small convenience store, but he knew they'd have soda.

They went inside, and as he went to the back, Lara wandered the aisles looking at the products on the shelves.

"Sam!"

He was just reaching into the refrigerated unit when he heard her cry out. He let the door slam shut as he raced to her side. Man, he shouldn't have left her alone. If some man had hit on her . . .

But she was alone.

"What?"

"I found the cure."

"What?"

"I've found the cure for the Elder."

Chapter 23

"I've found the cure for the Elder," Lara repeated almost to herself as it finally sank in. Relief . . . and sadness washed over her. She would have to leave Sam, and Earth. In a few hours, this would all be a distant memory.

"What?" Sam asked. "How could you find a cure in here? I thought you had to test plants."

She held out the small box for him to look at. "See, it says it relieves the symptoms of the common cold: nasal stuffiness, headache and fever, cough and congestion."

"The Elder has a cold? You risked your life and traveled to Earth for a cold?"

Why did he seem so surprised? "Yes, the Earthling said he was dying because he had a cold. When the Elder became infected, we knew she would also die if I didn't find a cure."

She shook her head. It was an amazing discovery.

"It was right here all the time. Of course, I'll have to test it—add the chemicals I brought from Nerak."

He ran a hand through his hair. "But people don't die from a cold, at least not here on Earth. They might feel as if they are, but they don't. I doubt the person from Earth actually meant he was dying."

"It was another figure of speech?"

He nodded.

She shook her head. "Torcara won't be happy. She might

decide to vaporize the Earthling for causing so much trouble," she said, speaking her thoughts aloud.

"Do you really think she'd do that?"

Now she'd worried Sam again. "A Nerakian figure of speech. I don't think she'd zap him."

"But you're not positive."

"Is anyone ever positive about anything?"

"Come on. Let's get out of here." He grabbed some more cold remedies for her to test, soda, and a bag of chocolate bars before going to the counter and handing the cashier a credit card.

They were silent on the way back to the cabin. The smell of the death by chocolate cake should've made her feel better, but it didn't. Now she didn't even have three days.

"What are you thinking?" he finally asked.

"That I have to leave."

"But you said you had to test the remedies, right?"

"Yes, but I'll know by morning. Once I am sure they work, I'll leave." The thought of never seeing Sam again, never seeing a deer or even a fish, never seeing the sunrise and the burst of orange and blue that came with it, never seeing any of the wonderful things Earth had to offer . . .

No, she couldn't think like that. It was very dangerous and disloyal. She raised her chin and squared her shoulders. She was a healer, a Nerakian, a superior being. Her duty was to the Elders, to her planet. That was more important than what she felt for Sam and everything else.

"I have no choice," she said, wanting him to at least try to understand.

"I know." His sigh was audible. "But we have tonight."

"Yes, we do have that."

As he drove over the metal pipes, she realized they didn't bother her as much as that first time. She could see how her cousin and sister would be able to stay on Earth. It wouldn't be so very hard to adapt. Earth had much to offer.

But there was also a lot to love about Nerak. Maybe the

Elders would relax some of their rules. Her planet could benefit from some of Earth's pleasures. Maybe then her people would want to stay rather than escaping to other planets.

Sam stopped the pickup, and they went inside, but her heart was heavy.

"Chocolate?" He held up the white box.

She shook her head. "I need to start the testing. Later." She took the bag of remedies to the kitchen and set them on the table as she gathered her glass plates.

She worked methodically, adding the chemical solutions she'd brought from Nerak and letting the two mix. One drop of the remedy, one drop of chemical. Another chemical, another remedy, then put a marker on each to distinguish it from the others.

By the time she had them all laid out, her back ached unbearably. How long had she been in the kitchen? It was still dark outside. The house was quiet. Had Sam gone to bed, tired of waiting for her? She wouldn't hold it against him.

But this was their last night together. He could've waited.

She stood, pressing the palms of her hands to the middle of her back to ease the deep ache. It helped, but that wasn't her only ache. There was a burning inside her chest. She had a feeling it would be with her much longer than the aches and pains she'd gotten from working.

Her steps were heavy as she made her way to the guest room, not wanting to disturb Sam's slumber. Maybe they would get up early and watch the sunrise together. The deer might come back, too. It would be nice to see him one more time.

She would say good-bye to Aasera and Lyraka before she left, too. If it was as Sam had said, then the Elder would not pass, her lifecycle would not end. Lara might even stay one more day.

But she knew she wouldn't. To delay much longer would make leaving more difficult. Not only for her, but for Sam as well, and she couldn't do that to him.

She pushed open the door . . . and smiled. Sam sat in a

chair beside the window. Of course, Sam wouldn't go to bed. He wanted this last night as much as she did.

"I thought you'd never get here," he said. There were candles lighting the room, casting a soft glow on everything. "I almost ate dessert without you." He nodded toward the bed as he came to his feet. In the center was the white box.

"I'm hungry."

"Me, too."

It didn't sound as if they were talking about the same kind of hunger, but as she watched him come toward her, she realized they might be talking about the same thing after all.

He stopped in front of her. His gaze scorched her body as it drifted lazily over her. The ache inside her increased; her nipples tightened, begging him to touch, to be kissed.

But he did none of those things. Instead, he pulled her hair over one shoulder before stepping behind her. His hands were warm on her back as he brushed them across the bare skin, then slowly lowered the zipper.

His breath tickled her neck, caressing it with the heat of his pent-up passion. He slid his hands beneath the straps, pushing the material off her shoulders. It slid down her body like a whisper and puddled at her feet. He came around to the front again.

"Have I told you how very beautiful you are?"

She nodded, unable to speak as she stood there wearing only a thong and her heels.

"You are." He pushed her hair back over her shoulder, running his fingers through the long strands as he did. "I love your hair. It feels like corn silk."

"I've never felt corn silk," she finally managed to get out.

"All you have to do is touch your hair, then you'll know." He took her hand and led her to the side of the bed, caressing his knuckles over her cheek before stepping back and removing his shirt. She reached toward him, but he captured her hand. "Not yet. Soon."

When he removed his pants and then his briefs, she wasn't

sure how long she would be able to keep herself from touching, caressing, tasting. His had better be real soon.

She admired his nakedness. Her gaze roamed over him from his wide shoulders to the sprinkling of curling hair on his broad chest. Past the muscles on his arms, to his hips. She breathed a deep sigh when her gaze rested on his erection. Magnificent. She reached toward him again, but he stopped her before she could touch.

"But I want to stroke you," she told him, pursing her lips. But as her gaze skimmed over him, her irritation vanished. "Oh, yes, I definitely want to touch you."

"First, the chocolate." He walked around to the other side of the bed.

It took a few seconds for his words to sink in. No, she could only stare. He had a nice butt, muscled legs, solid back, but a *really* nice butt. Her companion unit didn't even compare, but then, she hadn't had much to go on in the way of design. Sam was designed very well, however.

Kia had once let it slip that their cousin Mala had found a book of their grandmother's before she'd designed Barton, her companion unit. She'd also given him an attitude chip. Big mistake, if you asked Lara.

Lara hadn't had access to a book, though. Her companion unit wasn't nearly as well defined as Sam. The detail just wasn't there.

She snapped out of her daze. "Chocolate?"

Sam sat in the middle of the bed. He'd opened the box and waved his hand back and forth over it so the wonderful aroma drifted to her. She closed her eyes and inhaled. Umm, this was nice.

"Yes, chocolate . . . and sex."

"Or both," he said.

"That sounds intriguing." She slipped off her shoes and started to remove her thong, but he shook his head. But she wanted to be naked. It was a lot more fun not having any clothes between them.

"I'll take it off for you."

That was even better. She swallowed past the lump in her throat as she envisioned him slowly sliding her thong over her hips, his hands touching her body as he did. No, her companion unit had never done any of this.

She quickly moved onto the bed, not wanting to waste another minute. "We have nothing to eat the chocolate with," she stated breathlessly.

"We don't need utensils to eat cake," he told her with a wicked grin. "Watch." He broke off some of it and brought the piece to her mouth.

She automatically opened, taking what he offered, licking the icing off his fingers. "This is good." She closed her eyes, savoring the taste, running her tongue over her lips. When she looked at Sam, she could see the fire in his eyes. Her body grew warm.

She broke off a piece and took it to his mouth. He seized her hand, scooping the bite with his tongue, then sucking on each finger until they were cleaned of every morsel of chocolate.

He might have only had her finger in his mouth, but the sensation he'd started inside her shot all the way down to the junction between her legs. She wanted his mouth there. She wanted his hands on her. Pleasure and exquisite pain filled her because she had a feeling he was going to draw the moment out.

"I love watching you eat chocolate. You make it look very sensual."

He ran a finger through the icing. She opened her mouth, but he didn't bring his finger up so she could lick it off. Instead, he ran it across her nipples. She gasped, arching toward him.

"Lie back," he told her.

She did, her blood heating, anticipating what he was going to do.

He moved the box behind him, then leaned over her, dragging his tongue across each nipple. She whimpered.

"You taste sweet." He smiled. "I'm still hungry."

He took some more of the cake and smeared it across her stomach, right above the top of her thong, then followed with his tongue.

"Sam," she whimpered.

"What? Do you want me to go lower?"

"Oh, yes, I do, but first, I want to play, and you're having all the fun." She moved to her knees and reached behind him, scooping up half the cake and slapping it on his chest with a mischievous laugh.

She smeared it on him, sliding the rich dessert over his stomach but making sure she had plenty left for one other area of his body. She met his gaze before smiling as she ran it down his length.

He groaned.

"Do you like that?" she asked, already knowing the answer, but she wanted to hear him say the words.

"You know I do."

"Yes, I do," she said with a laugh. This kind of play was so much fun.

"I was going to make this night perfect for you."

"You just did," she said, then licked his chest. He sucked in a deep breath when she moved closer to his erection. "I love chocolate." She took one swipe across him, laughing as she straightened.

He sucked in a deep breath, closing his eyes. "I think you've caught on to the art of foreplay way too fast."

But when he opened his eyes, she saw the laughter mixed with the passion. Before she had a chance to react, he pushed her back onto the bed in one motion and slid her thong over her hips.

"I want to see all of you, kiss every inch." He tossed the thong onto the floor and scooted back up so he was sitting on his knees beside her. "You blow my mind sometimes."

He brushed his fingers through the curls between her legs. She moaned, automatically parting her legs so he would have better access to the heart of her need.

"Soft as corn silk," he murmured.

She reached out; this time he didn't stop her as she ran her fingers down his length, then grasped him in her hand. He closed his eyes and arched his hips forward. She watched him as she slid the skin down.

"Do you like my touch?" she asked.

"Yes," he moaned.

She smiled, enjoying that she could take back control of their lovemaking with just a simple touch.

"You look quite pleased with yourself," he told her.

"I am. I like being in charge. After all, I'm superior." But her words didn't carry the same connotation they once had.

"Then do your worst, or best. I give you control, my lady." He held his arms out as if to tell her, here I am, let's see what you can do.

She shifted to her knees. If he didn't think she would take charge, then he'd better think again. She was used to being a leader, not a follower.

"Do you have doubts that I can pleasure you?" She leaned forward, letting her nipples brush across his chest.

He shook his head. "You *are* pretty new when it comes to experimenting. I'm not sure you'll be able to impress me."

"You think not?" She licked down his body. "You're quite rigid, so much larger than my companion unit. I like taking you inside my mouth."

She ran her tongue down him, then back up before taking the tip of his erection inside her mouth and sucking gently. He tangled his fingers in her hair, pulling her closer, massaging her scalp.

She ran her hands over his hips, then behind him as she pulled him even closer, taking more of him.

Sam couldn't think. His brain had disintegrated a long time ago. "That feels so damned fantastic," he managed to mumble as her mouth worked a magic all its own on him.

The lights were back. Deep violets; fiery reds, their flames licking at him; oranges . . . the heat they gave off wrapped around him like a potent drug, charging through his body like an electrical sexual current.

Enough. He pulled her up, crushed her body against his, felt her hard little nipples scraping across his chest.

"And did I give you pleasure?" There was a knowing look in her passion-filled eyes.

"You know damn well you did."

"Yes, I do."

He swatted her bottom. She jumped, her eyes widening, then half-closing as she grasped his arms, snaking her hand upward and pulling his mouth down to hers. He lowered his lips to hers, their tongues sparring. She tasted like chocolate.

If he didn't have her soon, he was going to explode. He moved off the bed so he could get a condom out of the bed-side drawer.

She watched him, her breathing ragged.

"Spread your legs. I want to see all of you. I don't want you to hold anything back."

She didn't hesitate, opening for him. He drew in a sharp breath as he watched her open like a delicate flower waiting to be plucked.

"Now, Sam. I want you to bury yourself deep inside of my body." She raised her hips, beckoning.

"No more than I want to be there, nestled between your delicious thighs, but baby, I'm still hungry.

He got back on the bed, moving so he was situated between her legs. He stroked his hands over her breasts, tweaking her nipples between his forefinger and thumb, tugging slightly.

"Yes, Sam."

"Do you like what I'm doing?"

She nodded.

"Do you want me to do more?"

She nodded again, biting her lower lip.

"What do you want me to do? If you don't tell me, I won't know." He brushed his fingers over her abdomen, grazing the edge of her mound with his fingertips.

"Do you want me to stroke you here?" He ran his fingers up, then back down her clit. Her body jerked in response to his touch.

"Yes . . . that . . . that . . ."

"Do you want me to put my mouth there, stroke you with my tongue?"

She whimpered.

"Say it."

"Yes, take me with your mouth."

Her breathing was ragged. He knew she was getting close. One touch of his tongue, and she'd probably have an orgasm. He wanted her to have one.

He scooted back and lowered his head to her, running his tongue over her clit before sucking her inside his mouth. She cried out, her body jerking.

When her body stopped quivering, he gently spread her legs a little wider and entered her. She clamped her inner muscles around him. He sucked in a deep breath as wet heat surrounded him, contracting against him.

He rested there for a few seconds, gathering what strength he had, then moved out of her before thrusting back inside. She moved her hips, rotating them slightly in a circle as he continued to plunge inside her.

Maybe she hadn't had a lot of experience with sex, but she damn sure caught on fast. No inhibitions. She enjoyed making love, and it showed on her face.

But her eyes were closed. He wanted her to look at him. He wanted to see her when she came. He'd have to hold that memory close to his heart for the rest of his life.

She opened her eyes and looked at him as if she'd heard his thoughts.

"Now, Sam," she breathed.

He thrust faster. In and out. Their ragged breathing filled the room, blending with the colors.

Then everything seemed to explode at once. She cried out, grasping his hips. His body jerked as his orgasm rocked him to the very core of his being. He kept his eyes opened, watched as she came, saw her in the throes of her passion.

His whole body began to tremble as he collapsed to the bed, careful not to crush her with his weight. Then he was rolling to his side and taking her with him. He didn't want to break the connection. He couldn't break it, not without breaking his heart.

When had he fallen in love with her?

But he knew the answer. The minute he'd seen the hologram. Damn, how the hell could he give her up now that he'd found her?

"I can't stay," she whispered close to his ear, tears in her voice.

"I know, I know, but that doesn't mean I have to like the decision."

"I don't like it, either."

He pulled away from her, staring down into her eyes. "Then don't go. Mala stayed; Kia stayed. You can stay, too."

She stroked the back of her hand down the side of his face. "It's not the same as it was with them. I have to return."

He hugged her close. "I hurt so damn much."

"I know this pain you speak of. I feel it, too."

He knew she was going to leave. Gut instinct. And he knew there wasn't a damn thing he could do about it.

Sometimes, life wasn't fair. Not fair at all.

Chapter 24

Sam waited in the other room while Lara checked the results of her research from last night. It might not work, he told himself. Cold remedies only relieved the symptoms. They didn't cure the ailment. Three days was three days, and he'd take whatever he could get.

He stepped to the front porch, breathing in the fresh morning air. He loved it here. There was something clean and unsullied about his little plot of land. This was his piece of heaven right here on Earth.

There was a noise behind him. Just the soft rustle of her robes as she approached. He didn't turn around. Hell, he already knew what she was going to tell him. The connection between them was stronger the more they were around each other. She had said something about that happening between soul mates. But what would happen when she left?

The screen squeaked when she opened it.

"You found the cure." It wasn't a question.

"Yes. By using a combination of your medicine and Nerak's chemicals, I have the solution that will heal the Elder." There was sadness in her voice, but he knew it went far deeper than her words.

"Then you're leaving this morning?" He braced himself for her answer.

"I have to."

It didn't help. The pain reached deep, tearing at his heart.

"I'd like to see Aasera and Lyraka before I leave," she told him. "Is that possible?"

"I'll make the call." He started to go back into the other room, but when he was even with her, he stopped and wrapped her in his arms, pulling her tight against him. This was probably the hardest thing he'd ever had to do. He kissed her on top of her head before letting go.

He went inside to his room, retrieving his phone from the bedside table. He got the number of the colony from Information and called them, talking to Lyraka. Then he placed a call to Nick and told him they would be arriving in a few hours.

Everything was set in motion.

He went to the kitchen and got down the bag of chocolate bars he had bought last night. When he returned to the living room, Lara was bringing her suitcase out of the bedroom.

He held up the bag. "I thought you might want to take these back to Nerak. If you can get one of the Elders to try a chocolate bar"—he shrugged—"who knows what they'll allow."

Her smile trembled. "Maybe even slot machines?"

He chuckled. "Who knows?" He cleared his throat. "I guess you'll be glad to get home."

"I miss my home. It's not in my DNA to travel. I like where I live, although Earth can be very exciting."

She left her suitcase and went to the kitchen to gather her research, carefully putting one of the bottles into another bag. Apparently, this was the cure. She wistfully looked around the room. Her gaze stopped on the refrigerator.

"I wouldn't introduce wine though." When she looked at him, there was a mischievous smile on her face.

He relaxed for the first time that morning. "No, you'd better not introduce them to wine. I'd hate to be the cause of shorting out all the companion units."

There was the sound of a car pulling up out front, ending their laughter. He went to the door, Lara with him.

Aasera and Lyraka.

Lara went outside to greet them. He watched, marveling at how much Lara had changed since her arrival. But she was still revered, and she definitely looked like royalty as Aasera and Lyraka bowed before her.

Just as suddenly, he realized she didn't belong here. He finally understood what she meant. Earth wasn't her home. She was as much a part of Nerak as Nerak was a part of her.

Lara turned and motioned for him. He stepped to the porch. Now what?

"They will travel with us. Aasera and Lyraka want to see Kia. Lyraka asked if you could please drive her car. She's not accustomed to driving in a large city."

His first thought was no. He didn't want to share what precious little time he had left with her. Besides, Lara was acting pretty bossy again. Was she already trying to distance herself from him?

"Please."

He softened. "Yeah, sure. Nick can bring me back to get the pickup."

She smiled as she handed him the keys.

Going back inside, he grabbed the suitcase. Lara came inside, Lyraka with her, and they went to the kitchen for her satchel and the rest of her research equipment.

When he went back outside, Aasera gave him a look that would frost glass. What the hell had he done to her? He opened his mouth to ask what her problem was but then decided against it. She would have to learn to deal with it.

Maybe she did have something against men, but if she didn't learn to get a handle on her anger and resentment, Aasera would become her own worst enemy.

Still, he'd never been one to leave well enough alone. "I didn't hurt her."

She stiffened as he walked past her.

"Didn't you?"

He hit the button that popped the trunk and set the suitcase inside before turning back to her.

"You don't think I'm hurting because she's leaving? I don't want her to go."

"And if she stayed, what would you do? Promise to love her forever? She would give up everything for you if she stayed. Then, when things got rough, would you stay or leave her to fend for herself?"

"Is that what he did?"

Her face lost some of its color. "Who?"

He nodded toward the cabin. "Lyraka's father."

"Men are all alike. I wasn't the only one it happened to. Many women who come to my colony are escaping men who've hurt them."

"I would never hurt her."

She didn't look much like she believed him. He couldn't change her mind. At least, not in the next couple of hours. Maybe the next time he came to the cabin, he would stop by, and they could talk or something.

Yeah, right, who was he fooling? He didn't want to sever the connection with Lara, but going to see Aasera and Lyraka wouldn't bring her back to him.

Lara came outside with Lyraka right behind her. Together, they carried all of Lara's research equipment. He hurried to the porch and grabbed the biggest case, taking it to the trunk. Once everything was loaded, there wasn't anything else to do except leave.

"I would like to speak with you on the drive to your sister's," Aasera said when Lara started to get in the front seat.

Lara hesitated, then gave a nod of her head and got in the back seat. Sam had to take a deep breath to keep from telling Aasera to go to hell, that Lara would ride up front with him. He wouldn't play tug of war with her.

"I'll lock the cabin, and we can get started," he said.

Lara gave him a look of apology. He smiled to let her know it was okay.

He walked through the cabin, making sure there was nothing left out that could smell up the place. He'd come back next week and clean out the refrigerator.

Or not.

Suddenly, the cabin didn't hold as much appeal as it once did. Maybe that would change over time.

He went to the back door but hesitated at the last minute when he caught a flash of something moving in the woods. The buck? He narrowed his eyes, trying to see past the thick stand of trees, but whatever was there had left. Maybe it *had* been the buck.

"See you next time," he whispered.

He shut the door and locked it, then tested the knob before going to the front door and repeating the procedure. He met Lara's gaze as he walked to the car, then she turned to Aasera, and they began to talk.

Had he already lost and didn't want to face the truth? Maybe Kia could talk her sister into staying. And maybe it was just wishful thinking.

But he could feel her pain—it blended with his.

Lara couldn't look at Sam. Not when her heart felt as if it were breaking into a thousand tiny pieces.

"The Elders must hold you in very high esteem if they would take the chance of sending you down to Earth," Aasera said.

Lara focused her attention. "I'm close to them, yes. I have great respect for my leaders."

Aasera glanced pointedly at Sam as he started the car, then turned toward the road. "There are many dangerous distractions here."

"But not all of them are bad."

"You're Nerakian. A healer. You must not forget that," she warned. "The Elders would not like it if they discovered their trust was misplaced."

Lara raised an eyebrow. "You question my loyalty to the Elders? To my planet?"

Aasera bowed her head slightly. "Of course not. Forgive me if I have made it seem as if I was."

"I'll return to Nerak," she said.

She glanced out the window, ending their conversation. Why would Aasera even question whether she might leave? But maybe she knew the answer. She looked at Sam. He met her gaze in the small mirror.

Why had she agreed to sit back here? She didn't want to be in the back seat. She wanted to sit beside Sam, to feel the heat of his body, to touch his hand and have him touch hers. That was the way it should've been.

A healer wanting someone to touch her? Is this what she'd been reduced to? Forgetting her place in life?

But it was exactly what she wanted.

End it now, a voice inside her screamed. Stop thinking about what might have been because it's not meant to be. She was only delaying the inevitable. She clasped her hands together tightly in her lap. She didn't want it to end, though.

Her gaze moved to the window as she tried to bring her thoughts back under control. Sam drove past a sign that said there was a station up the road. She would miss exploring all the small businesses that were alongside the road. There hadn't been much time to see all she'd wanted to see. They all looked rather unusual and interesting.

Suddenly, she straightened. "Sam, please stop. I need to use the facilities." She had gotten very good at talking like an Earth person.

He raised an eyebrow but took the next exit.

"I won't be long," she said after he parked. "When I return, I'll sit in the front. A healer shouldn't sit in the back. It's not proper."

She saw Sam smile before he quickly straightened and looked out the front window.

"Of course, Healer."

Lyraka opened her door and got out as Lara hurried inside. People looked at her strangely as she went to the back of the store. She knew now it was because of the way she dressed. She couldn't help that. She was who she was.

She stayed in the bathroom for what she thought was an appropriate amount of time, then came out, quite satisfied with her maneuver.

Sam winked at her as she came back outside and climbed in the car.

"Will you be glad to get back to Nerak?" Lyraka asked when Sam was driving down the road.

"There are many things I'll miss about this planet." She moved her hand across the seat. Sam met her halfway, taking her hand in his and squeezing it.

She was grateful he didn't say anything. She reminded herself that on her planet, healers were above everyone except the royal family. They meditated, keeping everything in harmony. But Sam made her feel more alive than she'd ever felt her entire life.

She squeezed her eyes shut. How could she return to that life? Before, she hadn't known there were other ways to live. But now that she'd experienced a different way of life, would her memories be enough to make her content?

"Things have a way of working out," Sam said in a low voice. "Maybe someday, you'll return."

She wouldn't. They both knew this would be the last time they saw each other.

"What's your sister like?" Lyraka asked.

Lara smiled. At least this was a fairly safe topic. "On Nerak, she was a warrior code enforcer."

They hadn't visited that much. Kia and Mala had always been closer to each other. She'd always been on the outside.

Which was as it should be. Healers didn't mingle as much as other Nerakians. The same could be said of the princesses. She'd never realized how lonely her life had been.

The time passed too swiftly, like the scenery outside the

window. Soon, they were pulling into the parking area and getting out of the car.

Her hand trembled when she let go of Sam's, and coldness clung to her even though the air was warm. The emotions going through her right now cut deep. She didn't think she liked the feeling.

But she held her head high.

They traveled in the box that would take them to her sister's floor. It stopped, and they got out. With each step she took, a chant repeated over and over in her head: don't go, don't go. How would she ever be able to tell Sam good-bye?

How would she be able to leave her sister forever, not knowing what was happening to her here on Earth? Never would she play another slot machine or eat chocolate. The bag of chocolate bars she was taking with her would not last forever. Then what was she supposed to do?

No, she would go back to taking food capsules that had no taste, only nutritional value.

They stopped outside the apartment door, and Sam pushed a button. The door opened seconds later.

"Healer," Kia bowed.

"Oh, sister, what will I do?" She fell into her sister's arms.

Chapter 25

"Sam, what did you do to my sister?" Kia cast an accusing look in his direction.

He backed up a step. "No, I swear I didn't do anything." He looked at Nick, hoping he'd lend a hand, but his friend only shrugged his shoulders. A lot of help he was.

Kia looked behind him, her expression leery. "Who are they?"

Yeah, take the heat off him. "Your grandmother and her daughter."

Lara moved out of her sister's arms. Sam tugged her into his, brushing his lips across the top of her head.

"But . . ." Kia looked at them, then seemed to pull herself together. "Grandmother." She bowed respectfully. "Daughter."

"Kia, I remember when you were brought to our home. You were beautiful even at such a young age. And fierce. You were already showing your warrior qualities."

"The Elders said you were killed on a mission." Kia still looked like she was in shock. "Lara, how long have you known?"

"Not long. Sam told Nick."

Kia planted her hands on her hips and glared at Nick. "And you didn't think this was something I should know about?"

"I was going to drive you to the cabin to reunite, but after the research was finished. I swear."

"You have a private place to talk?" Aasera broke in and then looked pointedly at the men.

"I was just going to the store," Nick quickly supplied. "We're out of chocolate—again. Sam, go with me."

He didn't want to go without Lara. They didn't have much longer to spend together.

"Go. I won't leave while you're away. I need this time with them."

Sam reluctantly nodded. He didn't like leaving her for one second, but he had to give her time to say good-bye to her family. It wasn't as if he had exclusive rights on her or anything.

"I'll be back soon."

They went out the door and down to Nick's car. He opened the passenger side door, noting that it still stuck just a little. And no wonder—Kia had opened it, then a car had knocked it clean off.

He remembered that morning—Kia had told him earlier she was an alien. He hadn't believed her then. No, it had taken him longer than Nick to start believing.

He got in and fastened his seat belt. Instead of going to the store, Nick drove to the nearest bar just a couple of blocks from the apartment.

"I thought you might need a beer."

"A case would be nice." He scraped his fingers through his hair. "Do I look that messed up?"

"Yeah, as a matter of fact, you do."

"I feel even worse."

"I take it you and Lara like each other?"

"That's an understatement."

They didn't talk again until they were seated across from each other with a beer in front of them.

Sam stared down into his mug. "She's leaving."

"Yeah, I talked to Kia," Nick said. "She told me that as a healer, there's no way she could stay."

"How could I fall for her?" He started to take a drink but set his mug down and looked at Nick. "You saw how she was when we left your apartment to go to the cabin—all uppity and thinking she was better than everyone else."

"I thought when you two left, you'd either kill her or come back and kill me."

"I thought about it." He grimaced. "Then I realized it wasn't so much that she was uppity—she is that—but she just didn't know any better most of the time. I thought maybe if I showed her what living on Earth was like, then maybe she'd at least have a little different outlook and all."

"You did something to her, that's easy to see." Nick frowned. "I guess I should've told you about alcohol, then maybe you could've at least kept the relationship platonic. Does it really do what Mason told me it does?"

"Don't give Kia any. Take my word for it."

"You sure Lara can't be talked into staying?"

He shook his head, then took a long pull of the beer. It slid down his throat like liquid gold. He needed to drink enough so that it would numb him.

"You fell in love with her, didn't you?"

"It was more than that."

Visions of them making love, standing on the porch in each other's arms as they watched the buck, even her getting her first taste of addictions like chocolate and slot machines—it all flashed through his mind.

"What do you mean?" Nick asked.

"We connected in a different sort of way. As if I know what she's thinking, what she feels. Do you have that with Kia?"

"No, thank God. I don't want to know what women are thinking."

Sam raised his mug and drained the glass. "Let's get back. They should have everything sorted out by now."

"You don't look any better. I had hoped getting away from the apartment would help. I think you look worse, buddy."

Nick stood, dropping some bills on the table. He hadn't even drunk half his beer.

Sam made up his mind. "I'm not going to let her leave. That's it. I'll throw her over my shoulder and force her to stay with me. I can do that because it's her fault I'm in this shape."

Nick shook his head. "It wouldn't work. The Elders would come after her."

"Not if they don't know where she is."

"Have you forgotten about their locators? One drop of her blood, and they'll easily find her. I bet they have it all on file, too. Better than the FBI."

"Kia said they haven't zapped anyone in years, but try to keep a healer, and I'm pretty sure they'll bring zapping back into circulation."

"It's not fair."

Nick patted him on the back. "Yeah, I know."

Aasera sat on the sofa clasping her hands in front of her. "He left me when he found I was with child. He didn't know I was an interplanetary traveler. I'm thankful for that. After he left, I realized he wasn't a very good person. I'm not sure what he would've done with the information," she finished.

"I remember you from when I was young. I envied the life you led." Kia sighed. "Nerak has changed. The Elders have too many rules."

"They're only trying to protect everyone," Lara said. "You mustn't condemn them for that."

Kia turned to Lara. "Maybe they'll change, and maybe they won't. Are you sure you want to return to a life that stifles the spirit?"

"I have to."

Kia shook her head. "You have to do what you feel is right. Now tell us, what did Sam do to you? You're not the same person as when you left here."

"I fell in love with him," Lara admitted to the group of women.

"It's forbidden." Aasera came to her feet and began to pace the room. "You of all people should know this. You're not allowed close contact with anyone. You're a healer. How can you keep a perfect balance if you let anyone get close to you?"

She was right. Lara had turned her back on everything she'd been taught.

"She's a woman first," Lyraka said.

Everyone looked at her.

Lyraka stiffened her spine. "Everyone talks about how great Nerak is, but if you ask me, the Elders are holding everyone hostage."

There was a collective gasp.

"I don't care what everyone thinks. I would hate to live like that. It's as if you're all created for a certain purpose, but because no one is really living anymore, what's the point?"

"Lyraka is young. Please forgive her, Healer." Aasera bowed her head.

"You're just as bad, Mother," Lyraka whispered, ducking her head.

Lara looked from mother to daughter, holding her breath, waiting for what was about to happen. She didn't think it would be good.

"What?" Aasera asked, disbelief clearly on her face that her daughter would speak this way.

"It's true." Lyraka moved from her chair and knelt in front of her. "I mean no disrespect, Mother, but if you hadn't been able to travel to distant galaxies, how would that have made you feel? Even now, I see the trapped look in your eyes. I feel the same way."

Aasera drew herself up. "If I've been smothering you, then I'm sorry. If you feel this need to explore, then by all means, explore, but know that I was only trying to protect you."

"I know, Mother, and I love you for it, but it's time I found my purpose. I have gifts, and I want to use them."

"It's those very gifts that will get you into trouble," Aasera said.

"I'm careful. You know I am. And it's not as if we'll never see each other again."

Aasera was quiet. "I suppose I might have been a little stifling at times," she finally admitted.

"I do love you."

Aasera's smile was sad. "I guess I was afraid of being alone."

"I'll always be near."

She nodded, then turned to Lara. "And you, Healer, will you turn your back on all you know? Did you not hear my story? Men are evil."

"Not all men," Kia intervened. "Nick put his life in danger to save me and was shot. Not all men are evil."

"He did this?" Aasera asked with surprise.

Kia nodded her head. "That and a whole lot more. He's taught me how to live."

Aasera seemed to be taking this all in. She finally looked at Lara. "I guess you'll be staying, too?"

Duty warred against her feelings for Sam. "I have to return so that I can take the remedy to the Elder. I don't have a choice."

The door opened, and Nick and Sam came inside. Sam's gaze immediately sought hers, and she knew the exact second he accepted that as much as she cared for him, she would go back to her own people.

She came to her feet. "It's time. I can't delay any longer." She didn't add that each second made leaving that much harder. She came to her feet.

"We'll walk up with you," Kia said.

It was the longest and the shortest walk she'd ever taken . . . and it was the hardest. Once there, she pushed a button on the box she'd slipped inside her pocket earlier. The craft's invisibility shield disappeared, and the tube was there in front of her.

"A tube craft," Aasera whispered. "They were just beginning to build them when I left on my last mission. It's built for speed, and even though it's compact, it can hold at least six people. She's absolutely beautiful."

"You're right, travel is much faster in a tube craft," Lara nervously explained. She really hated flying.

"Lara," Kia said, "I will miss you."

Lara took her hands, then impulsively hugged her sister. Healer or not, she didn't care. This was her sister, and she would show her how much she cared.

Nick was next. She bowed, showing him much respect. "Make her happy."

"I will," he said, then stepped forward and kissed her on the cheek.

Aasera and Lyraka nodded respectfully.

And then there was Sam. Tears filled her eyes. She didn't care about what was proper as she went into his arms and one last time, felt his lips against hers. It was a gentle kiss, one that would have to last a lifetime in her memory. When she stepped away, her heart felt as if it were breaking into a million tiny pieces.

This isn't fair. Not fair at all.

His thoughts or hers? Maybe both. She turned and went toward the craft. Before she got inside, she looked one more time at Sam, committing his face to memory.

"I love you," he mouthed.

"And I you."

"You can't leave," an unfamiliar voice said from the rooftop door.

Everyone turned toward the man.

"Mr. Beacon," Lyraka said. "What are you doing here?"

"I'm here to stop the healer from leaving."

Chapter 26

"Who the hell are you?" Sam asked, reaching for his gun, then remembered he didn't have it with him. Great cop he was. Dammit, if this was someone looking for a big story or another jewel thief, then . . .

"I work for the government."

"Busted," Sam muttered.

"Great." Nick moved closer to Kia.

"It's not like you think," Mr. Beacon began explaining. "Not many people know of our group. You could say our agents are gifted with certain abilities."

"And what exactly do you do?" Sam wanted to know. He wanted Lara to stay, but if he hadn't been able to convince her, then what made this Mr. Beacon think he could?

Mr. Beacon shrugged. "You could say I'm a recruiter. We get the jobs others can't handle."

"And you want to recruit Lara. It's not going to happen, buddy." Yeah, he could see Lara fighting crime. What was she going to do—raise her eyebrows at them?

"I've had Aasera's colony under observation for some time. I know where she's really from." He nodded toward the craft. "This pretty much confirms it."

"I should never have let a man stay at the colony." Aasera cast a glare in Mr. Beacon's direction that would've brought most people to their knees. He didn't even flinch. In fact, he ignored her comment and returned his attention to Lara.

"You have stronger powers because you're a healer, untapped strengths that we've learned to bring to the forefront. Most of the Nerakians who are here don't realize the extent of their powers because they haven't been pushed to the limits. We can teach you. We have trainers who work with you to develop your skills, to control them."

Lara raised an eyebrow. "It sounds like we'd be test subjects put under an observation glass. Even if I could stay, I'm not sure I'd like that," Lara said.

"This is an elite force. The work would be dangerous, I won't lie to you, but you would be helping this country."

She shook her head. "I can't stay."

"I'll go with you." Lyraka stepped forward.

Mr. Beacon looked apologetic. "I'm sorry, I know you're only half Nerakian. I had hoped to ask Aasera, except the more I've been around her, the less I think she'd fit in with the group." He bowed slightly toward her. "Excuse my frankness, but I doubt you would want to go anyway."

Lyraka was standing by Nick one second, and in the next, she was beside Mr. Beacon. "I assure you that I have plenty of skills."

"Lyraka, no," Aasera cautioned her daughter. "He could be lying."

"You can check me out," Mr. Beacon told them, suddenly excited to discover what he wanted and to realize it had been right under his nose the whole time.

Lyraka looked with pleading eyes toward Aasera. "I want to do this, Mother. Maybe this is my purpose in life. Just as yours was exploring."

"We'll definitely be checking you out," Nick warned him. "If anything you've said doesn't fit, then I'm warning you now that you'll turn up missing and no one will ever know what happened."

"I have nothing to hide." He looked at Lyraka. "I just assumed your gifts would've been diluted."

"They're actually stronger," she explained.

"We can still use you," he told Lara.

She shook her head. "I'm sorry. I can't." She stepped into the tube craft. "Good-bye, Sam."

So this was it; she was leaving. *Don't go,* he thought to himself.

Her gaze locked with his. *I have to.* Her words were just as clear as if she'd spoken them aloud.

The door closed. Sam felt as if he was going to be sick. He couldn't watch. He couldn't . . .

The door opened. Hope leaped inside him.

"Something is wrong. I pushed the button to start the transport, and nothing happened."

Aasera stepped forward. "I'll take a look. They can't be much different than the crafts we used. Maybe a little more advanced, but they're the same design."

She stepped forward, then went into the craft, pushing a button that opened the back, and disappeared inside.

"My mother told me how she used to work on her craft, so don't worry, Healer, she'll be able to fix it."

They didn't have to be so blasted helpful, Sam thought to himself. Lara looked at him. Man, why did she have to look at him like that?

He had to hold her one more time. He walked to the craft and stepped inside, taking her into his arms. The kiss was only supposed to be a gentle good-bye, but when their lips met, fire ignited between them.

In the background, he heard the swish of the door closing. Good, he wanted this moment to be private. He leaned against the wall of the craft, pulling her closer. These were the last few seconds he would be able to spend with the woman he'd fallen so deeply in love with. When he ended the kiss, he pulled her tight against him.

"I wish you didn't have to leave."

"I know." There were tears in her voice. "I'll never love anyone like I've loved you."

"I think it's fixed," Aasera said, coming to the front as the door to the control room swished open. "You can make the journey home now."

"Good-bye," Lara told Sam and pushed the button to open the door.

He blinked several times, but everything was still a very bright white outside the craft. What had happened to the apartment complex roof? Where was Nick? And everyone else, for that matter?

Okay, what the hell was happening here?

He quickly scanned the area, noting the glass panels overhead that bathed them in white light. The walls sparkled as if crushed gems had been added to the mixture that had created the stone walls.

They were in some kind of landing dock, and there were women approaching the craft. They didn't look too happy.

"Lara?" Oh, man, he wasn't in Kansas anymore, or even Texas, for that matter.

"Oops," Lara said beside him.

"Oops? What do you mean, oops?"

Aasera stepped forward. "Nerak," she whispered, her eyes sparkling with unshed tears.

"How did we get here so fast?" he spoke in a low voice.

"It doesn't take as long in one of the tube crafts. I told you, we're a superior race. We've mastered the technology of interplanetary travel."

"Then get me the hell back home."

"Too late," Aasera said.

"Healer." The three women spoke in unison and bowed slightly, then turned to the other two occupants. "We have called warriors for your protection and the protection of Nerak."

"They've called for warriors? This is how your planet is

protected? By the time your warriors arrive, I could have taken over Nerak."

"Should we disintegrate him?" one asked as she pulled a small box from her pocket that looked suspiciously like the one Kia had carried.

"No!" Lara quickly intervened. "He's not to be harmed. He's a friend."

So maybe they weren't as vulnerable as he'd first thought.

"I will speak to the Elders. Prepare an aero unit." Lara raised her chin and looked down her nose at the other women.

She was a feisty little thing. He almost grinned but immediately stopped his smile from forming. Now might not be a good time to relax.

"He is an Earthman. We'll take him to decontamination." The woman covertly eyed him as if decontamination wasn't the only thing on her mind.

Okay, he wasn't too sure about these women. They were starting to look at him as if they wanted to eat him alive. He knew Lara said they didn't eat food, but maybe that's what had really happened to all the men.

He mentally shook his head. Too many sci-fi movies.

"You question my authority?" Lara asked. She glared at the woman who was still giving him the eye.

"Of course not, Healer. We will ready an aero unit."

A panel slid open, and two women emerged, weapons drawn. In their uniforms they resembled Kia, and they both had short black hair. And they looked excited about the prospect of taking him down.

"Move away from the healer," they commanded.

"Oh, great," he muttered.

Lara stepped in front of him. "He's a friend."

They looked at each other, their foreheads wrinkling. He bet this wasn't in their training manual.

"But he's human . . . and he's a man. We must eliminate him before he contaminates the planet."

"If we close the door, we can leave the way we came," Sam

whispered. They might look like Kia, but they sure didn't act like her. Or maybe they did. The first time he'd met Kia was right after she screwed up their surveillance, then started a barroom brawl. Maybe they weren't so different after all. "The sooner we leave, the better."

"Can't," Aasera told him. "We'd only get halfway. Not enough fuel."

"Right now, halfway is looking better than being zapped into oblivion."

The panel slid open again, and a woman in golden robes stepped out.

"Princess," Lara muttered and lowered her head.

The princess met his gaze, then raised an eyebrow. He bowed his head slightly in deference to her station, and the fact that he'd just as soon not get his ass zapped.

"I heard your arrival is causing quite a commotion, Lara," the princess said as she walked closer. She kept her gaze on him, though. He returned her stare.

"Forgive me," Lara said. "It was my fault he came with me. If anyone should be punished, then it is I."

"And you have brought someone else with you." She moved her gaze to Aasera.

"Princess." Aasera bowed.

The princess looked at her closely, then her eyes widened slightly as if she recognized her.

"You will come with me." She turned and strode back to the panel in the wall and waved her arm. It silently opened.

"That sounded like an order, not a request," Sam said.

"We must go with her." Lara grabbed her satchel as she hurried from the craft, then tugged on his hand.

He noticed the women's surprised looks. A healer had touched someone. Oh, my God, the world was coming to an end.

How had Lara survived all these years without touching anyone? They acted as if it was a crime. He frowned. As far as he knew, it might be.

How the hell had he gotten himself in this fix?

Now he knew a little of how Lara must've felt when she landed on Earth. But at least there hadn't been a bunch of people ready to zap her.

"Where are we going?"

"Shh," Lara hissed.

Lara knew she was in so much trouble. She didn't even think the chocolate bars would help. What had happened? They had been kissing, Sam had leaned her against the wall, she remembered her hand . . .

Oh, that must've been what happened. She'd leaned against the power button. Aasera had probably corrected the problem at the same time.

And here they were. On Nerak. Except men weren't allowed on Nerak. Poor Sam. What would they do to him?

She squared her shoulders. No, she wouldn't let any harm come to him. But her worry only escalated the closer they got to the princess's dwelling.

Each of the princesses had her own dwelling within the bubble on the outer edge. The Elders lived in the center. A clear bubble pipe connected communities, or one could travel by aero craft.

It was such a misfortune that Princess Shaedra's happened to be the closest to the landing site. She was the most difficult of all the princesses. Lara wouldn't put it past her to zap Sam into oblivion.

They came to the end of the hall, and the princess waved her hand. They went down another hall, and at the end, she waved her hand to open another door.

Her dwelling was furnished with lavish cloths in bright colors. Gems hung from the ceiling, catching the light from the windows and creating colorful prisms on the walls. Out of all the princesses, Shaedra preferred an array of different textures and colors.

But the softness of her dwelling didn't make her any more forgiving of a transgression to this degree.

"I'm disappointed, Lara." She sat in her thronelike chair, her golden gown fanning out beside her. "Not only have you brought a man into our midst, but you've also brought someone back from the dead."

"It wasn't her fault, Princess," Aasera said with her head bowed respectively. "The craft wouldn't start, and she has the remedy for the Elder. I was only trying to help, but the man and I were on board when it started. Before we knew what had happened, we were on Nerak."

"What do you think will happen when word gets out that the dead live and there's a man on our planet? Total chaos, that's what. The Elder, though better, is still quite ill. The damage could be irreparable."

"Then beam us back to Earth, and we'll be out of your hair," Sam said.

Lara stifled a groan. He didn't know who he was speaking to. She squeezed his hand in warning, then realized her mistake when she noticed the princess studying her.

"You touched him," she said. Her eyes narrowed. "Step closer, Man."

He frowned. "The name is Sam."

"Sam." She tested the word aloud. "It's a strange name. Quite ugly."

"I happen to like it."

"Step forward, I command you."

Lara could see by his scowl that he didn't like taking orders from the princess any more than he had from her. This wasn't good.

She watched as he further exacerbated the problem by planting his hands on his hips and glaring at the princess.

"Please, Sam," she whispered under her breath, but the princess heard and cast a glare in her direction.

"For you," he told Lara, and she breathed a little easier.

He stepped closer.

"Stop there." Shaedra narrowed her eyes as she looked him over. "Turn around."

"Your wish is my command."

"Yes, it is," she told him.

Sam muttered something under his breath, but Lara assumed if she couldn't understand what he'd said, then neither would the princess, and that was probably a good thing.

Sam turned in a slow circle, stopping when he faced her once again.

"Take off your clothes," she ordered. "I wish to see what you look like without them."

"Lady, I don't give a rat's ass who you are. I refuse to strip just so you can be entertained."

"He insulted me. Did you hear that?" She looked at Lara. "Your man insulted me."

"Please, Shaedra, he meant nothing by his words. It is the way of humans to wear clothing."

"Are their bodies horribly disfigured?"

"No, of course not."

She looked at Sam again. "Then why are you ashamed of your body."

"I'm not. I just don't go around taking my clothes off for women I don't know."

"Did you take off your clothes for Lara?"

"I don't think that's any of your business, princess or not."

"Sam, you're not making this any easier."

"No, he isn't." Shaedra reached in her pocket and pulled out a little black box, pointed it at Sam, and pushed the button. A red beam shot out.

One second, he was there, and the next he wasn't.

"He's . . . he's gone." She looked at the princess with accusing eyes.

She'd sworn to herself she'd protect him while he was on Nerak, but now he was gone—forever. No more Sam.

"How could you!"

Chapter 27

"What? Make him go away? It was easy," Shaedra said with a shrug. "I just pointed and pushed the button.

Tears filled Lara's eyes. Her Sam was gone. She would never feel his arms around her again. Would never taste his lips. She sniffed. And she would never love anyone like she'd loved him.

"You care that much for him?"

"Yes, not that it matters anymore." She hugged herself, trying to hold in the emotions.

"I did not disintegrate him, Lara. I only made him leave for a bit. He'll return in due time, and maybe he'll have a better attitude."

"You didn't disintegrate him?"

"Of course not. We haven't done that in years. You know this."

She breathed a sigh of relief. Sam would return shortly. She hadn't lost him forever. This was very good.

"When will he return?" She had to know positively.

Shaedra bit her bottom lip. "I'm not exactly sure. I've never made someone go away."

"Damn, damn, damn!"

"And what does that word mean?" Shaedra asked.

She frowned. "I'm not sure, but Sam says it a lot when he's upset."

"Damn." The princess tested the word. "Yes, I like the way it rolls off the tongue. We'll incorporate it into our system." Shaedra turned her attention to Aasera. "Do you know the meaning of this word?"

"I believe they call it cursing. It makes them feel better to utter it. The male species, especially, like to say it a lot."

Shaedra nodded. "The Elders said you were dead. That you were killed on a mission."

"I was exiled."

Lara noticed Aasera did not say the Elders had lied. That would be very disrespectful. The truth but disrespectful. Aasera still held true to the Nerakian values.

"Why would they exile you, then immortalize you on our meeting room wall?"

"Because I refused to eliminate the child within me," Aasera told her, standing tall.

Shaedra gripped the arms of the chair. "You were with child? But that's impossible. Nerakians cannot bear children. Not and live through the ordeal. The Elders have passed the stories down through the ages about the horrible pain women went through."

"It was painful, true, but I'm still here."

"And the child? Did it survive as well?"

"Her name is Lyraka, and her gifts are more powerful than what we have."

"You've fared well then . . . on Earth?"

"I've missed my home . . . my people, but I managed. It's not as bad as we were told."

"But there are so many men there. Did you copulate with one? Is that how you came to be with child?"

"Yes, but he wasn't a good man."

She nodded. "Then what the Elders said was true. Men are cruel. They prey upon women."

"Not all men, Princess. Sam is a very good man."

The princess looked at Aasera for confirmation.

"He seems good," she grudgingly admitted.

"And did you copulate with this male . . . Sam?" the princess asked Lara.

Her skin grew warm as she remembered the pleasure she'd shared with Sam.

She could lie. It would be much safer. But she was afraid the princess would know. "Yes, and it was quite different than copulating with a companion unit."

"In what way?"

At least the princess hadn't zapped her because of her admission. She might as well tell her all of it. "Sam made my body burn, but in a very good way. I enjoyed it immensely. He made me very horny."

"Horny? I don't know this word."

"It means I wanted to copulate with him very much."

She nodded.

There was a hiss and a pop, then Sam appeared, minus his clothes.

"Oh," the princess began, her gaze moving slowly over Sam. "We didn't get everything correct, I see. You look much bigger than the companion units."

"Damn, first Kia, and now you." He quickly grabbed a cloth off the lounging sofa and wrapped it around himself, knotting it at the waist. "Did you have to do that?"

"I'm a princess. I can do anything I want."

"Well, I hope all of you had a nice conversation while I was out in Never-Never Land."

"Yes, we did. Lara was telling us how she'd copulated with you."

"Lara!" Sam glared at her.

She cringed. Not talking about sex was a silly rule, and she'd forgotten about it. "They don't talk about copulating on Earth," Lara explained.

"They certainly don't mind doing it," Aasera muttered.

"Why don't they talk about it?" Shaedra asked.

"Because we just don't," Sam said. "And we don't run around without clothes, either."

"The Elders said Earthlings were rather odd."

"And you think Nerakians aren't?" Sam snorted.

Shaedra raised her chin. "Of course we're not. We are, after all, a superior race."

"Except you don't eat real food, and you had to build companion units so you can have sex."

"There is that," Aasera commented. "I did like the food on Earth, especially chocolate. Sex was exciting. Apparently, I chose the wrong male."

"What is chocolate?" Shaedra asked.

"I brought some along." Lara reached into her satchel and pulled out the bag of chocolate bars. Maybe the princess would see what Nerak was missing, and they could begin importing some of Earth's pleasures.

She ripped open the bag and handed the princess one of the chocolate bars. Shaedra brought it to her nose and sniffed.

"It smells . . . nice."

"You eat it," Lara explained.

She cautiously put one corner in her mouth, then took it out. "I taste nothing that tempts me."

"No, you have to unwrap it first." Lara removed the wrapping from one and bit into the chocolate, then closed her eyes and savored the taste.

"Why did you not explain?" Shaedra asked, but she was already removing the wrapper and biting into the bar. After only a second, she closed her eyes and began to chew slowly. In a matter of seconds, she had eaten the chocolate.

The princess's expression softened when she opened her eyes and looked straight at Lara. "You brought these for your princess?" The warmth of her smile enveloped everyone in the room.

No, she hadn't. They were her chocolate bars.

But then again, if it would soften the princess's heart toward Sam then she would give up the chocolate. She only hoped Sam realized the sacrifice she was making.

"Of course, Princess." When she bowed slightly, she caught Sam's eye. He gave her a look that said he knew exactly who she'd intended the chocolate bars for, and it wasn't the princess.

"Good, then I'll save them for later."

Lara's mouth watered as she watched Shaedra tuck the bag beside her.

"Did you find a cure for the Elder?" the princess asked, changing the subject.

Lara thought she just wanted to get everyone's mind off the chocolate in case they tried to get it away from her. Shaedra always had to have her own way. But then, most of the princesses were of the same temperament.

"The cure?" Shaedra prodded.

"Yes, I believe I've found a cure."

"Then you will heal the Elder. Go."

She looked at Sam, then Aasera. This wasn't good. And she could hear Sam's thoughts as he asked her not to leave him alone with Shaedra.

"I will not disintegrate this male, but I want to interrogate him."

"You promise?" she asked.

Shaedra raised an imperious eyebrow. "You question me?"

She bowed slightly. "Of course not."

"Good, then take Aasera with you. I'm sure she'll want to meet with the other Elders. They're gathered at Torcara's dwelling. Go through the tunnels. It might not be good if others recognize Aasera. The ones who have seen her and the male will keep their silence."

Aasera respectfully bowed before they left the room.

When they were a distance away from the princess's dwelling, Lara turned to Aasera. "Do you think she'll harm him?"

"Most likely not."

"But you're not sure?"

"The royals are notorious for doing whatever they want. It has always been like that. I doubt things have changed in that respect."

Lara's heart sank. Unfortunately, they hadn't.

"But I don't think she will. I didn't get the feeling that she would really harm anyone."

"I hope you're right." She watched as Aasera's gaze scanned every little detail as if she was committing it to memory. "Does it look the same?"

"Yes and no. It seems even more beautiful, calmer than I remember. I've missed my home, but even now, I would return to Earth. I fear for Lyraka's safety. I think I've been overly protective of my daughter, and she doesn't know Earth as I do."

"Kia and Nick will see that she doesn't come to harm while you are away."

"I know they will. Kia is a warrior and will protect her. And . . . I suppose if Kia says Nick is a good man, then I will have to accept her judgment. I should've taught Lyraka more, though. Her skills are not completely under control."

"I think you did teach her a lot. Maybe you don't realize it."

The nearer they came to Torcara's dwelling, the more she sensed Aasera's nervousness. What must she feel, meeting the Elders after so many years? It would be hard for her if they exiled her again, but even harder if she never saw Lyraka. It would be a choice Lara wouldn't want to make, but then she already had when she chose to leave Sam.

But her loyalty was with the Elders. Wasn't it?

They stopped in front of Torcara's dwelling and pushed a button, then waited to be admitted.

A few minutes passed before Torcara's companion unit opened the door and stepped back to allow them entrance into the massive chambers of the High Royal.

They entered with bowed heads as was the custom, but Lara could see that the other three Elders were in the room by the hems of the white robes, which it was their custom to wear.

Only one Elder would speak.

"Welcome home, Healer," a soft voice said.

She breathed a sigh of relief. Rabare was next in line to rule, but Lara thought she had more of a dreamer's DNA in her. She didn't think Rabare with her gentle soul, would be able to wage a war if the need should arise.

Not that she thought that time would ever come. After all, they were a peaceful nation.

Lara raised her head and looked into Rabare's soft yellow eyes. She could almost feel the warmth flowing from her.

"Who have you brought with you?" Rabare asked. "Raise your head so that I might look upon your face."

"I'm Aasera," she said as she stepped forward without waiting for Lara's introduction.

"Yes. I remember you. You were exiled for the safety of Nerak, yet you have returned." Her soft voice was more powerful, could cut deeper than if she had been harsh and scolding.

"It was an accident," Lara said. "She was working on the tube craft so that I might bring the remedy back for Torcara." She didn't want the grandmother or Sam to get into trouble because they'd been helping her.

"Apparently, you are still gifted at making things work. I must admit, I've missed your talents . . . and you."

"As I have missed my home and the royals."

"You know that we had no choice." Rabare clasped her hands in front of her.

"I accepted my fate."

"And the child, it is well?"

"Lyraka is quite special."

"Then you made the right choice."

"Yes, I would make the same one if I had to do it over again."

"Torcara will want to see you before you return to Earth."

Lara felt pity for the former interplanetary traveler. Rabare was letting her know that she couldn't stay on Nerak. It was as she had expected.

A companion unit entered the room carrying a tray. Rabare addressed Lara, "Shaedra let us know you were on your way, so we made sure we had your things assembled. She didn't mention Aasera. The princess has a rather odd sense of humor."

She did seem to like the dramatic, and she'd left Sam in her care. Not good. The quicker she returned, the better off he'd be.

She brought the remedy out of her satchel and placed it on the tray, then set her satchel on the floor before donning the protective gear. She nodded when she was ready to enter Torcara's chamber.

When she went inside, the Elder was lying on the bed, looking out the window.

"I never realized just how boring it could be when one is all alone"—she turned toward Lara—"nor thought about how lonely a healer must be since they have very little contact with others."

"You sound better, Torcara."

"It would seem the disease is running its course. I'm told the Earthling who infected me has recuperated."

"I brought a remedy that should hasten your recovery."

"And what else have you brought?"

Lara's eyes widened. Had she already heard about Aasera and Sam?

"Yes, I know about the ones who traveled with you. Did you think that I would not discover their presence?"

"No, Elder."

"Then tell me about them."

"It is Aasera and a . . . a man called Sam."

"Aasera . . ." Torcara closed her eyes, her features softening. "The hardest thing I ever did was to exile her. I was closer to her than to anyone. I loved to hear about her stories of distant worlds. I suppose I lived my life vicariously through her. I knew that I would never be able to leave Nerak. Not as the High Royal."

"She has missed her home, her people."

"But not enough that she would fight being exiled. She gave everything up for what? To have a child. I was afraid . . . I thought she might have died giving birth. Did her child survive?"

"Lyraka is a beautiful young woman with many gifts."

"Lyraka?" She sat up in bed. "That's what she calls her?"

"Yes." Lara wondered at the emotion showing on the Elder's face.

Torcara apparently realized she'd let her guard down and quickly sobered. "Lyraka was the name of my grandmother. We were also very close. At least, as close as we could be in our society." She drew in a deep breath. "And you brought a man back."

"His name is Sam, and I care deeply for him. Please do not hurt him."

Torcara frowned. "Tell me you don't think I'm going to have him disintegrated or anything."

When Lara didn't say anything, Torcara spoke again.

"Really, Lara, I do believe healers are left to their own devices more than necessary. You have too much time to think. It's not as if we've disintegrated the humans who came back in Mala's craft, although why we haven't I don't know. They're quite trying."

"Are you going to send them back?"

"Yes, soon, I would imagine, but we'll erase their memories of the time since they've been on Nerak. I suppose we'll have to do that with the male you brought back with you."

"But he'll still remember me."

"No, I'll make sure he has no memory left of you. It's best that way."

Sam wouldn't remember the time they'd spent together? A

sharp pain stabbed her in the center of her chest. The Elder was right, of course. He wouldn't miss her if he had no memory of her. It was the best solution.

Then why did it hurt so much to know he wouldn't remember what they'd shared?

Chapter 28

Sam didn't like the way Shaedra was looking at him—as if he were a chocolate bar, and she wanted to eat him up. There was definitely a predatory gleam in her eyes.

When would Lara return? It better be a damned fast trip.

"You look worried, Earthman." She removed a chocolate bar from the bag and slowly unwrapped it, but her gaze never left him.

"Yeah, well, if our positions were reversed, you'd be worried, too. It's not like I travel to a different planet every day and get zapped."

She laughed. "You amuse me. Sit. Tell me more about this place you come from. I want to know everything." She bit into the chocolate, a dreamy expression on her face as she savored the bite.

Great, now he was a boy toy to a princess. Well, she'd better think again. He wasn't about to become her concubine.

But if it would keep her from zapping him again, then he'd be more than happy to talk her head off. Man, being zapped was weird. It was like floating around in a dark place, actually living an episode of *The Twilight Zone*. It creeped him out, and he'd rather not go there again. So whatever made the princess happy, short of stripping.

She'd told him to sit, so he'd sit. He started toward a chair only a few feet away.

"Not that one," she said. "The one in the far corner." Her attention returned to the chocolate.

"What difference does it make?" But as he walked toward it, he heard her sigh. The chocolate? When he turned, her gaze was riveted on him.

Great, she wanted to look at his butt. Get an eyeful, lady. That's all he was going to give her. Damn, he sounded like a virginal librarian or something. No, it was more than that, and he knew it.

He dragged the chair nearer to her but far enough away so she couldn't bite or anything. He studied her, not so sure she wouldn't.

She looked pretty hot when he got past the royal treatment. Her reddish brown hair was short, and her eyes were a deep, deep green, but he wasn't about to be deceived by her looks. Besides, he was partial to longhaired blondes.

"I enjoy watching you move," she said after he'd settled himself in the chair. "Your muscles ripple quite nicely. Are you sure you wouldn't be more comfortable without that bulky cloth draping across your hips?"

"Yeah, I'm sure. I don't suppose you know when or if my clothes will return?" Not that they had when Kia zapped him. He'd had to wear Nick's clothes home. Damned uncomfortable, too.

"I don't know. I've never made someone go away." She brought her feet under her and leaned forward, her half-lidded gaze telling him exactly where her thoughts were. "You cause a reaction inside me that has never happened. My body tingles." She licked her lips.

Oh, Lord, he was in deep shit.

"I want to copulate with you."

He pushed with his heels, and his chair slid across the floor a good two feet farther away from her. Ah, damn, he had been afraid she was going to say something like that. Where the hell was Lara? Probably shooting the breeze while he was being fed to the lioness. He had to stall.

"Sorry, Princess, I'm a one-woman man, and right now, Lara and I have a relationship."

She sat back with a frown. "That's not possible—she's a healer. They can't bond with anyone. It would upset the harmony within them." She shook her head. "No, it's quite impossible."

"She's not dead." Damn, healers didn't have much of a life. He felt sorry for what Lara had had to put up with all these years, the enforced loneliness. He damn sure didn't like the idea of her returning to her former life. No, he'd do something to get off Nerak, and when he did, he'd be taking her with him.

"Of course she's not dead." Shaedra frowned. "If I commanded you to copulate, then you would be forced to comply," she changed the subject back to her own gratification.

He laughed. She sounded a lot like Lara did when she first came to earth.

"You laugh at me?" She drew her legs from beneath her and narrowed her eyes.

Uh-oh. He'd opened his mouth this time and stuck his size ten and a half foot in. "Not at you, just the way you think."

"And that's funny?" She quirked an eyebrow and didn't look a bit mollified by his explanation.

"Not at all," he quickly interjected. "But wouldn't you want to have your own man rather than one that belongs to a healer? One that she's been with?" He could tell she was pondering his words.

"Yes, you're right," she said. "You would be a used model, quite unworthy of a princess."

Thanks for nothing. Now he was being compared to a companion unit.

"But how will I ever get a man if there are none on Nerak?" She frowned. "Or more chocolate?"

Sam wasn't sure which meant more to her—men or chocolate. He had a feeling it would be a close race between the two even with women from Earth. A very disheartening comparison. Now if it was an ice-cold beer, he could understand that.

The door slid open. He breathed a sigh of relief when he saw Lara. He'd already started missing her. Her head was bowed as she waited for permission to enter.

Man, he'd get tired of this royal crap in a heartbeat. Too rigid for his way of life. Yeah, he had to find a way off Nerak and a way to take her with him.

He wondered if the government would give her sanctuary or diplomatic immunity, something to protect her. Maybe, if a bunch of warrior aliens didn't show up and zap a bunch of government officials—which might not be as bad as it sounded, come to think about it.

"Enter," the princess said. "You've returned rather quickly."

Lara stepped inside the room, raising her head. Was that pity he saw in her eyes? Damn, what was going to happen? Maybe they did disintegrate people on Nerak.

"The Elder has requested Sam's presence."

She didn't look at him when she spoke. This was bad. He closed his eyes. *What's going on?*

Stay strong.

He looked at Lara, knowing she hadn't spoken aloud, but he heard her words as clearly as if she had.

Shaedra came to her feet. "It's not fair. I wanted to question him further. We haven't spoken about Earth or their customs." She pursed her lips. "You may leave." She waved her arm, turning her back on them.

Lara judged the distance from where she stood to the bag of chocolate. She'd never make it, and then the princess would be furious that she'd tried to steal them back.

She motioned for Sam to follow her out of the room.

"What's going on, Lara?" he asked as soon as they were a good distance from the princess's dwelling. "And how come I can hear your thoughts more often?"

"It's the connection between us. The more you concentrate, the easier they come through." She nibbled her bottom lip. "But if the emotion is too strong, thoughts can be blocked."

He could feel how upset she was, but he had a feeling she had the ability to shut him out when she needed to. "What are they going to do to me?"

Lara knew Sam was trying to break into her thoughts, but she was stronger and she didn't want him to feel her anxiety any more than he already could.

"I'd rather hear it from you," he said, taking her hand in his and stopping her.

Her heart broke into tiny pieces as she looked at him. No, she had to be strong. "We can't keep the Elders waiting."

"What, Lara?"

"They will send you back to Earth." She didn't look at him as they continued down the private walkway of the royals. By going this route, no one would see Sam.

"Go with me," he pleaded. "You're not meant for a life this rigid."

She shook her head. "This is the life I was born to." She could feel him studying her as they walked.

"I think there's more to it."

"To what?"

"To me going home."

She hesitated but knew she had to tell him. Keeping the truth from him would only delay things. "They're going to erase your memory of me, of Nerak." When he didn't say anything, she looked up at him.

"They can't do that," he said.

"Yes, I'm afraid they can."

"But what about Nick? Are they going to erase his memory? Kia's?"

"No, they can't do that, but when Nick and Kia talk about me, you won't have any idea of whom they speak."

"What difference does it make if I remember you?" His words were laced with anger.

"It's not so much your memory of me; they don't want you to remember Nerak. It's to protect our planet."

"You think I'll give someone directions?"

"No, it's more than that." She hesitated, knowing some would think she betrayed her home, but she trusted Sam. "You've seen just how vulnerable we are. There are no wars here. We would not be prepared if we were invaded."

"And what's to stop them now?"

"We've fooled everyone. Our artists have created fierce holograms of mighty warriors. If dignitaries arrive to talk with the Elders, we drag out the holograms. They think we are many and that we're well trained."

"Why weren't they in place when we arrived? If you ask me, everyone looked ill-prepared to fight anyone."

"They knew the craft, and they knew I would be on board," she said.

"I won't let them erase my memory of you," he said. "And who the hell would I talk to about Nerak? If I did, they'd cart me off to the state hospital. Believe me, I have no desire to walk halls drooling and wearing a short white gown."

She had no idea what a state hospital was, but Sam wore a fierce frown and looked ready to do battle. She had a feeling the Elders didn't know what they were up against when it came to Sam. She knew he could be quite stubborn.

"I know you would have no one to tell our secrets to, but they don't trust you with the information. You'll have to give them a reason to believe in you." She approached the door to the Elder's dwelling and waved her hand, then bowed as the door silently opened.

"Enter," Rabare commanded in her soft voice.

They stepped inside. Lara looked up, noting Rabare was the only Elder in the room. Maybe she'd be able to convince her that Sam wished them no harm.

"I have never seen a man before," Rabare said. She

stepped closer, walking around him, then stopped in front. "Is this the way Earthmen clothe themselves?"

"The princess zapped me. When I came back, my clothes were gone. So no, this isn't the way we dress."

Not good. Sam looked quite upset that he didn't have his clothes. He had a magnificent body, so Lara really didn't see a problem.

"Torcara wants to eliminate your memory of Lara and our planet," Rabare told him.

"I won't let her." He straightened to his full height, curling his hands into fists.

Lara had to admire his obstinate manner. It made him come across as fierce as any warrior, and they were not to be taken lightly.

"You have seen more of Nerak than any outsider. That isn't good. You've put us in a vulnerable position. We know it's not your fault, and we hold no harm against you."

"What if others decide to test your strength, then where will you be?" he asked.

"You think like a warrior. Our defense council has also warned us of this possibility. Are you a warrior?"

"I'm a cop, so yeah, you could say I am. I put the bad guys away."

"And you have done this a long time?"

"Long enough."

Rabare sat in one of the chairs, then motioned for them to take a seat. Lara chose the lounging sofa. Sam sat next to her. She could feel his warmth, his strength.

"Tell me about Earth. It has been many years since we've allowed interplanetary travel, so we've had no stories of distant places."

"Why did you stop?" he countered.

"Because of Aasera. She was with child."

"Was that so wrong?"

"It would have changed everything about Nerak. We

couldn't let that happen. What if it had gotten out of control, caused an epidemic? Next, they'd want everything else that polluted our planet in the past. It has taken us years, and many Elders before us, to create the perfect place."

"And you think you've achieved that?" he asked.

"Yes, we do."

"No, we haven't," Lara spoke up. "We're not at all perfect. And we don't have any option except to live our lives as they are. Forgive me, Elder, but our freedom of choice was taken away from us."

Rabare's gaze swung to her, and for a moment, Lara wanted to call back her words, but it was too late and maybe what she'd spoken had needed saying.

"You question our authority, Healer?" There was a hard edge in her voice that Lara had never heard before, but she refused to back down.

"The Elders are wise in all things, but haven't you felt stifled? Everything is so . . . so perfect. Most of our jobs are obsolete."

"You have no pain," Rabare said.

"Nor pleasure."

"There are no wars."

"Nor victories."

Rabare frowned. "There is no death except by natural causes or choice."

"But there's no living, either," Lara sadly told her. "Sometimes, you have to suffer a little to experience the glory of being alive."

"You will leave us, Healer," Rabare said, her words brooking no argument. "Maybe you should meditate about the good things Nerak has to offer."

She stood. "Yes, Elder." Before she left, she cast a glance in Sam's direction. He reached out and took her hand in his, running his thumb across the back of it, then giving her a gentle squeeze.

She could still feel his warmth after she'd left the room. What had she done? She'd hoped Rabare would see the truth of her words, but Lara was afraid they had worked against her. Sam might be in more danger because of her. That hadn't been her intention at all.

She went to her dwelling, pacing back and forth across the room. Time slowed to a crawl.

Eventually, she stood beneath the beams of light, but it wasn't the same as the water cascading over her in Sam's bathing room. When she finished, her companion unit was waiting to help her don her robe.

She only had to put her arms into the sleeves of the transparent white robe. She waved him away when he would've belted it for her.

"I can manage to tie it, I believe."

When she looked at how her life had once been, she couldn't believe how little she'd done for herself. Sam had made the simplest task feel like a great accomplishment.

Was he already gone? Had Aasera left with him? No, she wouldn't think the worst.

"I'll meditate now," she said, dismissing him. But when she sat on her rug and crossed her legs, she felt her agitation more keenly.

Breathe in, breathe out.

She closed her eyes, forcing her mind to clear.

What if they erased his memory and sent him back to Earth while she had to remain here? What if he asked to see her one more time, and they wouldn't let him. Fear crept through her.

No, of course, they wouldn't do that. Would they?

"I'm detecting high levels of anxiety," the companion unit's voice came over the intercom. "Would you like me to prepare you a relaxation smoothie?"

"No." She gritted her teeth. Sometimes, the companion units could be quite irritating.

"They've risen even higher, Healer. It's not good for your levels to elevate this much. I can give you a massage if you'd like."

"I wouldn't like."

"Or I could hum a pleasing melody."

"Or you can go away."

"Yes, I can do that, too. I'll continue to monitor your anxiety levels."

If only there was an off switch. No, companion units lasted forever, and ever, and ever . . .

And the Elders had thought they were better than men? They didn't even come close. She wanted Sam.

"Damn, damn, damn!"

Oh, she felt much better using the words Sam had used. Already she felt more relaxed.

"I do not understand this word, Healer. Your anxiety levels have dropped, though. I would suggest you use damn as your mantra. If you are anxious, you'll be out of harmony with your mind and body and, therefore, will not be able to heal anyone."

"Go away!"

"As you wish. I'm here to serve."

Chapter 29

S am shifted in his seat. He didn't feel at all comfortable sitting there talking to Rabare draped in only a fancy cloth. And he'd been here for a while. She'd asked him about his life as a cop, so he'd told her.

"This Nick, is he of your DNA?"

"No, we're just friends."

"And Kia has mated with him."

"Yes, they're very happy."

Rabare sighed. "I do miss Kia. If we had ever had a war, she would've been a fierce warrior. And I miss Mala, too—so sweet."

She suddenly glanced around as if she didn't want to be overheard. "Tell me about this chocolate. I've heard of it, you know. Aasera mentioned it once long ago when she'd returned from one of her travels." She looked at him as if she was about to tell him a state secret. "I think Torcara has even tasted it."

What was it with women and chocolate? "Lara brought some back with her. Shaedra has it." That would teach her to zap him. "She loved the taste."

Rabare sat straight. "The princess has chocolate?" Her eyebrows veed.

She clapped her hands. A few seconds later, a companion

unit came into the room. "You will collect the chocolate from the Princess Shaedra."

He'd better stay far away from the princess while he was here. She wasn't going to like having to give up her chocolate.

Rabare faced him again. "It would not do to corrupt a princess. Now, tell me more about Earth. What do you do for entertainment?"

He shrugged. "We have movies and plays; Lara enjoyed the slot machines." He smiled when he remembered how much she'd enjoyed them. "There are competitive sports."

Rabare leaned closer. She reminded him of a child eager to explore but afraid if she did, she'd get into trouble. He almost felt sorry for her. He would, if she wasn't so eager to erase his memory.

"You know, all the royals have a bit of all DNA in them. Some tendencies are stronger than others." She tilted her head, and her eyes looked dreamy. "I think I would've been a great explorer.

His stomach rumbled.

She jumped. "Your body is making noises."

"I haven't eaten today. I'm getting hungry."

"Of course. I'll have my companion unit bring you a food capsule when he returns."

"I'm looking forward to it."

She arched an imperious eyebrow.

They had that look down pat.

"Are you being sarcastic?" she asked.

Okay, so she was smarter than he'd given her credit for. "I apologize."

"We used to think Earth beings were barbaric because they ate food."

"Don't knock it until you've tried it."

"Yes, you're quite right. I suppose that might be construed as rudeness."

Ya think?

The companion unit returned. There were only six chocolate bars left inside the bag.

"The princess was quite upset that you took her chocolate," he said.

Sam couldn't help studying the robot. He wasn't at all like Barton. This one looked . . . weird. Kind of like a walking, talking mannequin. No wonder Mala had done a little readjusting to hers.

Hell, Sam hadn't been able to tell Barton wasn't human when he'd met him. He'd been proper and stiff-acting, but Sam had just thought he was from England or something.

"You're dismissed," Rabare told the companion unit with a wave of her hand, then opened the package and brought out one of the bars and sniffed. She closed her eyes with a look of enjoyment on her face. "It does smell quite wonderful."

"It tastes even better, and this is just one little thing that Earth has to offer."

She turned it over in her hand, then looked over her shoulder. "Torcara wouldn't like me tasting one."

"I won't tell if you eat just one."

Yeah, he had ulterior motives. If chocolate made them happy, they might not zap him. They did seem to get addicted to it pretty fast, too. They would need more and more of the sweet bars. He could see himself now: ex-cop turned chocolate supplier. They could make monthly pickups, and maybe he'd get to see Lara.

"Just one then," she said.

"Unwrap it first."

"Of course." She peeled off the paper and laid it carefully to the side, then took a bite. "Oh, this is fabulous." She crammed the rest of the mini chocolate bar in her mouth. "I never expected . . ."

The door of the room behind her swished open, and a

majestically robed woman with blue hair stepped out. Not the old lady kind of blue that he normally saw. No, this was a vibrant blue that shimmered and sparkled.

And there were jewels draped around her neck. She could buy a country with the gems she had on: diamonds, sapphires, rubies, emeralds.

"Torcara," Rabare garbled, then swallowed the rest of the chocolate that was in her mouth and jumped to her feet, brushing at her robes in case there might have been crumbs.

But there was still a small smudge of chocolate near the corner of her mouth. He tried to warn her, but she turned before he could get her attention.

Rabare cleared her throat. "Torcara, this is the Earth male I told you about. The one who traveled here with Lara. He was telling me about . . . about . . ."

Torcara folded her arms in front of her and glared at Rabare. "You have chocolate on the side of your mouth."

"Oh . . . oh." She quickly dabbed it away.

When Torcara turned her glacier stare on him, Sam felt as if he were slowly turning into a block of ice. He quickly stood and bowed. "Elder." He kept his eyes lowered, but he could see a chair being brought for her. There was a rustle of her bright orange robes.

"Sit," she ordered.

He did, his eyes meeting hers. Okay, this woman was more than a little formidable. She reminded him of his captain, and his captain was as wily as a fox.

"You're here a short time, and already you are corrupting my people."

"It's only chocolate," he said.

"First, chocolate . . . then what?"

"You're a great ruler. I know because I've seen the respect Mala, Kia, and Lara have for all the Elders. But your people aren't happy."

She gripped the sides of the chair, her knuckles turning

white. Any second, he expected to turn into a pile of ashes. Well, she hadn't zapped him yet.

"That's why they're leaving. Their jobs are obsolete; the days stretch endlessly from one to the other."

"He's right," Aasera said as she stepped in from the other room. "You've known what he's telling you for a very long time. There has to be change, or you'll lose the favor of your people. That's not the type of leader I remember."

"Or we can erase his memory and send him home where he belongs."

"And before too long, everyone will find a way to leave," he said. "They can't continue to live in a tiny bubble. Are you going to erase everyone's memory?"

"Take him away," Torcara said, coming to her feet. "Lock him up. I will hear no more of this." She swept from the room as two companion units took him by the arms and began to lead him out of the room.

He tried to break their hold but couldn't. "Aasera, tell Lara; tell her what's happening."

Every movie he'd ever seen about alien probes came back to haunt him. This wasn't right. Not right at all. He could only hope Aasera would tell Lara. But he knew exactly what Aasera thought about him, about all men, and it didn't look good for him. Oh, God, he hoped they used lubricant.

They led him lower and lower into the bowels of the building. It grew more and more dim. Great, they were taking him to some kind of dungeon, and then they were probably going to cut him open and see what made him tick.

He'd never see Lara again. She would probably think he'd been sent back to Earth with no more memories of her.

"Hey, guys," he said to the companion units on either side of him, "if you let me go, I'll make sure I have a case of oil delivered to you. I won't tell a soul it was you guys, promise. All you have to do is take me to Lara.

Silence.

What he wouldn't give for a screwdriver. Clothes would be nice, too. The air was growing cooler by the minute.

One of the companion units waved his arm, and a door opened. They shoved Sam inside, and the door shut. He raced to it, pounding on what now just looked like one of the walls, but nothing happened. No knob to turn or bar to lift. He waved his arm—nothing happened.

"There's got to be a way out." He walked the perimeter of the room. Ten feet by ten feet. No windows. The walls were white. A cot floated in the center of the room, no wires, either. A toilet of sorts was in one corner, and a sink.

At least he had that much. He went to the sink, his mouth dry. He really needed a drink, but since there wasn't a beer close by, he'd settle for water.

No handles. Must be automatic. He stuck his hands beneath the faucet, and beams of blue and green lights shot out. He jumped back. Okay, this shit wasn't funny. He couldn't even get a drink of water.

He went to the bed and lay down. What the hell was he going to do now? He stared at the ceiling. It took a few seconds for the significance of the blinking red light in the corner to sink into his brain.

A camera? They were watching him?

That's all it could be. Great, now he felt like a monkey in a damned zoo! Okay, they wanted to observe the human? He'd give them something to look at. He came off the bed and bent at the waist away from the light. Let them get an eyeful! He raised the cloth he wore, then slapped his butt.

"This is what I think of you and your bullshit planet!"

"What is he doing now?" Torcara asked as she watched the screen on the wall.

Rabare squinted even though the screen took up most of one wall. "He's slapping his bottom."

"Why?"

"I don't know. It must be some kind of Earth custom." She cleared her throat. "He's quite handsome, you know."

"Yes, he is that."

"Lara seems to care deeply for him."

Rabare gave the impression she watched the screen, but Torcara knew her well and wasn't fooled. She knew exactly what the other Elder was doing.

"I'll not change my mind. If I let him go, he could cause trouble for all of us."

"But he was right." She let out a long sigh. "The people do love us, I'll not dispute that with you, but they feel stifled. We have to make some changes, or they may make them for us."

"I know."

"You do?" Rabare asked with surprise.

"Of course I do. I'm not blind. I can see what's going on."

"I have an idea how we can change all that." Rabare wore a self-satisfied smile.

Torcara didn't think she wanted to hear her idea. Rabare was a dreamer and had come up with a few slightly off-balance schemes in the past. She wasn't sure she wanted to hear her newest one, but something had to be done.

"Okay, tell me what it is you think will help Nerak."

Chapter 30

The door opened, and Lara's companion unit came to where she was attempting to meditate. She'd hoped to lose herself, maybe connect with Sam and find out what was happening, but she couldn't keep her concentration and failed miserably.

"Aasera to see you, Healer."

She jumped to her feet and quickly changed into her green robe. Maybe Aasera had news.

She hurried to the other room. "Aasera, where's Sam?"

When Aasera turned, Lara saw the pity in the grand-mother's clear gray eyes and understood the news she brought would not be good.

"They've locked him away . . . down below."

Lara grabbed the back of the lounging sofa to steady herself.

Not down there. Sam would go mad. The rooms were small, windowless. She remembered how much he said he enjoyed the outdoors, exploring. No, he wouldn't survive locked up.

"I have to help him." She began to pace the room.

"You can't. You know this. Torcara ordered the confinement."

She raised her chin. "And what about you? Are you going to be allowed to stay but never see Lyraka again, or will they exile you back to Earth?"

"I'll be sent home. They're only letting me stay a short time, and only if I wear concealment." She wandered to the window. "I have missed my home, the royals, but I couldn't live without Lyraka."

When she faced Lara once again, she frowned. "I don't like the idea of Lyraka working for Mr. Beacon. He said it was dangerous. I'll not have my daughter in harm's way."

"Take Sam with you," Lara pleaded. "I'll find a way to release him without their harming him."

"No, I can't. It would be too dangerous. You could find yourself locked away if you're not careful."

"I have to try." She clasped the edge of the lounging sofa. "I know you don't like Sam, so I'll not ask you to do it for him, but will you at least consider doing it for me?"

She frowned. "I've grown to . . . tolerate the young man. I've carried my anger at Lyraka's father far too many years. I blamed him for my exile when in truth, it was just as much my fault. It's time to let it go. I can see Sam cares deeply for you. I'll help you. We must hurry, though."

"Thank you."

"You'll go with us?"

She shook her head. "I might be able to pacify the Elders by staying. If I left, none of us would be safe."

"You have seen the Elders at their best," Aasera said. "I've seen their anger. I fear for your safety as it is."

"I'll be fine, but we must hurry."

Before they could leave, the companion unit came into the room. "The Elder wants to see you."

She could feel the color drain from her face. "Which one?"

"Torcara."

She closed her eyes and took a deep breath. This was it, then. They were probably too late to help Sam. Lara felt as if she couldn't even walk to the door.

"You are a healer, Lara," Aasera said. "Hold your head high."

Aasera was right, of course. Sam would want her to be

strong. They walked to a chamber where they boarded a multi aero unit that would take them to the Elder's dwellings. Aasera pulled the hood of her cape over her head, shielding her face from curious eyes.

As they boarded, heads turned Lara's way, then bowed.

"Healer, you honor us." They stepped away from her, giving her room so they wouldn't interfere with the harmony of her mind and body.

She closed her eyes and took a deep breath. This was what she had to look forward to for the rest of her life. She could only hope that it was a short one, or she'd go mad. She frowned at the four women in the unit. "I won't disappear in a puff of smoke if you stand near me."

"We're sorry if we've offended you in any way." They looked at each other, their foreheads puckered in confusion.

It wasn't their fault, though. They knew no better. "You haven't offended me. I'm not in harmony today, that's all."

They nodded in understanding.

She wanted to tell them what she really thought but knew they wouldn't understand. They were much like the companion units who served them. Almost as if *they* were programmed.

The aero unit stopped, and she and Aasera got off while the others continued on. She would've liked to be friends with some of them, but she doubted that would ever be possible. Everyone had a role to play here on Nerak, and unfortunately, they played it well.

She glanced around before she entered the majestic white building and couldn't stop the pride that swelled inside her. Nerak had its faults, but no one could say it wasn't beautiful. Maybe she wouldn't see a deer step out in all his glory, but there was beauty in the sun that splashed its rays down on the gem-encrusted buildings.

She inhaled, breathing in the fragrance the Elders had used this day. It was a pure, clean aroma.

"I'll miss my home, but there will be many new memories to take with me," Aasera said.

They went inside. A companion unit stood in the entry, waiting for them. "You're here to see Torcara."

They stepped inside. "Transport us to the cleansing area," the unit said.

She closed her eyes. The cleansing area. They had probably started the process. Then why even summon her? Maybe she would get one last good-bye.

Aasera squeezed her hand. She was surprised by the gesture, and maybe a little touched by it.

"We are here," the unit said.

They followed him. Not that she had much of a choice. When Torcara summoned, you went, no questions asked. The companion unit led them to a spacious and well-appointed room that had three lounging sofas . . . and it was quite empty.

"What's happening, Aasera?"

"I don't know."

Before Lara could question the unit, he left. She was too nervous to sit; instead, she walked to the window and waved her hand in front of it. The view of the city was beyond compare. But what was a view if you couldn't share it with the one you loved?

Lara knew what was missing in her life—had been missing for so long, but she'd never realized it. It didn't matter where she lived as long as Sam was in her life. But would the Elders allow her to leave with him?

A door opened.

"Lara." Aasera lightly touched her arm.

She dreaded turning around, but she finally forced herself to. If Torcara had entered, it would be a sign of disrespect not to immediately acknowledge her presence.

She bowed.

"That's what I like, a woman who knows how to treat a man," Sam said.

It was Sam! Her head jerked up. Her heart thudded inside her chest. He looked quite striking in black pants, a white shirt, and a long black coat belted loosely at the waist.

"You know who I am?"

"Baby, I don't think I could ever forget you."

She picked up her robes and ran to his outstretched arms. And when he enveloped her in his embrace, it felt as if it had been forever since he'd held her like this.

"What are you doing here, and wearing these clothes? Have you escaped?"

"You know as much as I do. A companion unit brought me the *Star Wars* clothes and then had me follow him here."

"I don't care how you got here as long as you're here. I've missed you. Kiss me," she said, raising her lips to meet his.

"Still demanding, I see." But he didn't argue as he lowered his mouth and kissed her.

His lips were hot against hers. He ran his hands over her body, drawing her closer still even when she didn't think they could get any nearer. His tongue caressed hers. He was fire . . . he was Sam.

Aasera cleared her throat. A flush of heat stole up Lara's face. She had forgotten Aasera was even in the room. Sam had blocked everything out.

He didn't let her draw away from him, not that she had even thought about doing so. No, she wanted to stay as close as she could for as long as she was permitted. And if the Elders never arrived, she would gladly die in his arms because she realized without him, life wasn't worth living.

"Are they going to copulate?" Torcara said as she entered the room.

"I'm not sure," Rabare offered. "I would like to know more about this touching of lips, though."

"It appeared to be a transference of germs." Torcara went to one of the lounging sofas and sat. "I can't imagine why anyone would want to know more."

"A very heated transference of germs, though, from what I could see. Aasera, sit since this involves you as well."

Lara moved away from Sam and quickly lowered her

head. "Forgive us. It's just that it's been a while since we've seen each other."

"What were you doing?" Rabare sat on the same lounging sofa as Torcara.

"It's called kissing. A sign of affection."

Torcara raised an eyebrow. "It looked to be much more than a sign of affection, if you ask me. You may sit also."

Damn, Sam really did hate all this royalty crap. If they hadn't come in when they had, he had been planning to try his best to escape with Lara. He would've convinced her to leave with him even if he had to kiss her all the way to the craft.

Too late.

Two of the robots stood just inside the closed door. There was no way they'd escape now. Man, he shouldn't have let testosterone rule. He could've grabbed her and been out of there before the Elders arrived, but he'd just had to kiss her.

Idiot!

When Lara tugged on his hand, he knew he didn't have a choice except to sit, but he was keeping her close to him this time.

"So, are you going to steal my memories or what?" He glared at the Elders.

"Wouldn't it be better if you had no thoughts of Lara?" Rabare asked. "Without memory of her, there would be no pain in your parting."

"I would rather suffer a million lifetimes than to go one day without remembering what it feels like to hold her near; to see her smile, hear her laughter; to kiss her, to make love with her."

"It's that important to you?" Torcara finally addressed him.

He took Lara's hand in his and squeezed it. "Yes. I love her very much."

"And you, Healer, how do you feel about this man?"

"I love him, too."

"But we can also erase your memory of him. That's always been a choice when a loved one passes."

"I would refuse."

"I had hoped it wouldn't come to this," Torcara said.

"Please, Elders," Lara pleaded.

"I'm not sure this is the right thing to do," Torcara continued as if Lara hadn't spoken. "I've seen what our society has become. The Elders before us thought to prevent fighting when the loss of their sons became too painful. They manipulated the DNA so only female children would be born into our society."

Rabare sat forward on the sofa. "And then they eliminated the pain of childbirth so it would make all our lives easier. Each thing they successfully eliminated took away a form of pain that went along with it."

"But they also took away what made you feel alive in the first place," Sam said.

Torcara and Rabare looked at each other, then at him. Torcara began to speak again.

"Maybe it's time we learned how to live again. Not all at once, of course. That would be too much of a shock. But maybe we could introduce a little at a time."

Lara squeezed his hand, having guessed, like him, where they might be going.

"And where do I stand in all this?" he asked.

"You would help us plan where we'll start. You would need to train everyone. We would begin interplanetary travels again. Aasera, are you up for the task?"

"Yes, Torcara." She bowed her head, but Lara saw the tear that slipped from the corner of her eye. She would have the best of both worlds—she'd be able to travel to Earth to see Lyraka, but she would also be doing what she loved. This was good.

"The companion units would have to be reprogrammed. We would need to bring"—Torcara looked at her hands, then back at him—"we would need to reintroduce men into our society, but not too many at once."

"And chocolate," Rabare said, nodding her head.

Torcara relaxed, then smiled. "And chocolate." She sighed. "There will be much that needs to be done. We would need help. Your help, Sam. Would you be willing to live on Nerak?"

He'd thought this might be where she was going, but when she actually spelled it out, the task was daunting, to say the least. They were giving him the chance to spend the rest of his life with Lara and help a new society form.

He studied her face and knew that she wanted him to stay, but she couldn't bring herself to ask him to give up his home, his friends, his job. It would have to be his decision.

Wasn't that what he'd wanted her to do, though? Give up everything she knew to live on Earth? Wasn't that what Mala and Kia had done? Could he do any less?

"I'll do it," he said as he looked into her eyes, and he immediately knew he'd made the right choice.

She threw her arms around him, hugging him so tight he could barely breathe. Yes, he'd definitely made the right choice because he was holding her just as tightly, and he wasn't sure he'd ever let her go.

One of the Elders cleared her throat. Lara immediately moved away.

"Thank you, Elders," she said, her words filled with deep emotion.

When he looked at the royals, they were smiling. Okay, so maybe they weren't all that bad.

"Where would you like me to start first?"

"Tell us about sex," they said in unison.

"Oh, he knows all about sex, and he's very good at it," Lara offered.

Was it too late to change his mind? He had a feeling the next twenty or so years were going to be very interesting.

Epilogue

Sam thought Lara still looked tense even though she had said she was fine. "Are you sure you want to do this?"

She nodded, burying her face against his chest and squeezing him so tightly around his middle he could barely breathe.

"She doesn't look fine," Aasera commented.

"I'm fine," she mumbled into his shirt.

"Okay," Aasera said and pushed the button. "Here we go, yee haw!" She pushed the button, and the craft roared to life.

"You were in Texas way too long," Sam told her.

"I'm just feeling alive for the first time in my life, and I like the way it feels. Want to see me do a double loop? I was the only interplanetary traveler that could pull off a double loop."

"No," they spoke in unison.

"You're right. I don't think this craft maneuvers as well as the old ones, but you can't say anything against the time that it takes to get somewhere."

What had happened to the stuffy Aasera he'd first met? Sam kind of missed her. Torcara had given her a string of young Nerakians to train for interplanetary traveling, and she was feeling like she probably had thirty years ago—God help them all.

"We're here," she said. "I can't wait to see Lyraka. She'll be so excited that Torcara wants to see her."

Aasera pushed the button that would open the door. Sam almost dreaded getting out. Nick was really going to razz him about the clothes. Now that he'd been wearing them for a week, he sort of liked the way they felt.

They stepped out.

Nick burst through the doorway of the rooftop at the same time. "Thank God," he said, sounding out of breath as he hurried toward them. "What the hell have you been doing? Man, I was worried. I thought they might have vaporized you or something!" He threw his arms around Sam in a bear-hug that knocked the breath out of Sam.

Kia and Lyraka were right behind him.

"Did you miss me?" Sam grinned as they stepped away from the craft.

"No!" he glowered. "Yes, dammit, I missed you. What the hell are you wearing? Looks like something out of *Star Wars.*"

"Mother, I was afraid for your safety." Lyraka hurried forward but stopped just short of throwing her arms around Aasera. "I'm glad to see you well." She bowed.

"And I you." Aasera pulled her daughter into her arms.

Sam knew this was a long time coming.

Aasera hugged her close, then stepped back and looked at Lyraka but still held on to her hands. "You didn't go with Mr. Beacon?"

She shook her head. "Not until I knew you were all right."

"But you want to?"

Lyraka hesitated. "More than anything."

Aasera nodded. "Then maybe that's your purpose in life."

Kia and Lara looked at each other and smiled.

"Lara, good to see you. Aasera." Nick nodded toward them. "I think I've aged ten years since you left."

"Sam was made advisor to the Elders," Lara said.

Sam shrugged. "I guess I'm finally getting to discover new worlds."

"Don't say it," Nick warned. "Don't even tell me I'm going to get stuck with Talking Trudy for a partner."

"Either that, or you can come to work for the Elders."

"For the Elders?" Kia said.

"We've got to bring Nerak up to date." Sam knew it would be a long shot, but it was worth a try. "There's so much to teach them, so many things to introduce. We'd be opening a whole new world to them. Just think about the possibilities. We'd be introducing them to so many things."

Nick shook his head. "I don't know about this, partner. Moving is one thing, but going to another planet—that might be pushing the envelope just a little."

He shrugged. "Yeah, I guess you're right. Working with Talking Trudy would be less taxing, I suppose."

"What exactly would we be introducing them to?"

"Chocolate," Lara spoke up.

"Yeah, food and stuff." He nodded. "You always said you wanted a little bar on the beach. This is your chance. Maybe not a bar exactly—you wouldn't want to serve alcohol. It's a chance to be your own boss. Just like you've always wanted. You could even travel between both planets."

Sam could see Nick was thinking it over. He figured it wouldn't take him long to decide after appealing to his friend's lifelong dream.

Nick glanced at Kia. She nodded her head. "I'd like to be able to live on Nerak part of the time."

Sam smiled and hugged Lara close to him. He'd told her he could talk Nick into returning with them. Later, he would tell Nick what the Elders had specifically asked him to import—chocolate and real men.

The chocolate would be easy. He just wasn't sure where they were going to get the men.

You'll think of something, Lara's thoughts came to him.

You think so?

I know so. You can do anything, Sam. You're my hero.

He kind of liked the idea of being Lara's hero. Yeah, life was good.

If you liked this book, you've got to try
HelenKay Dimon's HARD AS NAILS,
out this month from Brava.
Here's an excerpt from "This Old House,"
the first story in this three-novella anthology . . .

She dragged his mouth down and scorched him with a deep, drugging kiss. A kiss that wiped out good intentions and common sense. One that overpowered him, causing every nerve ending to flare to life.

Gone was the gentle assault. Restless energy radiated off her. Her lower body cuddled and inflamed him. Fingers tunneled into his hair as her hot tongue rubbed against his. Hot and wet, body against body, and mouth against mouth.

"Damn, Aubrey. Yes."

Air caught in his lungs, making breathing impossible. Every inhale breath hitched, every exhale breath caught and stuttered. When he finally broke off the kiss, he balanced his forehead against hers to hold on to the warm contact a few minutes longer.

"Better?" Her finger traced the outline of his jaw.

Damn, did she have to ask? "Magnificent."

"You do know your way around a kitchen."

"I'm pretty knowledgeable about every room of the house. Wait until you see what I can do with a shower stall."

Her laugh vibrated against his cheek. "I guess we can consider the kiss a down payment on my bill."

Her words hit him like a big bucket of icy water. If she wanted to kill the mood, she had succeeded.

He blew out a long, painful breath. "Aubrey, about that—"

"Maybe making these payments won't be so hard after all."

No way would he have her rolling over in bed tomorrow morning, looking up at him with those bottomless dark eyes, and accusing him of a new sin. Stealing was bad enough.

"Think of it more as a taste of things to come." He forced his hands to drop to his sides. The rest of his body shouted to stay right where he was.

"What are you doing?" A cloudy haze hovered over her eyes, and those sleek arms stayed around his shoulders.

"Stopping." He reached up and loosened her hold around his neck. Otherwise, she might choke him.

"Why in the hell are you doing that?"

Yep, haze gone. Anger firmly in place. He'd buried her desire all right. Scooped up the dirt and piled it on top.

Despite the strong pull he felt for this woman, the situation didn't feel right. Sex for a house. Sex to get out of trouble. Neither of those worked for him. Not on those terms. Sex for sex. Wanting him for him—not for the name or his finances—was the deal. For some reason, accepting less no longer sat right with him.

This "being mature" thing sure was a bitch.

"We need to call a halt," Cole said, as he separated their bodies the rest of the way.

"Are you a complete idiot?"

No mystery there. Yeah, he was. A master idiot. "I'm trying to be sensible."

"You're about to be killed." She shoved hard against his chest with both palms.

"That's not quite the reaction I was going for." Where was the gratitude for treating her like a woman and not just a body? For giving her the benefit of the doubt despite all of her accusations?

"What game are you playing? Clue me in, so I know the rules."

"No game, Aubrey. That's the point. When we have sex—"

"You blew your chance on that one, stud."

She didn't have to sound so sure. "When we have sex—and we will, so stop shaking your head—it will be because we both want it. Not because you need something from me."

She pulled back as if he'd slapped her. "What do you think I need?"

"Money. The house."

Somehow those black eyes darkened even further. "That's the kind of male nonsense guaranteed to get a plate smashed over your head."

"It is?"

"You make it sound as if I proposed we trade sex for money."

Uh-oh. Somewhere along the line he had lost the upper hand in the conversation. "Well, I thought . . ."

"You better deny it before you end up wearing those dishes," she warned.

Red face and puffing cheeks. A damned angry expression for a woman supposedly seeking a quid pro quo.

Cole tried to regain lost ground. "Look, let's back up a step."

"You can back right out the door for all I care." Her chest rose and fell in rapid counts.

"You mean you weren't saying . . . ?"

"I was kissing, you idiot." The words shot out of her and into him like tiny knife wounds. "And you were what, Cole, dissecting my intentions?"

"I didn't mean to—"

"Deciding I had a motive other than putting my tongue in your mouth?"

He knew enough to keep his mouth shut this time. Didn't help though. Her rage kept spiraling.

"I admit I'm new at the one-night stand thing, Cole, but I thought kissing meant kissing, not that cash needed to be exchanged."

Something that tasted like regret boiled up from his stomach. He'd been so sure a second ago that she wanted something from him. At least that's what he thought right up to the minute he started thinking something else.

He mentally composed a convincing apology. He refused to beg, but he could admit some responsibility for their misunderstanding. Cooking her something to eat would play a role. He'd need all of his skills for this one.

Sometimes it's okay to do something
JUST FOR HER.
Turn the page for a peek at
Katherine O'Neal's latest,
in stores this month from Brava.

"You won't find what you're looking for, I'm afraid."

He jerked around, into the moonlight streaming through the window from which he'd entered.

And as he did, she saw him more clearly—a tall figure, clad all in black, the fitted material clinging to a body that was muscular and sleek. A specifically fashioned mask, also black, concealed the top of his face . . . hiding his nose and cheeks . . . sweeping over his head to cover his hair . . . the only feature visible a clean-shaven jaw and the faint gleam of dark eyes through the slits of his disguise. He stood poised and alert, his hands at his sides, ready to pounce. The effect was both masculine and feline, calling to mind images of the jungle cat to which he'd been so aptly compared.

All at once, he darted for the open window. But she was closer. Instinctively, she stepped in front of it, blocking his path, reaching behind her to pull it closed.

He stopped in his tracks.

"I have a gun," she told him, her voice shaky.

She could see his head swivel as he quickly surveyed the room, looking for another escape. Two doors. One, behind him, led to the hallway, but it was closed. The other, the one connecting to her bedroom, was closer and open. He stared at it, then back at her. No doubt wondering if she would really shoot him if he made a dash for it.

Astonishingly, despite her advantage, she sensed no fear in him. His presence sparked and sizzled in the room, sucking the air from it so she could barely breathe. A raw, stalking presence, wholly male, predatory and sexual in nature, making her suddenly aware that she stood before him in nothing but a lace and chiffon nightgown. She could feel the vulnerability of her soft female flesh, of the swells and hollows of her body, in a way that made her feel it was *he* who held the upper hand.

For a moment—an eternity—he didn't move. He just stood there, his gaze locked on her. She could feel the heat of that gaze as though his hand was passing itself over her. She tried again to swallow. Heightened by the danger, it seemed to her that every pore of her skin radiated and throbbed with her awareness of him.

And then, like lightning—so suddenly she had no time to react—he lunged across the room and wrenched the pistol from her hand.

For a moment, he just stood there, the weapon aimed at her. Her hand aching, Jules could feel the frightened rasp of her breath. With her imagination running wild again, she pictured him pulling the trigger, heard in her mind the roar of the gun's retort.

The silence was deafening. Her nerves were raw.

But then—quickly, efficiently—he flipped open the barrel, let the bullets drop to the floor, and tossed the pistol aside. Jules felt a momentary relief. But it was short-lived. Unthreatened now, he skirted around her and started for the window from which he'd come.

In desperation, she sprang to block his exit, flinging herself back against the window, her arms spread wide to prevent his escape.

"Please, don't go."

He stopped at once, his instincts honed. She imagined him grabbing her and hauling her aside.

Instead, with a stealthy grace, he veered to his left and started for the open door that led to her bedroom and the terrace beyond. Realizing his intention, she ran after him.

"Wait!" she cried.

He wheeled on her threateningly, his hand raised. "Stand back," he warned, speaking in Italian—a deep, whispery, dangerous growl.

Switching quickly to Italian, she told him, "I just want to speak with you. That's why I lured you here."

"*Lured* me?" He glanced about warily, as if expecting a contingent of police to burst into the room.

"There's no one here," she rushed to assure him. "I don't want you captured. I just—"

He wasn't listening. She could feel his urgency to get away. He crossed the room, rounding the bed on his way to the French doors, the terrace, and freedom beyond.

Fueled by despair, Jules shot after him and grabbed him by the arm. Beneath the black sweater, it felt like iron.

He jerked free with a strength that sent her tumbling back. "I don't want to hurt you, but I will."

Jules was past caring. All she knew was that she couldn't let him walk out the door, and out of her life.

She grabbed onto him once again. This time he shoved her back onto the bed. "Don't you care what happens to you?" he snarled.

"No," she confessed. "I have nothing to lose."

"You're mad," he rasped.

"Am I?" She stood slowly, careful not to cause alarm. "Perhaps. All I know is that fate has brought you to me."

"Fate?"

"Destiny has sent you to me, Panther. You can't run away now."

"Can't I?"

He turned to leave, but she gasped out, quickly, "I have a proposition for you."

That stopped him. Slowly, he asked, "Now, what kind of proposition could a woman like you have for a man like me?"

Her eyes roamed the feral black-cloaked phantom before her. Unbidden, the first line of Byron's "Don Juan" sprang to her lips: "I want a hero."

"You want *what*?"

She took a breath and spat out the words.

"I want you to kill my husband."

And keep an eye out for Donna Kauffman's
THE BLACK SHEEP AND
THE ENGLISH ROSE,
coming next month from Brava . . .

"I only ask for one thing."

Felicity arched a brow and decided to give him the benefit of the doubt. "Which is?"

"Until the sapphire is in our hands, we operate as a team. No secret maneuvers, no hidden agendas."

Her whole life was a hidden agenda. Well, half of it anyway. "And when we have the necklace? Then what?"

"See? I like how you think. When, not if."

"Which doesn't answer my question."

"I don't have an answer for that. Yet."

She laughed. "Oh, great. I'm supposed to sign on to help you recover a priceless artifact, in the hopes that when we retrieve it, you'll just let me have it out of the kindness of your heart? Why would I sign on for that deal?"

Finn turned more fully and stepped into her personal space. She should have backed up. She should have made it clear he wouldn't be taking any liberties with her, regardless of Prague. Or Bogota. Or what they'd just done on her bed. Hell, she should have never involved herself with him in the first place. But it was far too late for that regret now.

"Because I found you tied to your own hotel room bed and I let you go. Because you need me." He toyed with the end of a tendril of her hair. "Just as much, I'm afraid, as I need you."

"What are you afraid of?" she asked, hating the breathy catch in her voice, but incapable of stifling it.

"Oh, any number of things. More bad clams, for one."

"Touché," she said, refusing to apologize again. "So why are you willing to risk that? Or any number of other exit strategies I might come up with this time around? You're quite good at your job, however you choose to label it these days. Why is it you really want my help? And don't tell me it's because you need me to get close to our quarry. You could just as easily pay someone to do that. Someone who he isn't already on the alert about and whose charms he's not immune to."

"Maybe I want to keep my enemies close. At least those that I can."

"Ah. Now we're getting somewhere. You think that by working together, you can reduce the chance that I'll come out with the win this time. I can't believe you just handed that over to me, and still expect me to agree to this arrangement."

"I said maybe. I also said there were myriad reasons why I think this is the best plan of action. For both of us. I never said it was great, or foolproof. Just the best option we happen to have at this time."

"Why should I trust you? Why should I trust that you'll keep to this no secret maneuvers, no hidden agenda deal? More to the point, why would you think I would? No matter what I stand here and promise you?"

"Have you ever lied to me?"

She started to laugh, incredulous, given their history, then stopped, paused, and thought about the question. She looked at him, almost as surprised by the actual answer as she'd been by the question itself. "No. No, I don't suppose, when it comes down to it, that I have." Not outright, anyway. But then, they'd been careful not to pose too many questions to each other, either.

"Exactly."

"But—"

"Yes, I know we've played to win, and we've done whatever was necessary to come out on top. No pun intended," he added, the flash of humor crinkling the corners of his eyes despite the dead seriousness of his tone. "But we've never pretended otherwise. And we've never pretended to be anything other than what we are."

"Honor among thieves, you mean."

"In a manner of speaking, yes."

"I still don't think this is wise. Our agendas—and we have them, no matter that you'd like to spin that differently—are at cross purposes."

"We'll sort out who gets what after we succeed in—"

"Who gets what?" she broke in. "There is only one thing we both want."

"That's where you're wrong."

She opened her mouth, then closed it again. "Wrong, how? Are you saying there are two priceless artifacts in the offing here? Or that you can somehow divide the one without destroying its value?"

He moved closer still, and her breath caught in her throat. He traced his fingertips down the side of her cheek, then cupped her face with both hands, tilting her head back as he kept his gaze directly on hers. "I'm saying there are other things I want. Things that have nothing to do with gemstones, rare or otherwise."

She couldn't breathe, couldn't so much as swallow. She definitely couldn't look away. He was mesmerizing at all times, but none more so than right that very second. She wanted to ask him what he meant, and blamed her sudden lack of oxygen for her inability to do so. When, in fact, it was absolute cowardice that prevented her from speaking. She didn't want him to put into words what he wanted.

Because then she might be forced to reconcile herself to the fact that she could want other things, too.

"Do we have a deal?" he asked, his gaze dropping briefly to her mouth as he tipped her face closer to his.

Every shred of common sense, every flicker of rational thought she possessed screamed at her to turn him down flat. To walk away, run if necessary, and never look back. But she did neither of those things, and was already damning herself even as she nodded. Barely more than a dip of her chin. But that was all it took. Her deal with the devil had been made.

"Good. Then let's seal it, shall we?"

She didn't have to respond this time. His mouth was already on hers.